The Third Hunter

A bloody folklore horror

PHILIP ALEXANDER BAKER

Artists:

Internal illustrations and design by Vanessa Baker

Front and back cover paintings by Mino

Editors:

Kathy Towns

Danielle Yeager at Hack & Slash Editing

Developmental Editing by Becker Jones at Jones Novel Editing

Paperback ISBN: 978-1-7392741-2-2

Ebook ISBN: 978-1-7392741-3-9

<u>The Hanging Hill Lane Trilogy</u>

The House on Hanging Hill Lane

The Third Hunter

Mother, Mother, Meat

Disclaimer

No human in this book is based on any real person. Any similarity is purely coincidental. The demons, however... are very real. One stands behind you right now, moving closer as you read, gliding silently across the floor. Do not look around. He'll be standing there as you read every word of this book. You may even feel his cold, close breath, or a slippery finger brush your neck. A wet warty tongue in your ear.

If you do, do not turn around. That's when they get you.

The Third Hunter

A bloody folklore horror

PHILIP ALEXANDER BAKER

Prologue

Late one night
As the piggy was dreaming,
There flew a duck, duck duckbill
gleaming.
And when it landed on the shore,
It pecked and pulled and slurped
some gore.
Something's not right, the piggy
thought,
Ducks don't eat gore.
And then it pecked and slurped
some more.

* * * * *

Three weeks later

* * * * *

Chapter One

DAPHNE'S FALL BACK DOWN to living hell was signalled by the freckled woman – a perfect empty shell
by the sea.

Her curly blonde bob artistically complemented the
freckles that speckled her button nose and glowing cheeks,
a natural fit for the front of any major magazine or bill-
board. But instead, the flawless freckled face was in the
background of a frantic news report on the gruesome and
fresh murders of six people on the rocky beach below. She
stood stock-still and dead-eyed behind the journalist on
the windswept clifftop under the midday sun, her curls
swaying in the soft sea breeze, framing her lifeless stare.
Behind the sea-blue eyes on the freckled face, there was
nothing. Nothing at all. Nothing but a terror-filled hollow
where a human mind used to be. The vacuous gaps behind
two perfect pools of blue stared deeply into the camera

lens, the pain and emptiness they held seeping into every lounge and bedroom the broadcast was beamed to.

In front of the terrified shell of a woman, news reporter Angela Shipman came through Daphne's television in perfect focus and clarity and centre frame, but it was the freckled beauty behind her that Daphne could not help but watch. She had never seen fear like it before – and she'd been at the centre of an attack by demons which had slaughtered her neighbours and driven three local police officers to suicide. This look of fear was otherworldly. This was unlike the look of a normal scared person. This was so much worse, and it shook Daphne's gut and her heart pounded fast and hard at the terrifying realisation.

This could not be the work of humans.

Three more women stiffly stepped into shot behind reporter Angela Shipman. All beautiful. All young, around twenty, the same age as Daphne. The same age as her friends. All petrified to the point that the spark of life in their young faces was drained and gone. The news camera slowly pulled back, revealing several more women on the clifftop and a familiar dirt pathway that revealed the location to Daphne as being just a few miles to the south. Those poor beautiful shells of women scattered around on the swaying grass, facing in all directions as the dark clouds of last night's brutal flash storm floated away. The women moved snail-paced and stiffly as if they knew they had to walk but were too scared to try. Some jerked and stopped, their expressions holding an anguish too deep to scream or cry. Too deep to even think. Too terrified for a human mind to do anything but hide somewhere deep inside the internal world and the skull in which it is eternally imprisoned. Daphne sat up slightly as she scanned the faces, in fear she might see an old classmate or friend. The freckled woman stepped slowly towards the camera, her dead eyes staring right through the lens, forcing a shiver down Daphne's spine. Her whole world went silent and dark as she dared not move her focus an inch from the screen, drawn into the black holes inside the blue irises on either side of the freckled nose.

A siren blared from the television speakers as another ambulance approached the grassy clifftop, and as the siren's sound grew stronger, so did Daphne's sense of responsibility for dealing with this, matched by the undeniable fear that she simply wasn't ready. She scanned the faces of the stricken women on her screen and unclenched her teeth slightly when she made certain she didn't know any of them. Perhaps it was returning anxiety that was making her leap to all the worst-case scenarios. As if any case could be worse than the return of the demons.

A speck of rain landed on the lens and wormed down the screen like a tear on a child's cheek. Daphne tuned herself out of the shell-shocked women and forced herself to listen to Angela Shipman.

A luxury superyacht had run aground in the storm, she reported, and six people had been found dead on the beach below. Police had already announced it was a murder investigation. Speculation was the yacht belonged to Brendan Burger, owner of the biggest social media company on earth and one of the richest people alive. Rumour was rife that he was among the dead.

Two police officers walked from the beach path onto the clifftop. One looked as white as a ghost. The other looked like she was fighting her stomach, attempting to hide her guttural retches from the television cameras.

But to Daphne, the murders, the beached yacht, the probably-dead celebrity, were all trumped by something far more worrying.

The young women.

Any slight happening – a police officer gently approaching, a leaf blowing softly along the grass – led to a startled flinch, the only time they showed any kind of humanness. It was fleeting, and after the brief reaction, they would return to catatonia.

Whatever this was, it was going to be big news. The biggest news since the six-eight-ten killings that had ravaged Daphne's street two years before.

Bigger.

Daphne did the only thing she knew when she sensed danger, and the world shifted and darkened. When her anxiety rose and bubbled.

She called her next-door neighbour and best friend, Sara, to come around and put the kettle on for a hot, sweet, nice cup of tea.

Sara always knew what to do.

Except this time, she didn't answer.

Chapter Two

THE NEW DOORBELL CHIMED an old-fashioned note that wasn't anything like the doorbell that had repeatedly terrified her two years before, which seemed to signal a danger that crept closer with every ring. Daphne answered the soft metallic tone to Sara and breathed easier the moment she saw her.

Sara held up her phone with the call notification. 'A step ahead of you as always, sister.' Of course she had been watching the same news report. The whole country probably was. Sara clutched sleepy two-year-old Alfie as she stepped in through the doorway, and Daphne smiled and ruffled his hair gently enough not to wake him. She often did that, and it normally felt fun and playful. This time, it somehow felt protective.

Three minutes after the kettle whistled, they clutched their teacups and sat in the lounge with the TV playing the news quietly in case of any updates. Angela Shipman repeated the story like a broken record, and the shell-shocked women flinched and stiffened as they were gently coaxed into ambulances. Alfie sat on the floor playing with a toy fox. Daphne watched him, wishing she could be just as oblivious to whatever was going on.

This could only be the work of something not of the human world. And if that was so, then it brought Daphne and Sara directly into the picture. Daphne felt a shiver at the thought, the nerves settling only slightly with her first sip of tea.

'This involves us, doesn't it?'

'I don't know,' said Sara. That was unusual. Sara always knew.

'Fuck.'

Daphne had shed much of her shyness with the killing of the demon two years before and along with her confidence, developed a bit of a potty mouth, partly in honour of her delightfully foul-mouthed late mother, who she was really missing right now. She'd always been a swearer in her head, but never out loud through fear of drawing attention to herself. Now, she didn't give a fuck.

But, as the world got scary again, her newfound confidence was fleeing, leaving nothing but a more colourful vocabulary behind. It wasn't going to be much help.

Angela Shipman suddenly looked animated on the television. Daphne reached for the TV remote, but Sara beat her to it, raising the volume with a small upward motion of her fingers through the air. Sara's fluency in magic was getting to be a bit of an annoyance, a reminder of

Daphne's lack of progress. The small pang of jealousy gave way quickly. The words coming from the television were too important.

'Police have confirmed we can now bring to you,' said Shipman, 'that the owner of the yacht was, as thought, Brendan Burger. We will bring you more on this as we get it, but we do now know, from a reliable source, that Brendan Burger, the second richest man in the world and owner of the world's largest social media company, is dead, killed on the beach below us, and this is being investigated as murder.'

'Fuck.'

'Yeah,' said Sara as she dropped the television volume with a downward curl of one finger.

'This isn't making sense though. Everything I've read, everything I've learned, all Mum's books said they'd find someone like that useful. Killing Brendan Burger doesn't sound like something out of the demon playbook. They've always used celebrities to manipulate, cause some trouble, they don't just kill them.'

'I guess. But they are demons, Daph. This is what they do. They make people kill each other, and themselves. Sometimes just for fun.' Sara squeezed Alfie tighter.

'The textbooks say—'

'I know what they say.' Wow, Sara was stressed. 'Demons don't always need a reason. They don't always follow the playbook that they didn't even write.' She took a breath, and paused. 'Sometimes, demons will just do what demons like to do.'

Sara seemed uncharacteristically irritable, her tone a little more coarse than normal.

Daphne softened her own tone to avoid any hint of conflict or friction. 'Then why not the women on the boat? Why just him? The one they should have kept and used?'

'Should? Demons don't understand *should*. They just do. Not everything needs to fit into a textbook box.'

'What do we do, Sara? I'm not ready. I tried. I'm still trying.'

'Let's just hope they got what they came for, right?' Sara paused for a moment in silence with a blank face that Daphne couldn't read. 'Trust me, Daph. Just keep your eyes open. I'm gonna go home, get this one some food.' Alfie belched and Sara stood as her face softened and she forced a small smile. 'It's okay, Daph. Keep practising. It takes a demon a decade to blink, they only came through our woods two years ago. Just keep learning, okay? And keep being okay. Message if you need me.' Sara stared at Daphne for a moment. 'And stop bloody worrying,' she said with an almost playful smile.

'Wait, what do I do?' Daphne's mind was blank.

Sara looked back and her smile grew. It gave Daphne a hint of confidence that everything was kind of okay. In the two years since her mother had passed, Sara, like a big sister, was beginning to blur the hole where her family used to be. No one would ever even start to fill the gap left by her mother's death, of course, but having a big sister figure helped in its own tiny way.

'I'll keep an eye on things, Daph. Seriously, if it was that bad, Mum would be back in a flash. Like, literally.'

Daphne's shoulders dropped a bit with Sara's assurances, and she smiled a silent goodbye as she closed the door.

In the two years since she'd learned that she wasn't human, she'd read all the textbooks but made almost no progress at all in the ways of the witch. She felt completely inadequate, and since watching the news report, felt like she was drowning. She jumped when her phone bleeped, and her heart pounded. A text message notification sat on her screen: NEARLY HERE?

It was Paulie. She had completely forgotten about their date, and while her mind replayed parts of the news report, she rushed to get ready, and the thought of his company replaced the thoughts of the news, washing away some of her anxiety as her face slightly softened and a smile gently returned to her cheeks.

Chapter Three

ALL DAPHNE WANTED TO do was have a nice, normal afternoon, pretend she was a normal human, pretend that the world was acting normally, and pretend she wasn't scared. It didn't feel like too much to ask. She'd had a lot of practice at pretending she wasn't scared.

After the killings two years before, she had worked out a whole load of what she wanted in life. Near-death experiences tend to assist such revelations. She'd read about that in books and now she knew it was true.

The downside was that over time, this threw up a whole load more confusion, as if solving one problem revealed ten more just as soon as the afterglow of beating demons had settled. Sure, she'd come out the other end having shed much of her teenage shyness – as you'd expect to if you had slayed a real demon and discovered you had magical powers. But the loss of the anxiety that plagued her old life was replaced by a new anxiety, more fitting to what she knew she was and how she now knew the world to really be. She felt like a tiny ant in a forest vaster than anything she had ever imagined. A forest with creatures she could not yet comprehend, and she was the smallest of them. She tried to learn. She tried to grow into what she was. Perhaps if she could learn enough magic, her anxiety would disappear. She was struggling. The step out of anxiety was always a small step beyond anything she had achieved. Magic was the answer. Sara could do it. Daphne couldn't. It made her feel stupid, though she kept that to herself.

But one good thing that had come of her newfound social abilities was Paulie. She'd met him one afternoon a few months before at the Old Gallows pub, not far from her house. She knew straight away he was a kind, gentle man, and his awkwardness was the kind that felt endearing and didn't detract from his looks. He had that ultra-rare kind of smile that was somehow both self-conscious and charismatic. The first time she saw him, his fumbling fingers were spilling his full pint awkwardly on the bar, accidentally pouring a gush of beer into his open packet of peanuts and looking around nervously to check no one had seen his ridiculous mishap. He saw Daphne, and their faces went as red as each other's. Matching rosy apple cheeks, matching awkwardness, and that was that. While she still struggled to give and receive even the slightest physical affection, she thought the world of him, and he understood to stay hands-off while she was still gaining confidence. He was a gem of a chap who worked at the animal sanctuary just beyond the woods. His obsession with superhero movies meant conversation never got too awkwardly personal.

Daphne arrived at the bar almost an hour late. She caught herself in the reflection in the window as she approached and disappointed herself, as every accidental reflection always did. The picture of how she walked, shown truthfully by the reflection in the window, never matched how she thought she held herself in any way. She cringed every time, and this wasn't the quick confidence-knock she needed right before she met Paulie. She walked through the entrance and scanned the pub for him.

'Daphers!' a loud voice boomed. It wasn't Paulie.

Before she knew it, she was being hugged tight by an annoyingly loud guy she knew from school and deliberately hadn't seen since. She always felt uncomfortable being hugged and normally managed to avoid it. But this had come out of nowhere. Since the demon had made her feel so violated, hugs felt even more uncomfortable. A hug from a stranger actually *disgusted* her. When he squeezed her tighter and moved his hand under the back of her hair, she found a fist forming and checked herself. She pushed him away gently and relaxed her hand as they looked at each other with expressions that couldn't be more different.

'How are you, Daphne?' he grinned, brimming with life.

The real answer was a mix of terrified about the news on the television, excited to see Paulie, and pissed off about being hugged like that. 'Fine.'

'I'm good,' he replied without being asked. 'Seen the news? It's proper mad.'

'You shouldn't just grab people,' she said, and he just turned to look back at the screen. 'I said you shouldn't just grab people.'

He looked back at her, surprised. 'Sorry Daph, was just nice to see you.'

Daphne didn't have time for this, and didn't know if she was just stressed or rightfully annoyed. She walked away across the bar leaving the man staring at the screen as if he had forgotten her already. And then she saw Paulie and the world suddenly weighed less.

Paulie was sipping on a full pint, an empty peanut packet and dirty glass on the beer mat in front of him. He was sitting on a barstool, swinging his feet nervously while reading the subtitles on the television news that played behind the bar. His face lit up when he saw Daphne arrive and he wiped the froth from his lip and patted down an invisible tuft of messy hair on the top of his head.

'I'm so sorry.' The words rushed out of Daphne's mouth. 'I got distracted.'

'That's okay,' said Paulie, ever lovely. He nodded to the TV on the wall. 'Have you seen this? Brendan Burger got killed at the beach we keep talking about going to. They reckon he was having a party on his yacht and someone killed him and his whole crew.'

'It's crazy, right?' This was the last thing Daphne wanted to think about.

'Drink?'

'Just a lemonade, please.'

'Is everything okay? You seem a little nervy. Did I do something?' Paulie looked worried.

'I'm okay. I just got out of breath rushing. It's nice to see you.'

It really was nice to see him. When Daphne set eyes on Paulie, breathing felt easier. She was still scared of intimacy and had no idea why, but Paulie understood. And if she could get through it, she knew he would be the one to help her. Somehow, despite being wafer-thin and never having been in a fight in his life, he made her feel safe. She'd almost made up her mind to get so drunk someday soon that she thought she could cope with a kiss and a cuddle at least, and after she had done it once, perhaps it would come easier when sober. But now wasn't the time. Something sinister was happening. The last thing she needed was for the demons to return and for her to be smashed out of her skull on vodka. Cuddles could wait. And Paulie was a patient man. Perhaps he was nervous about it himself.

Daphne turned from the bar. A lack of human chatter in the normally very social pub just didn't sound right, and every eye in there was fixed firmly on the television. It wasn't often that a superstar celebrity got murdered just down the road. The only being in the building that wasn't watching the screen was the regular pooch in the pub, who lay quietly on her back, paws up as if wondering why no one was giving her belly rubs today.

As Daphne looked around at the faces of the people watching, she couldn't help but notice her fear creeping back into her stomach, up her back and into her stiffening shoulders. This really was serious. It didn't just concern her and Sara, but the whole world. This was huge. What-ever was brewing was filling her with dread. She felt some-thing cold touch her upper arm and almost jumped out of her skin.

'I'm so sorry,' said Paulie, a look of devastation and regret on his face as lemonade spilled down the glass, drenching his fingers. He held up her pint of icy lemonade.

Daphne breathed again and smiled. 'Sorry. The news is just making me jumpy. Can we go outside? Away from the telly.'

'Isn't it a bit cold?' asked Paulie. He studied her face. 'Of course,' he said, and they stepped out into the deserted beer garden and sat at an old, semi-rotting picnic bench.

He was right. It was cold. Colder than it had been for weeks, and Daphne felt her anxiety intensify and her shoulders raise some more. She sat at the table and disap-peared inside her head, worrying about what the hell was happening. Worrying that her life was about to descend back into chaos and horror. And then she looked up at Paulie, who was stiffly sitting down with his typical lack of coordination, and as he did so, knocked his pint into his peanuts, taking her right back to the moment they'd met. She felt her face relax and the air return to her lungs a little more easily every time she saw Paulie's distinctive, awkward smile.

'I like your hair,' Paulie said as he fiddled with the soaked packet of peanuts.

Her hair was different only because she had rushed out and for the first time, met him without making even the slightest effort with it. And he liked it anyway. For the first time ever, someone had mentioned her hair and she hadn't got self-conscious about it. As long as he didn't try to touch it – she *really* hated that – but he never would. Paulie loved superheroes, but it was like his own superhero strength was recognising boundaries and making Daphne feel comfortable. She was happy with that. They were getting through their awkwardness together, and it felt wonderful. It felt perfect.

'Well, I've spilt both our drinks and ruined the nuts already,' Paulie said with an embarrassed smile. 'What else could go wrong today?'

Daphne knew the answer and she hated it. If only her mind hadn't flown to a logical answer instead of hearing the playful rhetorical question it was intended to be. His mouth moved for a while after that, and sounds were no doubt coming out.

The demons were coming back. She could feel it in the chill air. Their marks were all over that news report. And she was going to be the one to deal with it. If they were coming, just like last time, they were coming for her, Daphne Locke, the vulnerable witch.

Paulie stared at her with concern in his eyes. 'You weren't listening, were you? What's up?'

'I'm sorry. I'm listening.'

'It's nothing. I was just talking about movies.'

'That's unlike you.' Daphne smiled. 'Sorry. Tell me.'

'Least favourite movie trope?' he asked.

Daphne was fighting her mind from wandering. Wandering back to the news, wandering back to wondering what on earth was going on with the women on the clifftop.

'I don't really know.'

Paulie looked serious. 'I hate witches.'

Daphne's attention snapped back, her eyes scouring his face. Did he know? Surely not. No, he's just talking about movies. Damn her returning anxiety, pushing her mind into making ridiculous jumps like that.

'A bit ridiculous for me.' he continued. 'And then there's that one from Spiderman and all the others, where the superhero can't have close friends because that puts them in danger. I've been thinking about that one. Like, it's true and I don't know what else they can do, but I just don't like it. I mean, everyone's gotta have friends. Especially superheroes.'

The anxiety fuelled Daphne's thoughts. *Does he know? He can't know.*

But he was right. He'd answered his own question. What could go wrong? *That. That* is what could go wrong. Daphne stared back at him, her mind racing but her face stone still.

'And then there are the horrible romance ones, where the abuser becomes the lover, and just because he's good-looking and got a six-pack, all gets forgiven. That one has implications beyond the book or screen. Which, I guess, witches at least don't. Sorry, I'm such a geek.' He grinned shakily and somehow managed to hide behind his pint glass. 'I just don't like witches.'

Daphne watched Paulie and could feel her heart tug. That stupid trope was right. What if he was in danger because of her? Of course he was in danger because of her, just like her dead neighbours from two years ago. It would be so selfish to stay with him. And yet he made her feel so safe. As if he could protect her from the demons. It would break her heart, but to keep Paulie safe, she'd have to leave him. End it before it had really started, just like in the stupid movies.

'Daphne!' Paulie snapped gently in a way only he could. 'You're miles away. What's wrong?'

'I'll think about it,' said Daphne, realising too late what she'd said.

'It shouldn't take much thought. Just the stuff you don't like. Okay, tell me next time.' Paulie looked deep into his glass, as if it held all the answers to all the questions in the universe, and then looked like not a single answer had come. 'What's wrong?'

'I'm sorry.' She could feel the first tears forming but knew she still had a few moments before they fell. 'Shit. I'm so sorry.'

Confusion washed over Paulie's face.

'I left the iron on. I'm going to burn down the house. I've got to go.'

Paulie stared, disappointed but understanding. He stood with her.

'Gotta run. I'll text you.'

She got up and walked quickly through the pub. Not a person murmured, their eyes still fixated on the screens. On the news. The news that had already ruined everything.

Chapter Four

DAPHNE'S FEAR STRAINED HER face all the way to the top of Hanging Hill Lane, where her phone pinged. It was Paulie: SOGGY PEANUTS. It was dumb and mundane. But that's what she liked about him the most. Everything about him was safe. By the time she was halfway down the hill, she was smiling again.

She reached the bottom and stopped, taking a moment to concoct a witty reply. But as she paused to think, her thumbs hovering over her phone, it wasn't a witty reply that came to her. It was a shock. Something gripped and tightened around her ankle. A plant from a front garden wrapped itself tightly around her foot, while another vine snaked from the plant towards her other leg, wrapping around her ankle and stopping her from moving. Thick tendrils from a second plant edged closer, crawling along the pavement like giant caterpillars. Daphne looked up and across the road, her heart pounding in her chest. Then she laughed.

Sara stood in her doorway, giggling, her hand motioning with the movement of the plants. Prank magic was becoming a regular part of their life now.

'For God's sake, Sara.' Daphne laughed and said with a smile, 'It's like the set of Harry fucking Potter round here now.'

Sara laughed and dropped her hands to her side, and the vines gently retreated back to the garden. 'How's Paulie?'

'Good guess,' said Daphne. 'Have you found anything out about the news?'

'Nothing to worry about still. It's nice to see you smile. Try to relax this evening, sister.'

'Thanks, Sara. Give Alfie a kiss for me.'

Sara disappeared into her home and the door closed. Daphne wondered if things in the world were good after all. If she needed to worry, Sara wouldn't be playing around like that. And she was feeling good. When she thought of Paulie, she felt safe and happy. And, unusually, somehow soft and warm inside. When she realised where she recognised the feeling from, she giggled all the way to her doorway while a nostalgic tear formed in one eye. She walked in, closed the door, lay on her bed, and enjoyed one of her favourite memories of her beautiful mother.

It was still so clear. It played like a movie.

* * * * *

The kitchen of number two Hanging Hill Lane had always displayed the most incredible herb and spice selection, with neat rows of jars immaculately labelled in swirly writing. But the really pretty stuff was always kept well out of reach of young Daphne. The spice rack below the herbs contained all the regular flavours you might expect in a well-used kitchen – parsley, paprika, salt and pepper – and a varied selection of others in beautiful hand-crafted jars of stained glass and vintage wood.

When Daphne was thirteen, she'd picked up some fish and chips from the old chippy on the way back from school for her and her mother. When she got home, she sprinkled on some vinegar but the salt shaker ran out, the last grains falling on her own chips. To save her mother from going without, Daphne climbed onto a stool and searched through the beautifully ornate spice rack to find more salt. She found a substance labelled 'love salt' – close enough. She sprinkled just a little on her mother's chips and carefully placed the love salt back onto the rack. Daphne watched her mother taste the first chip, just to check her reaction was no different from normal. Then Daphne went upstairs with her own chips to get her homework done early.

An hour or so later, music reverberated from the lounge. Then the volume picked up. It was most unlike her quiet mother. Daphne crept downstairs and peered through the small gap between the door and doorframe.

Her mother was in the lounge, slowly dancing alone to the music. Daphne had never seen her act anything like it in her whole life. She was using her full body, swaying with the music, occasionally stroking her own face, grinning and somehow looking like she was filled with love, and showed huge affection to any object she picked up, cuddling the cushions, kissing the candlesticks, rubbing the television remote on her cheek. At one point, she pointed at a cushion and said with a loving smile, 'You're so fucking soft.' Daphne covered her mouth to hide her laugh.

Then her mother picked up a framed photo of the pair of them and danced with it, hugging it tight to her chest, and turned the volume dial up a little more. Daphne's giggle was drowned out by the loud music, and her mother danced on without a care in the world. After a good waltz with her eyes squeezed shut, she carefully placed the picture down and approached the mirror hanging over the fireplace. Daphne watched on in secret as her wonderful mother put her hands over her eyes and played peekaboo with herself in the reflection, laughing with herself and playing like she was both adult and child. She looked like she was in love with the woman in the old mirror, and the woman who looked back looked like she was in love with her in a pure, beautiful way. Daphne hid away, not to be spied in the reflection too, and wondered what on Earth had got into her mother. And then she realised.

The love salt.

The penny dropped. Her mother had drugs in the house, and she had inadvertently put some on her dinner.

Oops.

The incident was never spoken of. It was only recently that Daphne had put two and two together and realised that those spices weren't drugs, as such, but for witchcraft. And definitely not for flavouring fish and chips.

As Daphne had grown a little older, having seen the effect of the love salt, she wanted to try it for herself. One night, at sixteen, when her mother was out of the house, she had put a bit on the end of her finger and licked it off. It tasted salty, and she wondered if it *was* just salt in that jar after all. An hour later, she felt like a new person. The carpet under her bare feet felt like a light, fluffy, perfectly warm cloud. She couldn't help but put some music on the stereo, and immediately discovered why her mother had danced that night. Each move made her fall in love with the music a little bit more. When she peered out the window and spotted a hare hopping down the road, she felt a new kind of love for wildlife. It looked so soft and pretty as it bounded happily and gently along. She wanted to hug it. The trees looked like they glowed with an aura of life and she felt like she was floating in a soft cloud made entirely of pure and fluffy love. When she closed her eyes, she even noticed a little love for herself. It was a memory she had kept as her private little secret forever.

The last time she had eaten the love salt was a few months after her mother had passed. The realisation that her mother and so many others had died as a means to get to her had started to hit hard, and the guilt was weighing heavier every day, bringing with it feelings she had never felt before, and she had no idea how to cope. She'd tried everything – meditation, articles with crappy advice about coping with guilt, distractions with books and movies, a therapist called Dr Bohn – and one day, while cleaning the kitchen, had found the pot again. Perhaps it could make her feel better, if only for the evening. It felt like cheating, but she was desperate. She was panicking about where her mind was heading. She only poured a few grains onto her palm and licked it off.

A few hours later, she found herself looking through the photo album of her mother with her heart full of love. She went to bed that night and closed her eyes, and her attention seemed to scan through the vastness of her mind as though it were an enormous world of its own. But with the help of the witches' special seasoning, she was peering around every corner of this new internal world with her sight coloured with love. That's when she found some forgiveness for herself. When she learned the killings of her mother and her neighbours were *not her fault*. She'd felt a little better ever since.

When she woke up the next day, she saw she'd sent a few messages, too, and felt a weird mix of embarrassment and happiness. She'd been looking at old photos and ended up staring at a picture of herself with her college best friend, Olivia, and messaged her for the first time in months. Perhaps it was largely the love salt talking. It simply said, I LOVE YOU. A reply was waiting when she woke up. LOVE YOU TOO, MISS YOU. They hadn't messaged since.

Daphne hadn't taken the love salt again, however much she'd adored the feeling. Witchcraft wasn't something to be abused. She'd never felt anything like it before or since.

Until now.

When she thought of Paulie, there it was. That same feeling of gentle warmth and softness, if just a tiny little bit.

He made her feel safe like her mother had, too. The feeling of love, safety and nostalgia compelled Daphne to do something she hadn't done for a long time. She walked into her mother's bedroom. A room where four clothed mannequins stood, the plastic occasionally – just for a minuscule moment – coming alive.

One would even smile.

Chapter Five

OVER THE LAST TWO years, Sara had learned so much and could do so much more than Daphne in their shared dark arts. It made Daphne feel so inadequate, like nothing she did was ever good enough. Sometimes, she felt ready to give up. Sometimes, she'd feel a wave of determination, which would get quashed by a few hours of failure. It wasn't right. Daphne had read all the textbooks. Sara had barely read three books and still was miles ahead.

Sometimes, stupid Daphne just couldn't do it. Sometimes, a voice of strength would call from within and tell her she could. If only that voice hadn't somehow felt caged.

After two years, it almost felt like the threat was over. Now it was back. Worse, the three old witches from the street stood as little more than monuments in her dead mother's bedroom, in the form of affordable plastic, just clothing on mass-produced dummies. She'd moved them from the living room into her mother's room, out of sight, so she could live a life without constant reminders of her darkest days. But she'd still been hoping to one day bring them back to human form.

When she had first put the old witches' clothes on the mannequins, it had been in a semi-dazed state of shock, a way not to feel so alone while she made sense of what had happened. And then, a few days later, the twitching had started. That's when she had decided to try and push further, read a load of textbooks, and see if the old witches could fully return. Looking back, they were both terrifying and exciting days. Now, the kind of magic ability that she'd expected to gain felt like an eternity away. The mannequins would occasionally move, murmur, or twitch, bringing a little hope, but the life of the old witches was buried deep inside. The mannequin in her mother's clothes hadn't moved once. She was the furthest away of them all.

Only one mannequin showed any true progress. Dressed in Gugwana's bright and colourful clothes, its white plastic tone was shifting to darker, and it would smile with real life. And yet, Daphne knew in her heart that it was Gugwana who was doing it, not her.

In the art of witchcraft, Daphne felt like an utter failure. An embarrassment. Stupid.

But it was the witches' job – and that meant Daphne's job – to protect the world from the demons that entered the world through the doorway in Hanging Hill Woods. Witches had lived on the lane for centuries, the first line of defence. Now, only Sara and Daphne remained, and Daphne had no idea why the demons didn't just return now. Their route into the world was guarded by only two inexperienced witches. One of them had a two-year-old child. The other may as well have been a stupid, weak human. They'd have been walkovers.

It would have been easy.

Maybe the demons didn't like easy. Maybe easy wasn't enough fun. The textbooks said all kinds of things, and none of it really made sense.

Daphne could almost feel the darkness descending on her, her chest constricting as her anxiety returned, and every tiny creak of the house amplified and gave itself a dark meaning once through her ears. As she stared at the clothed mannequins, it hit her that these women – these witches – were the only thing that had saved her from death the last time the demons had come. And now, they were useless. She had Sara, but otherwise, she was on her own.

She took the hand of the mannequin wearing her mother's clothes and looked at its clean, unblemished white face. She stared, scouring the smooth plastic, as if staring for long enough would reveal a hint of movement. Desperation filled the vacuum left by hope as it fled. The anxiety in her chest was joined by a painful sadness.

The mannequins of the other three witches had made very slow, but very real, progress. Her mother's had made none. The one woman she needed the most might never be coming back. Perhaps it was the sliver of hope that made it more painful. It was making it impossible to properly let go.

Daphne's trancelike stare was broken by a sound that rattled through the window. A tin can rolling and clattering down the hill outside, blown by the breeze.

The wind was rising.

A storm was coming.

She felt it.

Chapter Six

DAPHNE WASN'T HUNGRY BUT served herself a simple dinner of sausages and microwaved mash. She'd burnt the sausages a bit because her thoughts had been occupied with Paulie, and the stupid film trope of superheroes protecting their loved ones from danger by distancing themselves. She didn't know what to do. The demons had long shown they would kill the people closest to her to get to her. Her mother, her neighbours, even some local police. One minute she was sure she knew what she had to do, and that was to end things with Paulie. Then she'd spend a few minutes justifying not doing that – perhaps she could protect him, or perhaps they wouldn't know about him or wouldn't think it would work – but every time, she realised she was just making things up because she didn't want to do what she knew she had to do. And then the sausages were black.

The TV news was always a good source of information from a human perspective, but every time she switched it on, she was hit by another gut punch of anxiety, dreading what she might learn next. The reports had so far been revolving takes on the story of Brendan Burger and the murders of his crewmen on the beach. But this time was different.

The local news had switched focus from the murders to a missing person – an unrelated case, with the authorities appealing for witnesses.

The newsreader's voice slipped behind a photograph of a blonde woman in her mid-twenties. Described as outgoing and likeable, it was a face far too familiar to Daphne. A face that had helped her through thick and thin in her college days before they were cut short by Daphne's mother's strange death and the terrible events that followed. The pretty face belonged to her college best friend and roommate, the young woman who had been an inspiration and support throughout her awkward college days. The woman she had texted while under the influence of the love salt.

It wasn't Paulie the demons had targeted after all. They'd hit her in another way. Daphne burst into tears the moment she saw the picture of Olivia's face.

Chapter Seven

Daphne had first properly met Olivia on the south coast of Cornwall, on a beautiful stretch of sand not far from where Brendan Burger would be murdered. It was a hot day and the pair had started their college course just three days before.

Ever since Daphne had first laid eyes on Olivia in the college's car park, she had somehow been drawn to her. But teenage Daphne was very shy and hadn't dared speak to her, not even to say a simple hello. People flocked around Olivia like she was some kind of a celebrity. She was beautiful and effortlessly attracted people to her. She'd have drawn Daphne to her, too, if only Daphne's shyness hadn't won every time. While her eyes and thoughts and hopes moved towards Olivia at the college induction day, her social anxiety worked through her muscles. The moment she had the slightest whisp of an idea to approach her, anxiety pinned her feet to the floor like they were nailed down. Only the confident kids got to talk to Olivia. And the creeps.

Now, as Daphne looked up from her book on the semi-crowded beach, there she was. Olivia, in her swimsuit, chatting to a couple of besotted passers-by. Daphne sat and stared, completely in awe of her new classmate, desperately wanting to go and say hello. This was her chance to make a very cool friend on her course. Olivia looked around and caught Daphne's eye, who looked straight back into her book as a bolt of totally unnecessary adrenaline shot through her, making her feel like there was something wrong with her. Like she was failing at life.

Daphne had always been nervous around people, but this was something unusual. She was starstruck by her classmate, but aside from a couple of years in age and some undeniable physical beauty, she was her equal in every way. She chastised herself for her stupid feelings and looked up to see Olivia again. Another couple of passers-by had stopped and were laughing at Olivia's jokes. Daphne watched on in awe of how she could command a conversation like that and be so free chatting with strangers. The fact that she could do it in a swimsuit just made it even more amazing. She was in complete control of a cheeky salaciousness that onlookers couldn't help but be drawn by.

Daphne refused to be beaten by her nerves and gathered her courage, her floppy sunhat and her book, and stepped shakily towards Olivia. Her legs felt like jelly, which made no logical sense, but at least they weren't nailed down. Perhaps if this young woman had been a pop star or famous actress, she would have understood – but she wasn't. This was just a new classmate. After a few wobbly paces, Daphne dropped back down to the sand and opened her book to peer over and watch as a pair of middle-aged passers-by left with huge smiles. Olivia continued to laugh and joke with two besotted men who stood looking ridiculous in their swim shorts, like dogs desperate for a command to obey just to show how submissive they were. The whole thing was ridiculous.

Ridiculous but fun, and Daphne wanted in, if only her damn anxiety wouldn't stop her. She forced herself to her feet and made it another few paces before her anxiety activated her freeze stress response, sticking her to the sand. She slumped down again and hid behind her book, berating her stupid self for her stupid inability to do something so stupidly simple and human. She felt so disappointed with herself that she wanted to cry. But, as if a caged strength was calling from somewhere deep in the back of her mind, she refused to be beaten. She watched as Olivia shooed the men from her and they finally skulked away. Olivia dropped her sunglasses back over her eyes and lay back down, facing the sky, one knee pointing up towards the white fluffy clouds. One of the admiring men looked back around at Olivia. He looked crestfallen.

Yup, ridiculous.

Daphne had recently been reading about how horror stories could actually help with anxiety, and there were even studies to prove it. So she'd brought along to the beach the scariest horror book she could find, MJ Mars's

The Suffering, and ended up hiding behind the scary book of monsters from something that shouldn't be scary in the slightest. A young woman. A friendly classmate. As her eyes scanned the pages about ghosts and evil, she again realised the absurdity of it all.

She could do this. All she had to do was get up and walk a few paces and say hello. Just introduce herself as a classmate. This should be easy. But her stupid legs had other ideas and didn't want to cooperate. All they wanted to do was run away. And yet she saw a potential new friend, and a very cool friend at that. She'd never had a cool friend before. It took her several more minutes of pretend-reading and self-talk to be able to stand and wobble another five paces towards her, but then she sat back down, beaten, clutching *The Suffering* like a comfort blanket, ready to cry, a stupid failure. And now she'd got sand in her book.

She bought herself some time to prepare. First, she lied to herself. She told herself she had just started the book and needed to read at least a chapter or two. Otherwise, someone might see where her bookmark was and judge her for reading too slowly. So she told herself she would read a chapter and then would go and speak to her. Then she berated herself for caring so much about what other people might think, and decided to get up and go and talk to her anyway. Her legs did not oblige. So she stared out over the sea and felt her guts churn up sadness, fear and disappointment into a new painful feeling that would teach her there and then for being so stupid.

She knew she was shy but had no idea that her anxiety would run so deep when she wanted to act differently for something so stupidly simple as meeting a new classmate. She'd lost. She gave up. The stone steps off the beach invited her to escape and go home and beat herself up about her stupid insecurities. She wanted to feel the safety of being with her mother. At seventeen, that just made her feel even more stupid. Her relaxing reading day at the beach had become one of the most stressful days of her life, and it was all pointless stress of her own making. All in her head. But she wouldn't let herself be fully beaten and promised herself that the next time something like this happened, she would conquer her fears and do it. Next time, she would win. Next time, for sure. She prepared to stand, but as she did, she couldn't help but see Olivia's head shift in her direction.

Olivia was looking right at her and pushed her sunglasses up onto her beautiful blonde hair. Woah. She'd noticed her. No one ever noticed her.

'Are you coming or what?' asked Olivia with a smile that removed almost all of Daphne's anxiety in one swoop, while a wave of excitement whooshed in to replace it. Daphne got up and shuffled over shyly, her legs shaking now with excitement rather than fear.

'You're on my course, right?' asked Olivia.

'Yeah. Fashion. I thought I saw you at the induction. I'm Daphne.'

'I'm Olivia.'

'I know.'

'Nice to meet you, Daphne.' Olivia smiled at her like Daphne was the only person in the world, and Daphne was suddenly almost at ease. She could actually feel the adrenaline drain from her body. Olivia dropped her sunglasses back down and lay on her back with one knee up, looking like a glossy magazine model, and Daphne awkwardly copied the pose. They lay like that in silence for half an hour, and it was lovely. It was as though they'd been friends forever and Daphne felt more relaxed than she had in years as the sun warmed her face and the waves rolled in and out slowly, pulling Daphne's breath into a slow rhythm with it. She'd never felt so relaxed with a stranger. That was until Olivia started humming a tune in a beautiful, almost magical voice, leaving Daphne wondering if there was anything at all about this woman that wasn't out-of-this-world beautiful.

Her humming had caught the attention of two lads, who approached, using the tune as a way into a conversation. Daphne didn't want an interruption, certainly not from strangers. Her warmth and peace disappeared, and she felt her shoulders stiffen, although at least the lads seemed to ignore her entirely.

'Guess that tune?' one of the lads said with a cockiness that didn't fully cover up his nerves.

'Have a nice day, boys,' said Olivia without moving her head, dismissive but somehow not rude.

The men stood above her, staring.

Olivia turned toward them. 'Are you both okay?'

'What's your name?' asked one of the men through a giggle. Daphne felt uneasy, like this man wasn't quite right. He was saying friendly things, and no doubt would say he was just being friendly if questioned, but there was some desperation there coming out as aggression masked by a smile, and Daphne didn't like it one bit. The other stared at Olivia, and Daphne counted down the seconds until she expected the dribble to come from his mouth. They didn't budge.

'You're hot,' giggled the other man nervously.

'You're right, I could use an ice cream,' said Olivia.

The men jumped to action as if commanded by a superior. 'What flavour?' the near-dribbling man ejaculated.

'Anything. And one for my friend.'

The men scuttled away across the beach towards an ice cream van.

Friend. Daphne stifled the small, proud smile the word brought.

Olivia sat up and raised her sunglasses. 'Run,' she said with a giggle and eyes that twinkled like the sun on the sea.

'What?'

'Run!' The girls jumped up, grabbed their things, and ran into the crowd near the steps up off the beach. They watched from the top of the steps. Their grins matched.

The men had bought the biggest ice creams Daphne had ever seen and run back to where they had been lying. One of the men kicked the sand in anger, showering a nearby family with a small child, who broke into tears with sand in his eyes. The other man looked almost ready to cry too, and threw an ice cream into the sand. Olivia laughed, setting off Daphne, and the moment they became best friends was etched into Daphne's memory forever.

✽ ✽ ✽ ✽ ✽

And now Olivia was gone. Missing right when the demons had returned. There weren't many dots to connect and Daphne was the middle dot. They'd taken Olivia to get to Daphne. It was just like Paulie had said. Olivia was in danger, or, more likely, dead, and it was all Daphne's fault.

Her fault.

Her stupid fault.

Again.

Chapter Eight

Police Constable Joanne Bach salivated at the thought of her packed lunch back at the station. She hadn't used the station canteen for two years now. Too many memories there.

Today, she had been sent out alone for a police welfare check on a woman whose family was frightened she was about to end her own life. It wasn't the first time for this lady. An army veteran who'd served in Afghanistan, the poor woman suffered from depression and post-traumatic stress disorder, and her flashbacks would take her to a frantic and dark place, which she said felt just like a fragmented reality of a real experience of being back there. She refused therapy, likely in a fruitless effort to avoid ever having to think about those memories again, and so her family would call the police to attend whenever they were worried she might be close to ending her stay on Earth.

Joanne Bach was often the officer called on for welfare checks. She was good with people. She was likeable and had a calming persona, and she really, actually, cared. She'd last seen this lady on bonfire night the previous year, when the fireworks brought on flashbacks of missile fire and mine explosions and vivid memories of her friends losing limbs, intestines and heads. The poor woman's descriptions had been intense, then suddenly stopped as if the conversation had never happened.

Constable Bach could spot trauma when she saw it.

Unofficial counselling should have been beyond the remit of a police bobby without mental health training, especially one as young as twenty-five, and though her superiors had complaints about it being a job for psychology professionals, Joanne Bach volunteered for this kind of job when she could.

This time, she left the lady full of tea and feeling a little better, as confident as she could be that she would be okay, at least for now. This was why she'd joined the police. She was making a difference.

Five minutes later, she was sitting at a red light, handbrake on and car in neutral, indicator ticking away in the background, allowing her mind to relax for just a few seconds, and feeling the warmth of the sun through the windscreen on her cheek before the light changed. Like a perfect shower, the warm sun felt like it was washing away the stress and transferred-trauma of the last hour or so, and dissolving the images in her mind of the stories she had just been told.

As red turned to green and she dropped the handbrake, a car flew across in front of her at breakneck speed. She swung the car around and followed, giving a quick radio message back to the station. As she whipped around the corner, she saw the offending car well ahead, speeding towards the signs for the primary school. Her foot feathered the brake. She couldn't give chase and risk the offender speeding up, or distract the driver and risk the car hitting a child, so she held well back and waited for instructions.

It wasn't a kid that caused the speeding car to swerve.

It wasn't clear what did. It all happened so fast. Within the blink of an eye, the offending car was a crumpled steaming wreck up against an old oak tree right by the school entrance. Joanne Bach accelerated gently and carefully, then slowed and pulled in behind the smoking mess of crunched metal that still crackled.

The car bonnet was fully wrapped around the tree, steam and smoke pouring from the cracks, crystals of glass all over the pavement and grass. Small faces bunched up behind a classroom window, staring. Joanne Bach jumped out of the car, keeping the info flowing to the station and requesting an immediate ambulance. She stopped at the driver's side of the crashed car and looked in through where the window used to be.

There sat a man, perhaps forty years old. Dark hair with a streak of grey. The airbag was deflated and hung limply on his lap. The man looked to be surprisingly healthy, if unconscious, aside from a small cut on his cheek.

'Sir, can you hear me?'

Nothing.

A little blood speckled his chest under a hundred small chunks of glass. His face was clean, if a little stubbly. His hair was styled in so much product that the impact hadn't changed it at all. The only thing that stood out about the sight was the man's strange neckwear. Perhaps some kind of primitive ornamental tribal wear from a place far away, it was thick and made from inch-long pieces of something hard and shiny that looked like ivory. It shone as if covered in a thick varnish, and blood began to ooze into it, gap by gap, from behind him. It took a moment for Joanne Bach to realise. It wasn't neckwear. It was part of the man's own skeleton, the vertebrae from his neck's nape now wrapped neatly around the front of his throat like a vicar's dog collar made of his own spine. Bach jolted away and then stopped still as the shock grabbed hold and froze her mind and body. She barely registered the blazing siren of the ambulance as it arrived. She didn't warn the paramedics of the sight they were about to see. She could almost see the trauma thread its way into her brain and take hold, as if watching from the eyes of someone outside her, numbness preventing her from doing anything.

The image seared itself into Joanne Bach's brain. So did a clear picture of the surroundings. The old school made of yellowy-grey stone blocks, paint peeling on the window ledges. The faces of the children looking out and the bespectacled teacher peering over their heads, confused. The pattern on the trunk of the oak tree bark that kind of looked like a heart. It was like a huge snapshot that would ingrain itself into her brain, but none so clear as the dead man, thick red blood oozing from behind his neck crawling forward, filling the gaps in his spine, vertebra by vertebra. The memory would last forever.

And yet she didn't even remember how she got back to the station.

Chapter Nine

PAULIE ARRIVED AT NUMBER two Hanging Hill Lane less than an hour after Daphne had seen the news that her friend was missing. Daphne had immediately called round to Sara, but, unusually, she wasn't at home. Feeling herself starting to panic and feeling very alone in the house, she had called Paulie and invited him to her house for the first time. In a way, it was progress. Further signs she was developing the ability to trust. It was also the complete opposite of what she thought would be the sensible thing to do for his safety. The doorbell chimed and Daphne opened the thick wooden front door.

Paulie stepped into the old house and smiled. He held two bundles of paper with grease seeping through at the corners.

'I brought chips. I hope you like mushy peas. But first, you have to show me around this super cool house.'

Daphne hadn't intended to do a tour of something that felt very normal to her, but to a new person, the old house was fascinating and Paulie couldn't stop grinning.

'Okay. Kitchen first.'

The stone walls of the kitchen looked old and the spice rack immediately took Paulie's attention. The white modern oven looked a little incongruous with the otherwise charmingly rustic feel, but Daphne had replaced the old one a few days after the events of two years ago. Any time she looked at the old oven, the memory of that poor policeman's head inside it slammed into her consciousness, skin blistering and popping, scorched eyes bulging, just one of the many things the demons had done to try to break her and take her as a possessed witch. The old oven had to go. She bought a brand-new bright white model that looked a little weird sitting in the old stone kitchen and somehow managed to remind Daphne of the horrible events in its own way. Andrew, his name had been. Another innocent victim of the demons. Andrew Foot. His friends had called him Casper.

Vintage knives still hung on a rack.

An inscribed iron bar spanned the back door making sure no one – or no thing – could get in. Daphne ran her finger over the inscriptions as she passed it. They made her feel safe, but they also reminded her of what was being kept outside, and the fear that managed to push up from her stomach reached her head and pushed a tear to form in her eye. She didn't normally cry that easily.

Paulie dropped the chips near the sink and looked at Daphne with awe in his eyes. 'Beautiful. You never told me about this place.' His face changed when he noticed her tear. 'What's wrong?' Paulie leant forward barely an inch, a subtle and gentle offer of physical comfort, but withdrew when he sensed Daphne's tiny flinch. 'What's wrong?'

'Can we sit down?'

They walked through to the lounge and sat on the sofa with half a seat space between them as Daphne composed herself.

'I have this friend. I used to, anyway. Still do, I think. I don't know.'

Paulie looked concerned, trying to work out what she may have meant. 'A "friend"? What do you mean, "friend"?' His skin suddenly looked paler.

'She's missing. She's on the news.'

His relief was noticeable. 'The blonde girl on the news?'

'We lived together at college. We kind of fell out but we shouldn't have done. She was so amazing to me for so long. The police are looking for her.'

'Oh no. Can I do anything?' He looked so genuine, so kind and caring, and Daphne worried that just by being here, he was in danger. It hit her that if he hadn't been in danger before, bringing him here may well have put him in it. She suddenly felt so stupid, ready to kick herself hard for it just as soon as she had some time alone.

'You know most missing people find their own way back?' Paulie said, ever lovely and supportive. 'There's normally a very simple explanation. She'll almost certainly turn up absolutely fine.'

'Yeah, but...' Daphne stopped herself. She knew this was no ordinary missing person case. She had worked out from the news reports that the beach killings had happened at the same time as her last reported sighting. And those poor shells of women nearby. Those women were all pictures of perfect beauty. The only woman Daphne knew who was that beautiful was Olivia. Olivia was her friend, and the demons had a history of murdering people who were close to her to get at her. These were all dots that were starting to connect. If Olivia was alive, she would be in a kind of trouble unknown to almost any human, and little Paulie wasn't going to be able to help. But if Olivia was dead, surely the demons would have shown her by now. God only knew what state her body would turn up in. And she couldn't mention any of it to Paulie. She fumbled around in her mind for a moment to work out exactly why she had asked him over when he couldn't offer any kind of help. But then she tuned out her thoughts and found her attention back on Paulie's face – a picture of empathy – and realised again that he made her feel safe, and that would have to be enough.

But it wasn't right.

She'd asked him round and put him in danger so she could feel safe, even though she wasn't. How stupidly selfish. She would kick herself again when she got that minute alone.

'Wanna check the news channel? See if there's an up-date?' Paulie asked gently. Daphne didn't want to. She knew there wouldn't be. But she thought they could watch the screen in silence for a few minutes while she composed herself.

Angela Shipman presented from the clifftop again. The pair watched in shock as the report came through. Details of the six deaths on the beach had been revealed. Three crew members and Brendan Burger made four. The other two victims were each newsworthy in their own right.

Murdered: Boddy, one of the most influential pop stars in the world. The Korean-American had just landed a string of number one hits but was getting better known for her outspoken social media presence. She had one of the biggest followings in the world in both languages.

That wasn't even the biggest news in England.

Murdered: William Head, the deputy prime minister of the United Kingdom. He'd been in the news a lot recently, always for scandals and sleaze, some complaints of inappropriate remarks and groping of young female civil servants, and photos in the press of him drunk in nightclubs and a high-end strip bar. The papers had been a never-ending reel of his latest debauchery and on the news, clip after clip of him denying wrongdoing and refusing to resign. Now he was on the news because he was dead.

'Woah,' said Paulie. 'I had tickets for Boddy.'

'Yeah,' replied Daphne, the dots connecting quickly in her head. She knew the demon playbook off by heart now. She'd been reading about it for the past two years in preparation. They'd try to possess influential figures to create chaos. These three people – the most influential pop star in the world, the owner of the world's biggest social media company, and the deputy leader of the United Kingdom – would have been perfect targets. But they weren't possessed. They were dead. Why would the demons do that?

It made no sense at all. Especially as all three were doing a perfectly good job of creating chaos without any help from other realms. The dots slowly disconnected and their links in her mind dissolved.

The three crew members were also named, all men. Several likely witnesses, all women, seemed completely unable to speak and had been taken into psychiatric care. Piecing things together, Shipman reported that there had been a party on Brendan Burger's yacht, he'd invited Boddy who was on a not-so-secret holiday in the area, and several women had joined the party.

Burger was known for his regular entourage of pretty young women, considering himself a bit of a Leonardo DiCaprio-type character, though the rest of the world cringed and saw him more likely a Jeffrey Epstein. Still, where he and his money went, some pretty girls followed, and where pretty girls went, William Head crawled his way in. Now, the three celebrities were dead, murdered brutally, the three crew members slaughtered too, and the fun-chasing women on board somehow mentally incapacitated. Daphne recalled the freckled woman on the cliff. She tried to piece it together again. Lots of dots. Few connections.

Olivia was a dot that still didn't quite fit.

They both stared at the screen until it suddenly went black. Paulie put down the remote and Daphne looked at him.

'That isn't helping,' he said. 'I'm sorry to hear about your friend. Let me know if there's anything I can do.'

'You're here. Thank you.'

'William Head is dead. Shit. Political, I guess. I suppose that makes it terrorism. Wow. Terrorists in quiet old Cornwall. I didn't know terrorists came this far west.'

'Something like that,' Daphne replied.

'Not a lot we can do.' Paulie looked at Daphne and smiled. 'And, worse, the chips will be cold and soggy.'

Once again, she felt safer. And once again, she knew she'd messed up.

The chips were cold, but they poured them out onto plates anyway. They were doing their best to enjoy them when Daphne's phone dinged. It was Sara suggesting she go round. She had to go. This would have been about the news – and possibly urgent.

'I'm sorry, Paulie. I have to go. Someone's got an emergency.'

Paulie tried to hide his disappointment. 'Your missing friend?'

Daphne shook her head.

Paulie smiled. 'But cold mushy peas are so delicious. You're bumping off me and the soggy chips? Sure?'

Daphne almost laughed.

'See,' said Paulie. 'I love how you always find something to smile about. I hope your friend is okay. I'll help in any way I can.'

'Thank you, Paulie. I really have to go.'

As she arrived at the front door and pulled it ajar, Paulie looked at Daphne. 'Are you sure you don't want a hug?'

It was weird. For possibly the first time ever, she did.

And so she hugged him.

It surprised her that she liked it. Paulie felt warm and Daphne felt butterflies take flight as she squeezed him tight. In the middle of everything that was going bad in the world, she somehow felt more than comfortable. She felt safe. She absolutely hated herself for putting him in danger like that, but somehow couldn't help it. She felt like she needed him and couldn't stop herself.

Paulie gave Daphne a kiss on her cheek. The first she'd ever had from a romantic interest. She liked it. He gently kissed her cheek again, her cheekbone, then just under her ear.

And Daphne fell into a dark abyss.

✴ ✴ ✴ ✴ ✴

Daphne, lying in bed unable to move, feeling the demon creature's weight on top of her. She feels the rough, stinking tongue on her cheek. On her earlobe. The tip of the demon tongue inside her ear.

She smells the rancid stench of rot and death.

Daphne, sitting with her back to the front door on the floor, an invisible creature in front of her, licking her face, her eyes full of chemicals, streaming. Feeling the tongue like a leathery verruca-covered wet foot dragging up her face and poking into her ear.

Daphne, believing it is time to die.

The smell of death.

The deepest of fear.

Under attack.

She has to fight.

* * * * *

The flashback felt so real. It felt like it was happening all over again, in real time but in dreamlike fragments, experiencing it again as if it were right now. At least for the first terrifying moment.

Then she'd been half watching herself like she'd somehow drifted from her own head, viewing herself from outside herself, like the flashback had been so real and terrifying that she had actually left her own head to escape it. All the memories and feelings from the time the demon had terrorised her and her neighbourhood flooded back all at once, and the fear was just as intense as it had been the first time. Paulie's soft kisses on her cheek and ears had set off a chain of neurones somewhere in Daphne's mind and taken her right back as if she were living that moment of hell again, Paulie's soft face touching the very places the demon's disgusting tongue had licked. Fragmented but very real visions of the demon appeared and hissed right in front of her eyes. The physical feeling of the demon tongue in her ear. Adrenaline and stress hormones raged through her mind and body, stiffening it and forcing her fists to clench. She didn't just feel fear. She felt anger. Anger like she'd never felt it before. Anger towards the person who made her go through it again. The urgent and desperate need to fight back.

How dare Paulie do that? How dare he get so close? She yanked the door open and pushed him forcefully away down the short garden path. Rage filled her and she stepped after him and pushed him back again, barely registering the upset, confused expression on his kind, befuddled face.

'I'm sorry,' he pleaded, but that just made the anger hit harder.

'Get away from me!' she yelled and stepped towards him as he backed away. This anger was out of control. This anger was new, from somewhere else, like a cage inside her mind had opened and a beast had got out.

Paulie tripped and dropped, falling on his back on the pavement by the road. Daphne raged forward, regaining just enough control not to hit him while he was on the ground. She fought the urge to kick him while he was down. She raised her foot to stamp, and screamed. She was barely in control.

He scrambled back, then to his feet, desperate and confused.

'I'm sorry,' he blurted out, and tears followed before he turned and swiftly escaped up the winding hill, wiping his face with his sleeve as he hurried away.

Daphne watched him go with anger and tears in her eyes, feeling it with every part of her. She'd never felt anger like it. It had completely taken over. As Paulie disappeared around the bend out of sight, the rage started to dissipate, making way for confusion and upset. Regret fell fast. What on earth had she done? In that moment, she didn't know her stupid self.

But then, across the road, she noticed a small pair of eyes looking back at her.

Someone was staring at her.

The girl looked around ten or eleven years old. She wore a green school dress that was filthy and too small for her, like she was ready to burst out of it. The shoulder fabric had snapped and broken, replaced by straps made from raw green vines from a plant or tree. She had long black hair down to her waist. In one hand she held a short black, very straight stick.

The two held each other's gaze for a moment, Daphne's anger making way for confusion. Then the child turned and ran down the hill and disappeared into Hanging Hill Woods.

The girl's face was familiar. Daphne knew it, she just couldn't remember how, her mind still confused and horrified from her flashback. Her phone pinged. It was a text from Paulie: SORRY.

Daphne walked back to her front door, and as she did, saw her hands were shaking. She wanted to go back inside and compose herself and try to work out what that reaction had been about. The flashback had felt so real, and it had been Paulie who had set it off. But he was only trying to be sweet. He was so sweet. He was the sweetest man alive.

She already wanted to apologise and sort things out with Paulie. He was amazing. But what had just happened was horrific, and part of her mind still held him responsible, even though another part just wanted to cry and say sorry. She opened his message and her thumbs trembled as she replied. SORRY TOO, TALK TO YOU ABOUT IT LATER X

First, she had to see Sara. Whatever had happened to her, however she'd messed up, if the demons had killed the celebrities as she suspected, she needed to know. She gave herself a minute to regain some composure, aided by some breathing techniques she had learned from Dr Bohn, and walked up to Sara's door. She raised her hand to knock, but Sara answered it before her still-shaking fist made contact with the old wood.

'What's wrong, Daph? You look a bit flustered.'

Daphne didn't want to say what she had just done. She already felt shame and guilt and wasn't ready to go there. 'I'm okay. I just saw a child staring at me. It was weird.'

'Child?'

'Yeah, a girl. She ran off into the woods. She didn't look right, something was off there.'

'Dog walker's kid, I guess. I still find it funny that people walk their dogs around a gateway to literal Hell with absolutely no idea.'

'What's going on then, Sara? I saw the news. What the actual fuck is going on?'

'Language, Daph, jeez.' She looked over at Alfie, snoozing on the sofa.

'Sorry.'

'But yeah, it's mad, right?

'Doesn't make sense. Not according to Mum's books. Why would the demons do that?' Daphne wrestled her attention away from what had just happened and back to the problem at hand. The murders.

'The books tell us what we think a demon would do. They don't read them and follow them. You get angry ones, mean ones. Most care little about strategy and more about bringing evil into the world just for demon fun. I'm not sure how useful the books are really.'

'That doesn't make me feel better.'

'It shouldn't.'

I'll still win though. There it was again. That voice from somewhere within Daphne, calling from some kind of mental cage hidden deep in the darkness of her mind. It scared her a bit that she trusted it. It meant she would have to fight. She snapped her attention back to the present.

The interior of Sara's house was very similar to Daphne's. They'd been built at the same time and lived in by witches for over a hundred years, there to guard the demon's entrance to the world in the woods. The walls were made of the same stone, the layout identical, and the back door also had an inscribed iron bar across it. The toilets were on the ground floor down a small corridor from where they had begun as outhouses and then joined with the house as building in the area modernised. It was another quirk of living in an old house. The garage outside was the only modern part of the building and the only part that made it substantially different from Daphne's, which was so close to the woodland edge that there was no space for any kind of garage or driveway.

Sara walked towards her garage and looked at Daphne to follow. 'Sorry sis, I'm in the middle of a clear out. But then the news came on and I thought we'd better chat. Excuse the busy hands.'

They stepped into the cluttered garage and Sara reached up and pulled a box down. 'It's Dickhead's stuff. Decided it's time to get rid of it. Make some space to move on, ya know?'

Daphne watched Sara steady the cardboard box in her arms. If that's her priority, then surely things – the unearthly things – couldn't be that bad. Surely.

'Can you grab those please?' Sara said, nodding at a couple of fishing rods. Daphne picked them up and followed Sara back to the main house.

'You don't seem too worried still?'

'Honestly, things seem okay. If they were on a boat, they didn't come through the woods. Not our business. The others can deal with that.'

'You know so much more than me about all this stuff, Sara. I don't know how you can read so quick.'

'Video calls with Mother, Daph. It helps to have a supportive mum.' Sara's face changed and saddened as she immediately realised her mistake. 'Oh, I'm so sorry. I didn't mean... you know. How are you doing? I miss her too. Really. A lot.'

An image of the mannequin dressed in her mother's clothing flashed up in Daphne's mind. Any magic she tried was a futile attempt to bring her back in any form she could, the mannequin remaining as lifeless plastic. And again, her lack of magical ability made her feel worthless. Stupid.

'I hate that she's not here. But she's not. I'm trying to bring her back but I don't know if I ever can or ever will. Not her, not the others. I'll keep trying but I'm still so clueless, you know that. Maybe your mum can help when she's back.'

They stepped into the lounge and stopped. Sara looked at Daphne.

'And that, right there, Daph, is why I'm not worried.' Sara gave a lovely, peaceful smile.

'Why?'

'Because, Daphne Locke, if we were really in trouble, Mum would be back here running the show. She was here two years ago, you know? Watching out for us.'

'She was here?'

'Yeah. But apparently we had to learn or we'll never learn. And you learned, right? You know what Mum's like.'

'Shit.' Daphne knew exactly what Sara's mother was like. She was a huge terrifying woman who insisted on discipline. Learning the hard way was very in-keeping with her difficult ways, but even so, Daphne felt annoyed. She made sure not to let on. Half her mind was still on what she'd done outside to Paulie, and she wasn't ready for any more friction.

Sara looked strangely calm. 'I couldn't have chased off the third hunter demon without her. Even she couldn't kill it. Anyway, Mum's not here now. And if things were going to hell, or hell was coming to us, she'd be here, and we'd know what to do.' Sara put her box down and dragged the coffee table to one side. She got on her knees and pulled the carpet back at the corner, revealing a wooden hatch in the old floorboards.

'Woah,' said Daphne. 'You have a basement?'

'Yeah. Quicker than a trip to the rubbish dump, I'll just throw all Dickhead's crap down here.'

'How big is it?'

'Big,' laughed Sara. She stood up and dropped the box of her ex's belongings down the square hole. Daphne didn't hear it land. She walked over and peered down into the darkness. 'Chuck 'em in,' said Sara, and Daphne dropped in the fishing rods and listened.

Nothing.

Still nothing.

'How far down does that go?' Daphne asked as she peered into the black.

'All the way,' said Sara with a grin as she dropped the hatch and the bang echoed around the stone walls and old wooden finishings. 'I'll chuck the rest in when I get half a minute. He's been gone years and he's still getting in the way. Men, eh?'

'Yeah. Men.' Poor Paulie.

Sara stared back.

When Daphne continued, it wasn't about men. 'About the news. I know you said not to worry, but I am worried. I'm sure this is going to concern us.'

Sara pushed the carpet back to the corner and toed the edges into the skirting boards.

'Did you see the story of the missing woman?' asked Daphne.

'The pretty blonde?'

'Yeah. That's my roommate from college. Olivia.'

'Oh no.' Sara stared back as she stood, her face focused in deep thought before looking at Daphne and softening with sympathy and compassion. Then her face changed again. 'The one who left you in the stink.'

'I think I've worked it out, and it's not good. It's scaring me.'

'Go on.'

'You said how these demons come in threes, right? And I got one. The old witches got one too. So there's still one out there. The one your mum chased off.'

'Somewhere. Not our fault we didn't get it, we're kind of short-staffed.'

Daphne didn't acknowledge Sara's humour at all. 'What if it's back?'

Sara looked thoughtful. 'You think the third hunter demon did that on the beach? The politician, Burger and the pop star?'

'And the crew. It killed six.'

'I don't know why it would. But then, demons will be demons.'

'But that's just it. It didn't fit to me either. But now Olivia's gone and it's making sense. Look at all they did last time to break me down. All the poor neighbours they killed. My mother. All to hurt me, because I'm the weakest witch and their best chance of possessing one of us. Now it's at it again. Killing celebrities on the beach near where we live. One of my favourite singers. Taking my old house-mate. I'm so worried she's going to end up dead in some horrible state designed to scare me. And I don't know how to help.'

Sara looked back and drummed her fingers on the coffee table. 'I'll check in with Mum later. Things aren't exactly making sense. You're right. But you're strong now, so stay that way. Don't let it get to you, will you?'

Daphne looked back at Sara straight-faced. She knew it already had got to her. She'd had a terrifying flashback. She'd physically attacked the one man she'd ever felt close to. Despite her brave face with Sara, she could feel she was losing it already. She felt like she was losing before the fight had even begun. 'I'm okay,' she said, it hitting her there and then that she would have to be and had no choice in the matter.

'She'll turn up,' said Sara.

'It'll be okay,' said Daphne, remembering what Olivia said almost every time things got bad. 'It'll be okay. Things always turn out okay. Every time.' That was Olivia's phrase whenever things got bad. But she didn't feel it. Her nerves were building stronger. 'And what about those women?'

'What women?' asked Sara, as Alfie started to cry.

'Sara,' said Daphne, looking at her old friend seriously, knowing she needed to know whatever Sara knew. She couldn't afford anything to be withheld this time. 'Why didn't you tell me?'

'Tell you what?'

'When the demons came last time. I was so scared. I could have died. And you knew. Why didn't you tell me? Why didn't you warn me?'

Sara sat down and rocked Alfie, who fell quiet. 'It wouldn't have been a good idea. I'm sorry.'

'But why? You could have prepared me. You could have come and stayed with me and helped me. But you didn't. I trust you. I just want to know why.' It was something that had been on Daphne's mind for a while, but she always felt too awkward at the thought of bringing it up. Now, she was being driven forward by fear, and the awkwardness sat aside.

'Daphne,' Sara said, 'we do things the way we do for a reason.'

'Mum used to say that exact thing. Except that was about cooking, cleaning, all the most normal boring stuff.'

'Okay, I'll explain very quickly, and then we move on, right?'

Daphne looked back at her and felt herself trembling.

'The demons did what they did to break you. To make you think you were going mad, or to actually send you crazy. That's how they could take you. And we could not and cannot let that happen.'

'I know, Sara, I know that. So why no warning?'

'Daphne, if I had come round and told you that I was a witch, and so are you, and there are demons out there trying to possess you because you are, so they can wreak havoc on the world using the ultimate weapon of a possessed witch, would you have believed me? Knowing what you knew then?'

'No, but you could have proved it. You could do magic. I'd have had to believe you then.'

'Exactly. So you think that if I'd told you about what we both are while standing upside down on your ceiling doing some really creepy shit, you think that would have helped stop you thinking you were going mad? It would have played right into their hands.'

'You could have explained.'

'Explained, done a whole load of weird magic stuff so you believed me, then left you in your house all alone to grieve your mother while the locals were getting massacred. I'm sorry, Daphne, but that is not a way to keep you sane.'

'You didn't need to leave me alone.'

'I had things to do.'

'Like what?' Daphne snapped.

'There were three demons out there that night, Daphne. The ladies helped you with two. Someone else had to keep the other one away. If you knew what I went through that night, you would not be asking me this. The third hunter was the most dangerous, the most devious, the most clever. And I had to do that with a newborn fucking baby, Daph, so I suggest you don't push it.'

Daphne looked back, blank-faced, no thoughts coming to help her push her point, which was rapidly losing power as fast as she felt she was.

Sara softened. 'I had a newborn baby, Daph. Probably why they picked that time, while I was weak. Look, we had a plan. It worked as best it could. Some things happen because they were meant to be that way.'

'You really do sound like Mum sometimes.'

'I'm sorry. I wanted to tell you. I really did. Look, I'm not supposed to tell you this, so tell no one, please. Mum told me not to. She said it would have risked everything. She said we do what we can. You don't argue with Mum, Daph, you know that.'

She knew it well. Agatha Hunter had terrified her since she was a small child. 'Promise me you'll tell me anything you know next time.' Daphne thought for a second. 'This time. It's happening again, isn't it? It's the other demon from before, isn't it? Down on the beach.'

'I don't know.'

Daphne looked at Sara and plucked up the courage to ask a question she'd been dying to ask all along. 'Is Paulie going to be safe?'

'I don't know.'

Chapter Ten

Sergeant Jason Cox, now a little past middle age but still beaming with muscle and quiet charisma, ushered Joanne Bach into his office and gestured to her to close the door. She had the familiar feeling she was there because she was in trouble. She always had that feeling whenever a superior called to see her. Always.

He looked at her compassionately and asked, 'How are you doing, Jo?'

'Bearing up.'

'I'm so sorry you had to see what you saw. I'm going to make you an appointment with the psychologist, okay?'

'No, sarge.' Joanne Bach had only recently stopped seeing the police psychologist and had started feeling herself again. Returning to therapy would feel like a step backwards. She had the mental tools she needed to cope now, to survive, if not yet to thrive. 'I'd rather just keep busy. And there's a lot to focus on right now.'

'Get yourself booked in in your own time, Jo. In the meantime, we've got a new spot for you. Something a little more gentle.'

'I'm okay.' Her hidden shaking hands said otherwise.

'That may be so, Jo, but we need you on the new team. Unless you wanted some time off, and that's completely okay. I'll get it arranged.'

'I'm okay, sarge.' That came out quieter than she had expected as Joanne Bach sensed what was really up. It was a sad part of the job, seeing dead people like that. Normally, people didn't get taken off their cases or moved to something 'gentle.' *Gentle.* That was code for something else. There were six bodies recently found on the beach in far worse condition than the poor soul she'd just seen, and no one else was being moved to *gentle* duties. She was being singled out. This was an excuse to move her and get her out of the way. She knew exactly why.

The strangeness of the killings on the beach had set off alarm bells and connections in her head, taking her back to the six-eight-ten killings, as the press called them. The residents of Hanging Hill Lane weren't the only deaths involved at that time. Three police officers had died too. All suicides, none of which made any sense.

One had been her fiancé.

She'd struggled to recover, and after returning to work had, for a while, wanted to link every violent or unexplained crime to Hanging Hill Lane. Her superiors had to tell her gently but firmly to stop and to seek help. The police psychologist hadn't made her feel much better by calling it a 'trauma-induced delusion', later softened to a 'lens of trauma', but she eventually accepted that her thinking stemmed from her personal struggles rather than the facts.

It had been a painful realisation that left a burning feeling of unfinished business inside her. The burning hurt.

When she saw the details of the six brutal murders on the beach, stress rose inside her and she'd made that old connection again and dared to mention it. She could have felt the thick pity swamp the room when she did. It was no coincidence she was now being asked to get back to the psychologist or take some time off and move away from the action to something more *gentle*.

Gentle means *unimportant*. *Gentle* doesn't make a difference.

She squeezed her shaking hands under the table and said, 'Where are you hiding me?'

'It's not like that. But if you want to keep working, the opportunity is there.'

'I'd rather keep busy, sarge.'

'Okay. Whatever is helpful to you. So, we've set up a brand-new dedicated misper team. I think it could use you and the good things you bring.'

Mispers. Missing persons didn't sound so bad. Sure, there were suicides involved in that, and very rare kidnappings. But otherwise, some cases would indeed be fairly gentle. Actually gentle, and not just *gentle*. She felt herself relax a little. And then it hit her.

The image of the man's bloody spine flashed through her mind. She blinked and shook her head instinctively to try to clear it, to force it aside, and when she looked up, noted the expression on Cox's face, then realised that gentle actually did sound sensible. 'Okay, sir. Mispers sounds good, thank you. When do I move?'

Joanne Bach walked into the newly dedicated missing persons room minutes later, where a small team sat around a large square table. They'd all worked on mispers before as part of their caseloads, but this was the first time a dedicated team had been set up. Sergeant Cox sat alongside a whiteboard. Joanne Bach looked at the six faces who turned to eyeball her as she entered, and the room went quiet.

It wasn't a bad team. She wasn't being put out to pasture at the age of twenty-five after all. She was good with this. It felt both gentle and important, although the photos of the local missing people on the wall felt imposing and a little uncomfortable. She felt proud to be given the opportunity to bring them back.

Constable Beverly Trevithick smiled a welcome. Aside from Cox, she was the oldest person in the room by about two and a half decades, with wispy grey hair and smokers' wrinkles that added at least a decade more. She scooted her chair over and pulled another out with an inviting nod. Trevithick had been there forever, an old sweat who was now part of the furniture, never climbing official rank but becoming the unofficial mother of the station. She always seemed very happy with that. Joanne Bach sat. To her left, two younger uniformed men greeted her and she realised she wasn't as much the new girl as she still always felt.

Bach said, 'Hey Tim, hey Jim,' and the young men nodded together.

'Nice to have you here, Jo,' said Detective Oliver Ovary from across the table. If there was a detective in the room, it meant somebody on the misper list was vulnerable. A high-risk case that needed solving fast. 'You're doing okay, right?' He'd meant it sincerely, but it brought an elephant stomping into the room. Everyone knew that Joanne Bach's suggestion that the beach murders were somehow linked to Hanging Hill Lane was from a relapse into personal obsession rather than based on any kind of evidence. Everyone knew that's why she'd been moved off the case and on to mispers. No one needed to mention it.

'I'm good, thanks. Are we starting?' The room – the four uniformed officers, Detective Ovary and a couple of bespectacled civilian case workers – turned to face the sergeant.

Sergeant Cox moved minimally, but everyone knew the room was his. 'Thanks, team. You all know there have been a whole load of new mispers recently. New names, new faces, and that's why we're worried. We've been struggling to help. And right now, there's always a more newsworthy priority with what's happened on our doorstep with the Burger boat, and that's been pulling our resources and our attention away from these good ladies and gents on the wall here. So now maybe you can do this with a bit of peace. All okay?'

Beverly Trevithick smiled and said, 'Thanks, Lance,' causing some rare annoyance to flash over the sergeant's face.

'Over to you, Oliver,' he said without acknowledging Trevithick's mischievous grin.

'We've currently got some high-priority cases, including a couple of vulnerables we're hopeful for good outcomes for, and of course a child we all know about and we're not so hopeful for, but has a father who runs the local gossip rag. The numbers have been up and down a lot over the last few days. There's plenty to be getting on with, hence the dedicated team.'

Joanne Bach knew exactly who the child was. They all did.

Penelope Pengilly had gone missing two years before, disappearing the same week as the Hanging Hill Lane killings, and from a street not far away. There was no evidence linking the two, but Joanne Bach had her suspicions. She kept them quiet now.

A child missing for two years very, very rarely comes back, and they all knew it. Penelope Pengilly would have been long dead or trafficked to Eastern Europe by now, with no hope. Probably the former. It didn't matter to them anymore. It was incredibly sad but there wasn't any more they could do. The problem was that the girl's father, Peter, hadn't given up hope where there was none. He'd often be seen in his own newspaper mouthing off about the uselessness of the police and even occasionally on the local television news. Far too often, he'd be at the station kicking up a stink and using up officer time that could have been far better used elsewhere, getting special treatment to avoid another shitty article in the local press. As such, Penelope Pengilly, who would now be nine years old, was still permanently buzzing around on the list of active cases, with enough effort put into the case to show willing but without genuine hope within the walls of the police station.

Ovary continued. 'High-priority, we have Mr Mattey again. He's vulnerable and we need to find him quick before he ends up smeared along some train tracks. We've been close a few times with Mr Mattey, so there's plenty on the misper report. Last time Mattey disappeared, he was talked down off the railway bridge up at Lostwithiel by a passing paramedic. We're pretty sure he'd have jumped if the ambulance hadn't passed when it did. We've got cars swinging by that bridge when they can, but so far, nothing. No phone activity for four days, officially missing for five. That's a new record for Mr Mattey.'

He wrote the name on the whiteboard, then another name underneath. High-priority again. 'I'll be taking this one. He has his baby with him and any one of you might get pulled off what you're doing to help if I need you.'

Everyone nodded as he wrote another name on the board, and Joanne Bach realised this wasn't going to be that gentle after all.

'Medium-priority, we have Olivia Merrigan. Twenty-four, missing for over a day, no leads, no explanation. We're not really sure what's going on with this one, and she's not been gone that long, but it just feels weird.' He passed a printed photo to the team at the table who all leaned in to take a look. 'She's not down as vulnerable, no history of mental illness nor going missing. Nothing on the file at all. We're bumping her to medium because she fits the profile of some trafficking victims of a gang up north. If it's them, it would mean they've arrived here in Cornwall. She also fits the profile of the women found on the beach after the Burger murders, but we can't see any other link. So far, we have nothing.'

'Nothing?' asked Joanne Bach.

'Nothing. Response have checked the hospitals, visited the family, called friends and leads. Everyone said she was as happy as always. No recent bank withdrawals. There's a misper report on her but it's pretty empty beyond basics.'

'Fuck,' said Tim under his breath, acknowledging the beauty of the woman in the photograph. Jim nodded in agreement. Joanne Bach couldn't help but notice she looked vaguely familiar.

'Assuming it's not the gang, any admirers we should know of?' asked PC Beverly Trevithick in her soft, croaky voice. 'Aside from these two idiots?' Tim and Jim stopped smiling.

'About every male in the town who knew her,' said Ovary. 'Everyone the response team spoke to absolutely loves her. A few said she has a certain draw.'

'Meaning what?' asked Trevithick. 'Promiscuous?'

'We don't think so. But we don't know.'

Jim said, 'She's stunning,' and Tim nodded in agreement.

'There's no evidence for kidnapping,' said Cox. 'But then, there's no evidence for anything at all. Last phone ping was the south coast masts.'

'The cliffs?' asked Beverly Trevithick. The whole room knew a mobile phone ping on the south coast masts would often mean a cliff jumper asking for help or saying a final goodbye.

'That area, but we don't think she jumped. We've searched down there and found nothing. Plus, Olivia Merrigan lives near the sea down that way. A message sent from her bedroom would ping on the same masts.'

'So she sent a message from home and then vanished?' asked Joanne Bach.

'From her home or nearby. She's top priority after Mr Mattey and the dad with the baby. I'd like them all back, in one piece, please.' Cox paused and turned to the whiteboard. 'Low-priority,' he continued, drawing a dotted line under the Olivia Merrigan case space on the board. 'As of this morning, we're down to eight.'

A phone rang. Ovary answered. It was a short conversation before he turned to the group. 'Seven. Old man Terrance came back again.'

'He does that,' said Cox. 'Good. Seven. Details are ready to go, misper reports are all up to date and we hope they'll rock up back at their own front doors within a day or so, but if the trafficking gang is here, we're not really considering anyone completely low-risk right now. We've still got nothing on the beach murderer, and this town has a bit of a history with unsolved serial killers.'

'Same killer? Any link?' asked Joanne Bach.

'Who knows, but there are teams on that. Our eyes are on the mispers.'

Beverly Trevithick said, 'That's eleven mispers. I heard there were around twenty.'

'A whole load got mopped up already,' said Cox. 'All on the Burger boat, now all in the psychiatric hospital. All young women in a terrible state. Lord only knows what is going on there. We'll let you know when we know more. We've got a psychologist and two officers there working through it. But yes, the pretty women on the picture board up there have all been found alive, if not exactly well.'

Beverly Trevithick held up the photograph of Olivia and said, 'All the pretty women but one.'

'We're pretty sure she wasn't on the boat,' said Cox, 'though she was last seen on the same day. As I said. Weird.'

'What would a message from the boat look like? Coastal masts ping?'

'Yes, the same.'

'Can we write "hot woman" as an official connection?' said Jim. 'Feels wrong to write that on the paperwork. But my eyes see a connection.' No one responded.

'Do they all have socials?' asked Joanne Bach, desperate to get cracking.

'Mr Mattey doesn't, not since MySpace. Nor does the father. Olivia Merrigan has the full set. All on the misper reports. Joanne and Beverly, you start on Miss Merrigan for now, please. Tim, Jim, you guys on Mattey. Act on whatever you find as soon as you can, and keep on at those cars to get eyes on that bridge. We'll get to the others when we can. And, of course, myself and Ovary on the father and baby.'

'There's one more kiddy, right?' said Jim, rolling his eyes.

Tim raised his shoulders and put his arms out like a gorilla and said, 'She'll be with the nonces by now,' exaggerating an impression of someone Joanne Bach had never met.

'That's enough of that,' said Cox. 'Yes, the Penelope Pengilly file is still open. Low-priority, obviously, but if we close that file, the press will be all over us. Watch out for hoaxes on that one because we're still getting the odd lunatic. Right. The misper reports await you. Get on Olivia Merrigan's socials first, and Mattey's mental health history. Any leads on Mattey, drop Merrigan for now and get on it. Any questions?'

'All good thanks, Lance,' croaked Beverly Trevithick, drawing annoyance from Sergeant Cox as he turned and left.

Joanne Bach and Beverly Trevithick logged on to their computers. Joanne Bach clicked on links to Olivia's social media as Beverly Trevithick scrolled through her misper report – more photos of her, details for friends and family who'd already been contacted, data for that last known phone ping. The section for known recent actions was blank.

Bach looked over to Trevithick and quietly asked, 'Why do you call him Lance? He doesn't like it at all, does he?'

Trevithick replied with a wink, 'He hates it. I'm just one of the old guard, he knows better than to mess with me.'

'Yeah. But why "*Lance*"?' Jo pressed.

'Why "*Baton*"?' asked Jim from across the room with a smirk, knocking the grin from Joanne Bach's face immediately. It was something she didn't find at all funny.

'You know.' Bach turned to face her screen.

'Come on, Baton, tell us.'

Joanne Bach flipped. 'Just fuck off, alright? Seriously. Fuck off and do your fucking job.' Her hands shook as she slid them under the desk. Sure, being called Baton always upset her, but until now, she'd always hidden it and hoped it would go away. Today, she was more on edge than she'd realised. That car death had really shaken her up.

'Woah. It's only banter,' said Jim as he retreated to his work.

'It's dickishness.' Joanne Bach swivelled around and glared at her screen and tried to compose herself, unsure what to do after an outburst unlike anything she'd had before.

But then something on her screen grabbed her attention. She nudged Trevithick. 'This one on Merrigan's socials friends list. Daphne Locke, she's known.'

'Oh really? She's not on her list of friends on the misper report.'

'I've been to her house. Lots of us have.' Joanne Bach hushed her voice and looked around before continuing. 'She's at Hanging Hill Lane.'

Beverly Trevithick glanced over her shoulder at the rest of the room. No one was taking much notice of them now, hiding in their work. 'Fuck.'

'Yeah. Number two. That's the woman.'

'Keep that one quiet in here,' whispered PC Trevithick. 'We can follow it up if we need to.'

Joanne Bach breathed deeply and said, 'I need some air anyway. You're driving.'

Chapter Eleven

OCTOBER, 1647. AN HOUR before noon. Three rough ropes waited at the gallows, a hungry noose tied at the ends, as three trembling women stepped forward. All had been accused of witchcraft. None had admitted guilt. In the middle of the three stood twenty-four-year-old Iris Carter, watched by her son, John, nearly five-and-a-half and happy, sitting on his father's shoulders in the crowd.

Young John smiled as, one by one, the nooses were hung around the women's necks.

'What's happening, Daddy?'

'God is removing evil from this town, son, and that means your mother, too.'

The three women stepped forward. In the middle, Iris Carter looked out at the crowd, young John poking out above the heads. She didn't look at Daddy.

All three women had been tried by a professional witchfinder. He had pricked them with a pin. Had they bled, he would have let them go. Not bleeding was the sign of a witch. None of these women had bled. The witchfinder had been paid twenty shillings for each. It had been a good payday. He was a professional. An expert. And he was doing the Lord's good work.

Young John watched his mother. He didn't know why one of the women next to her was crying. He loved his mother, and was fascinated by her being up on stage, the centre of attention, the star of the show.

Mummy's special!

Iris Carter did not cry. She stared back at her son with nothing but love in her eyes. It would be the last few seconds of her life and she would spend it in magical love. Poor little John still had no idea what was to come.

The executioner was ready and stood tall, enjoying the knowledge such a crowd had gathered to see him work. His best numbers yet.

Young John, up above the crowd, was secretly excited to go home too. He had made a horse shape out of stones and wanted to show his mother just as soon as they all returned. It was a good horse. It was black with an off-white nose and a tail made of pebbles all the way from the sea. It even had a mane. There was beauty in that horse, the gift to the mother he loved so much. Their mother-son bond was perfect and always would—

Crack.

A silent crowd and three gentle women swinging.

And a small gasp of a child named John, wondering what his mother was doing now and why she was going to sleep. His eyes moved gently, smoothly, and ever so slightly, to the left, to the right, to the left, to the right, and stopped. That's when his expression changed. That's when he realised.

Sweet young John grew up into a big, strong alcoholic. He married Mary, who he beat up when he was three drinks in. He didn't remember seeing his mother's execution, but the moment remembered him well. It never let him go, not until the day he hanged himself. Their own son, Timothy, had watched his father abuse his mother and cried, and he got a beating too when he grew up a bit and tried to interfere.

Timothy also grew up to be a big strong alcoholic who beat his own son, James. Trauma doesn't stop until it's stopped.

James never drank when he grew up. He barely spoke and, too filled with trauma and anxiety to find real work, lived in poverty. He eventually married an equally shy woman named Henrietta, and they had five children. Four died from living in poor, filthy conditions. The survivor, Peter, never got over his sibling's deaths and grew up living on the dirty streets. There, he impregnated a homeless girl called Sally, fourteen, who gave birth and left the child at the roadside. It was adopted by a middle-class family who already had four of their own beautiful children. As such, it was treated as a servant, a workhorse, and never shown any love or attention unless something was needed. It turned to drink at thirteen and lashed out at anyone and everyone. When it finally calmed down a little, it married Jane. They had three kids. It never showed a single one of them any love. It didn't know how. The children all grew up into alcoholics. The most volatile was the middle brother, Alfred. Alfred became an unapologetic wife-beater who spent much of his miserable life in prison.

Ten more generations followed, and nothing changed. The chain of trauma beginning with the brutal hanging of the woman accused of being a witch stayed strong and manifested in various ways, from violence to extreme social withdrawal and alcoholism, as if it were written into the DNA of each and every one of them. If it wasn't alcohol or violence, it was other substances. In 1966, it was a mutual love of heroin that brought together another pair who, in 1970, gave birth to a direct descendent, John, and in 1971, John was beaten for crying. He escaped his brutal father in 1980 and started to improve his life. Social services helped house him, moving him back to the county of Cornwall, the home of his ancestors, where he was given a new surname. Locke. There, he had a string of girlfriends but never married. The Cornish lasses were too savvy to marry such an abusive, vile drunk. Until, in 1995, he met the love of his life, Martha, and married her three years later. Martha had a magical, gentle charm about her, a way that made sure he was never angry, and lived on a lovely little countryside lane next to some woods a few miles from the sea. He started to feel guilty about the way he'd treated his old partners. He was determined he wouldn't treat anyone else in the way he had been treated himself. In 2003, Martha gave birth to Daphne. John was delighted and cried happy tears for the first time. They confused him greatly.

Daphne was a loud, needy baby, and John's tiredness and stress levels boiled over. When Daphne was two, she kept him up all night, and he finally flipped, lashing a fist at Martha while Daphne was in her arms, accidentally hitting Daphne on the side of the head, and then, deliberately, Martha's. Little Daphne watched as her father pushed her mother against the wall and pushed himself close. She had no idea why he licked her mother's cheek, or why she looked so scared as he did. It was a memory that never resurfaced for her to work out.

John disappeared that day and was never seen again. No one knows how. No one knows why. Perhaps there is still a toad living in Hanging Hill Woods who knows a little more about it.

Chapter Twelve

Daphne spread raspberry jam thickly across her breakfast. She had only recently bought a new toaster, having thrown the old one out two years prior, after a demon had used it to drive fear into her by having it eject and spray a dead policeman's fingers across the kitchen. That was one of the memories she hated the most. Andrew Foot had been a lovely man, and he was one of several people who had died because of her. She had counted sixteen people dead at the hands of the demons to get at her. To try to break her. She was finally coming to terms with it, in a way. Logically, she knew it wasn't her fault. But the feeling of guilt still hit hard, especially when reminders showed up.

Now it was happening again. Six more deaths, and Olivia may quickly become the seventh. She wasn't ready for that kind of guilt. She'd never asked for any of this. The realisation struck that the demon, probably the third hunter demon, was out there killing again. And that if it was going for people she loved, both Olivia and Paulie were in huge danger. She felt sick to her stomach, and as she cut the slices of toast and dropped the knife into the sink, she realised her worry had forcefully displaced her hunger. When the doorbell chimed moments later, adrenaline shot through her. She was back on edge, a place she hadn't been for months. Her peace was gone.

People rarely used the doorbell now. The last time it had been used regularly was two years before, during the killings. The street had been very quiet since then, aside from a few macabre photograph hunters. Dark tourists, the local press called them. Houses six to ten, the homes of those slaughtered in the killings, remained empty. No one wanted to move in. The houses were listed for having historical value and couldn't legally be pulled down. They just remained as empty shells and dark reminders every time Daphne walked up the hill. They'd been secured with boards since some ghost-hunting idiots had started breaking in to try and find evidence for their weird delusions of the supernatural.

Daphne approached the door and dreaded looking through the spyhole. Adrenaline flowed harder as she leaned forward to peer through, the closeness of the wood reflecting the soft sound of her shaking breath. Two police officers stood outside. This hadn't happened since the slaughters. Since she'd been attacked by the demons. Since the time she was so desperate to forget. An officer pressed the button again and the bell chimed and echoed through the old house. Daphne opened the door slowly and looked at the vaguely familiar face of the young police constable in front of her.

'Hello again,' said PC Joanne Bach. 'I don't know if you remember me.'

Daphne stared back, hearing the words, her mind too frozen to respond.

'Sorry to bother you. Could we come in for a chat?'

Daphne looked at Joanne Bach and finally, the memory twigged. She had been the lovely officer who had sat with her in her room while she got dressed. One of the few warm faces of the officers that had swarmed through her house. Daphne looked at the other officer. She looked around sixty years old, or perhaps a little older, with grey hair. She was kind of familiar, not because they'd met, but because she reminded Daphne of someone she used to know, perhaps.

'We won't be long,' croaked PC Beverly Trevithick with a smile.

'Cup of tea?' asked Daphne meekly.

The two officers sat in Daphne's lounge while Daphne used the time alone in the kitchen to compose herself as the kettle boiled. Had they come with the news that Olivia was dead? Surely not, those visits were probably reserved for family. Had they been investigating the killings on the street for the last two years and found a whole load of things that didn't add up? Surely to the human police force, a whole load of it would have been confusing as hell. Perhaps they still wanted answers. Was Daphne in trouble? Oh shit... Was it Paulie? Had Paulie called the police after she pushed him over? She hadn't meant to. She had no idea what had happened. She wasn't fighting Paulie. She was fighting the memory of the demon that still apparently lived in her head. As the tannin seeped from bag to brew, Daphne's anxiety seeped from her mind and through her body, and when both were saturated, she carried the three mugs to the lounge with shaking hands to where the two officers quietly waited.

As she stepped towards them, she tripped, her foot hitting something on the floor, and fell forward, spraying hot tea all over the room, spattering the policewomen and smashing one of the mugs into several pieces. Daphne had never felt so embarrassed and stupid in her whole life.

'I'm so sorry,' she said, feeling like she wanted to curl up and die.

'Are you okay?' asked PC Bach.

'I'm sorry,' repeated Daphne, completely struck down with the feeling of stupidity. How could she have been so careless around the police, of all people?

'Nothing we haven't seen a few times before,' said PC Trevithick with a calming smile that helped.

'How can I help?' Daphne asked as a sticky lump of anxiety half clogged her throat as she picked up the pieces of the mugs. 'I'm sorry.'

Constable Bach leant down and picked up another. 'I'm PC Bach, if you remember, and this is PC Trevithick. We're from the missing persons team. We've got a few questions about Olivia Merrigan. You know her, we understand.'

Daphne didn't know what to feel. Relief she wasn't in trouble, sure, a bit. Relief she didn't have to explain any holes in the police's understanding of the killings from two years before? Definitely. Worried about Olivia? More so. Suddenly a broken mug didn't seem so important.

'We lived together at college. We haven't seen each other since, well, since I last saw you, I suppose.'

Joanne Bach looked at her with sympathy. 'Have you had any contact? Phone calls, text messages? Has she been active on social media? Hers is very private.'

'She gets weirdos,' said Daphne, pulling out a handful of tissues from a box and dropping to her hands and knees.

'Weirdos?' came a croak from PC Trevithick.

'If she makes her pictures public online, she gets weirdos. Men, mostly. When her photos are private, they stop. We message occasionally. But not like we used to. Maybe not for six months now.'

'Falling out?' asked PC Trevithick.

'Not really,' said Daphne, ludicrously thinking she might be incriminating herself as her anxiety took over her thoughts again. 'Nothing bad. We just drifted apart. But I'm worried. I'm really worried.'

'You realise who your friends are when they're gone, right?' said PC Trevithick.

'She's gone?' asked Daphne.

'No, I didn't mean that.'

'We don't know where she is, but there's nothing anywhere to say she's been hurt,' reassured Joanne Bach.

'Nothing?' asked Daphne.

'Nothing at all,' croaked Beverly Trevithick.

Daphne scanned their faces to see if they betrayed any details at all, any knowledge or worries. They seemed to be telling the truth.

'I don't know anything. I wish I did,' said Daphne, pulling another load of tissues from the box.

'There must be something,' Bach said to Trevithick quietly, failing to mask her frustration with feigned over-curiosity. They both looked to Daphne. 'It doesn't matter if the details are small. You might know something without realising it's important.'

Of course Daphne knew something. But she couldn't very well try to explain to the police that she was worried her friend had been taken by a demon from another realm to personally scare her into a breakdown to leave her defenceless to allow it to possess her because she was a witch, and a possessed witch would unleash all sorts of terror into the world. That's not the kind of thing you can tell the police. 'I don't know anything.'

'Okay,' came the friendly croak.

'Do you think it may be linked to the beach murders?' asked Daphne. The two looked up at her together.

'Why do you ask that?' said Joanne Bach.

'No reason,' said Daphne, feeling the dots must surely be connected and fishing for something that might help her join them. 'It's just they were both on the news. I'm a bit scared.'

Beverly Trevithick stood and smiled. Joanne Bach stayed put, looking mildly frustrated.

Trevithick put her hat on. 'Don't be afraid, you're not in any danger. None at all. Thank you for your time. Take this card, it's got the number straight to us at missing persons. Just ask for PC Bach or Trevithick. It's written there.'

Constable Bach stood reluctantly and half-smiled at Daphne. 'Nice to see you again. You been okay?'

'Yes, thank you.'

'Have they given you the help you need?'

'Yes, thank you.'

'Me too,' said Bach, then looked a little awkward for a microsecond before her face of friendly authority returned. 'Call any time. Nice to see you.'

'Nice to see you, too,' she replied, although it wasn't. There was no problem with PC Bach, but any authority figure brought Daphne a sense of unease and always had.

The other reason it wasn't nice to see her was more pressing. Last time she had seen her, it was because of the demons. Now she was back, just as it appeared the third demon was. There were too many dots connecting, and they were terrifying.

The two officers left and Daphne's heart finally started to slow. As she cleaned up the spilled tea, she kicked herself again for tripping like that. It was probably over one of her old toys from her childhood toybox she had brought down for Alfie. It was nice seeing Alfie play with her old toys, even if she was forever clearing them up like her mother had once done for her. But when she looked to find the offending article, the object that tripped her, she saw nothing. Nothing at all. And yet she had felt her foot make contact with something very real. The nothing on the floor in front of her brought in a new sense of unease. Of course there wouldn't be any toys on the floor. Alfie hadn't been over alone since Sara had dropped him off in a hurry for an impromptu babysit the evening before the news report that turned her life upside down.

No one seemed to know anything about what was going on. Not Daphne, not Sara, and not the police. They hadn't seemed to know anything about Olivia at all. But the uniformed presence had sparked some kind of connection in Daphne's mind, which came to her in a dawning realisation and a quick intake of breath. There was someone, perhaps, who might know something. A police officer who had been possessed himself. The man who had locked her in her house and told her she would burn when under the control of the demon. Surely he might know something. Perhaps he may have learned something from the demon that took over his mind. He wouldn't be hard to find. It was in all the local papers at the time. Detective Inspector Bright had been put on leave for mental health issues after saying he'd been possessed by the Devil, then investigated and fired for all sorts of dodgy behaviour over the course of his long career. He'd been taken into a mental health hospital and the story went quiet. Perhaps he would still be there. Even the gutter press tended to stop bullying people once they were institutionalised – although their last headline had been 'Mad as a Hatter' with a large photo of a policeman's hat.

A quick online search found one psychiatric hospital in the small town. The Gwydhenn Centre was a twenty-minute walk away. Daphne took a look at the route on her phone map, grabbed a coat and her keys, patted her pocket, and walked out the door.

Chapter Thirteen

THE POLICE CAR CRAWLED back up Hanging Hill Lane, Joanne Bach's muscles constricting and pulling in tightly as Beverly Trevithick drove.

'A bit brown for this time of year,' said Trevithick.

She had always been a kind lady who Joanne Bach had looked up to. But Bach didn't want small talk today. She had a busy mind, occasionally tortured by the flashing image of the man in the car crash, his spine filling with blood. As they passed number six, Joanne Bach stared out the window at the boarded-up doors and windows, the house a shell of what it used to be before trauma had come and taken the street.

Trevithick stared at Bach for as long as was safely possible while driving and said, 'You shouldn't let them know it gets to you, you know. The Baton name thing. If they know, they'll start using it more. Bloody children.'

'I know. I shouldn't have reacted like that. It's been a tough day.' She could feel tears welling up in her eyes. She could tell Beverly Trevithick had noticed.

'Wanna tell me? Just between us. What's this about?'

'I lost my baton. You know that.'

'Well, everyone knows that. You can expect to get some stick for that. If you'll excuse the pun.'

'It gets worse. A witness, who was clearly completely off their rocker, said he saw a small child making off with it. Which is ridiculous and everyone knows it, but adds to the hilarity of it all, apparently.'

'That is quite funny,' smiled Trevithick, 'and everyone knows that too. So why the reaction? It's not like you, we know you can take a joke.'

'I lost it right here on this road when the murders were happening. Daz died a couple of days later.' Bach noticed the smile gently falling from Trevithick's face before she continued. 'When I lost it, he teased me all night about it. Just silly gentle pillow talk teasing. We laughed a lot. It was one of our happiest nights, he made me feel so much better about it, about everything, see the ridiculousness of it so I could stop kicking myself. Taught me to be gentle with myself. It was my birthday, actually. And then two days later, he killed himself. Because of what happened here but no one really knows why. It still makes no sense.'

Beverly Trevithick simply and gently replied, 'Oh, Jo.'

'So yeah. Now it hits me right in the gut when someone calls me that. But I can't tell them to stop or they'll just do it more, like you say.'

'Children.'

'I don't know why I snapped like that. I've kind of done myself over with that, haven't I?'

'I'll have a word with the little boys. Leave it to Mother Bev.'

The car turned onto the main road through the town, a slightly different way to the most direct way, and it didn't go unnoticed that Trevithick was taking Joanne a way she wouldn't pass the school where Joanne had seen the accident, and all without mention. It was silently appreciated.

'You want me to keep your birthdays quiet from now on at the station? If they feel a little difficult after that.'

'No, birthdays are still special. More so, really. He always said birthdays weren't a time to worry about getting old. They were a day to forgive all your fuck-ups of the year, because everyone in history has made them. So, on our birthdays, we forgave each other's and our own fuck-ups. It was our little thing. It kept us strong.' The car turned a slow corner towards the station. 'Don't tell them, please. It's so personal, really. When someone calls me that it hurts. Today, I don't know why it suddenly made me so angry. I guess I still have some forgiving to do, somewhere. Still, I don't know why I let it get to me. It's like there's something missing in my life and that just points at that hole.'

'The real reason is, my young friend,' said Beverly Trevithick as she turned the wheel gently, 'because those guys can be complete six-inch dicks.' She smiled a smile that quickly subsided back to soft sympathy. 'I don't want to overstep, and tell me to piss off if you want, but is that why you always end up on Hanging Hill? Figuratively. Looking for something that's missing? Because that's where it started?'

'The last time I saw him, he was walking into number six to get the family out. He turned to me and smiled as he walked in. He seemed relaxed. And I never saw him again. The police psychologist thinks I'm constantly searching for an answer to put it all to bed because it doesn't make sense, and some part of my brain thinks I'll find closure on Hanging Hill Lane because, as you say, that's where it all happened.'

'And *you* think?'

'I think it's police intuition and I'm good at it.'

'I think you are too.'

Joanne found herself smiling. She looked at the side of Beverly Trevithick's ageing, wrinkled face, such a wonderful lady. She smiled and said with a cheeky grin, 'So why Lance?'

'You little bugger,' said Trevithick with a grin. 'Now that, that really is funny as hell.' Bach leaned forward with a smile of expectation as Trevithick said, 'But I'm not telling you.'

Chapter Fourteen

DAPHNE WAITED NERVOUSLY IN the reception of the Gwydhenn Centre psychiatric hospital with no idea what to expect inside, but hoping she would find DI Bright in there. A receptionist arrived, her reek of a freshly smoked cigarette coming under the glass that separated them, and looked at her impatiently. Daphne suddenly felt guilty, like she shouldn't be there. Visitors should be friends, not strangers. So, feeling under pressure, she lied.

'I'm looking for my friend and wondered if she might be in here. Olivia Merrigan?'

'Not by name. What's she look like?'

'She's twenty-four, blonde, super pretty.'

'Lots of pretty ladies in here right now,' she said without the slightest hint of a care. 'You can go in and look. Sign in.' She slid a lanyard through the hatch as Daphne signed a sheet of paper, and the receptionist pushed a button as if she'd had the whole world asked of her. A light flashed up with a click. Open. Daphne pushed the door, stepped through, and was greeted by a long, sterile corridor. She didn't know what she was supposed to do or where she was supposed to go, but as she'd been buzzed in and given a pass, she guessed she'd just keep walking and work it out.

Several doors lined the dull corridor. Posters adorned pinboards on the old walls about mental health and how to get help. A huge drawing of a penis took up the whole of one poster, undermining the artwork's message about acting responsibly while inside the facility.

A few plastic chairs stood at the sides of the corridors, all empty but one, where a staff member sat looking bored at his phone. He looked up and saw Daphne, dropped his hands into his lap, and tried to look awake. 'Can I help?'

'I'm looking for my friend, Olivia. She's blonde, twenty-four, tall.'

'Head on down to the end there, through the double doors and turn right. You'll get to the communal lounge. That's where they normally all are.'

'"They"?'

'The pretty ones who don't speak.'

Daphne hurried on with a nervous smile, wondering why she was being sent to the mute ward, if there was such a thing. If there was one thing that Olivia was not, it was quiet. She walked up the long corridor towards the double doors, where she pushed, expecting to walk straight in. The doors barely moved, a little stuck. She tried again, pushed a bit harder. They moved an inch and then pushed firmly closed again. She looked back down the corridor to the man, who looked up from his phone and gestured back with his hands to push hard. She pushed harder. They moved two inches, then thudded shut. She looked back again, where the man got more animated and gestured to give the door a good hard shove. She did, and flew through into the next corridor, where she saw two old women sitting on the floor by the doors, laughing.

Daphne turned right and hastened along the corridor as a lone old man looked at her and blew her a kiss as she passed. Then just up ahead on the ceiling was a sign, LOUNGE, and a little arrow to the right through more double doors. She stood at the doorway looking through the glass into the lounge. The term 'lounge' wouldn't normally apply to a space like this, but there were soft chairs, tables and a television, so it came kind of close. A few members of staff hovered at the edges and a few more mingled. Then, walking so very slowly past the glass just the other side, was a beautiful woman with a shell-shocked look on her face. She noticed Daphne on the other side of the glass and jumped back in shock, sending Daphne jumping back too. Then the woman cried where she stood, and a nurse shuffled over to comfort her.

A few other ladies walked around inside with the same look on their faces, walking slowly or sitting down with an occasional jerk or twitch of a face but otherwise seemingly numb to their surroundings. They were all as beautiful as they were confused. And then, walking amongst them, a familiar freckled face. The stricken lady with the button nose and blonde bob walked slowly past, her expression unchanged since the day she was filmed on the clifftop, though already her hair was a little grey right at the roots.

A television played and a few people sat and watched. It was the news, continuing the story of the murders on the beach, pop star Boddy's scantily clothed photograph taking up half the screen.

Daphne pushed tentatively through the doors and stepped into the lounge to check for Olivia. Perhaps she would be there after all. It all felt connected somehow.

A couple of nurses looked at her, making her feel self-conscious, then one of the shell-shocked ladies flinched, taking Daphne's attention for a second before she scanned the room. Olivia wasn't there. But another familiar face was. The man she had come to see.

Sitting at a table alone, looking a decade older than the last time she had seen him two years before, now with long scraggly hair and skin starting to peel from the sides of his face, was the man in charge of the police during the six-eight-ten killings. The man Daphne recognised instantly as Detective Inspector Bright. Adrenaline filled her body and her vision turned to black.

✴ ✴ ✴ ✴ ✴

Daphne, sitting in her chair in her lounge looking up at DI Bright as his eyes glow red and his sockets sink back into his skull.

'You. Will. Burn.'

Daphne, sitting with her back against her front door. The Demon monster right in her face, revealed by a layer of police pepper spray. The monster, licking her face, covering it in stinking sticky slime. The tongue touches her cheek and slides up to her earhole. It slides slowly inside.

Daphne, looking at a painting in her room that should not exist. A painting of a demon monster that no one had painted.

Daphne, looking at a blistering head in the oven in her kitchen, eyes bulging and ready to burst.

Panic. Darkness.

✴ ✴ ✴ ✴ ✴

Daphne opened her eyes, her first sight being her own hands shivering and shaking, feeling terrified to her core. Three mental health nurses surrounded her in a private room. Two nurses left while one crouched with her, and minutes must have passed while she got her breathing under control because one returned with a cup of tea seemingly immediately. As she started to slowly feel like herself again, and her breathing slowed and calmed, she managed a small smile for the nurse.

The nurse smiled back. 'You chose the right place for that to happen. You won't find a member of staff here who doesn't deal with panic attacks most days. Clutch that hot cuppa and let it warm you and you'll feel better. Just feel the warmth and breathe. You're okay, my lovely.' She was so calm and reassuring and Daphne felt much better quickly.

'Who are you here to visit?' asked the nurse.

'I'm looking for a friend, but she isn't in there,' she said, continuing the lie that got her through the front door.

'You're really worried about her, aren't you?'

'I am, but that wasn't why that happened. Something reminded me of something but I'm okay now. Really, I'm okay.' Daphne leant over to see through the glass in the door, where she could see the once-Detective Inspector. It was him. Bright. 'That man over there, is he a policeman?'

'I can't give information about the patients, I'm sorry,' said the kindly nurse.

If anyone had answers, it could be him. This was a man who had been possessed by a demon – the third demon that was responsible for the chaos surrounding her – and now, in this psychiatric unit, he was either driven mad by the demon or was sectioned for telling the truth. If there was anyone who knew anything about what was happening, if anyone could start connecting the dots, it was Detective Inspector Bright. But she was terrified of him and the memories he brought.

The nurse spoke softly, bringing Daphne's attention back to her. 'You're allowed to talk to the residents. What's your name?'

'Daphne.'

'Well, Daphne, this isn't a prison or like the horrible old places you see in films. This is a modern hospital, even if the building is a little rickety. We encourage visits and contact. It's good for the people here. I'm sorry your friend isn't here, but it wouldn't be a waste of time to say hello. He could use a visit. It would be lovely for him to have a chat with someone new. Up to you, of course. If and when you're feeling better.'

The man had barricaded her in her house with not one but two demons. The man had told her he was glad her mother was dead. The man had tried to destroy her. Except it wasn't the man who did any of those things, was it? That was the demon inside him, controlling him, that eventually changed him from a Detective Inspector in the police force to a live-in patient at a psychiatric hospital. The same demon that was now probably back, preparing to rain havoc on her life. Daphne had something in common with that man. They had both been the victims of the events two years before.

Yes, she'd planned to come and speak to him. But now that she could actually see him, the prospect felt terrifying, and she felt her anxiety return to pin her feet to the floor. It was like being seventeen again.

The whole atmosphere felt the same as two years before. Now and then felt very much connected. And if they were connected, then this DI – *ex*-DI – Bright might know something about it. Something about Olivia. Something about the women who slowly jerked around him. Something about what the hell was going on. She had no choice but to talk.

'Are you okay?' asked the lovely nurse. 'You're starting to look a little pale again. Sip your tea. You want some sugar? Sweetness can help.'

Daphne looked down at her drink. The fingers on her right hand were white from gripping the mug handle so hard, so she relaxed herself to avoid pulling the handle clean off. She was deeply frightened, and she knew it. But she had to do it. That man was the shell where a demon used to be. Empty shells aren't scary. Or they shouldn't be. 'No, thank you,' she said to the kind nurse, then looked back at Bright, who had a glazed look on his face as he peeled off a two-inch flake of skin from his cheek and popped it disgustingly into his mouth.

Daphne stopped sipping her tea. 'Thank you for your help. I'll finish my drink then say hello.'

The nurse smiled and stood, walked to the door, and turned. 'Gordon's harmless. Everyone here is. Nothing to worry about.'

The nurse left and softly pushed the door closed. Daphne stood and walked to the glass, clutching the comfort of the warm mug in both hands as she looked out across the room to Bright. *Gordon* Bright. How could anyone called *Gordon* be scary? Especially as in the last two years his chin and neck had grown downwards and flappy, and now looked a little like the wattle of a chicken. That thought made Daphne smile, and with it, the fear faded a bit. The Detective Inspector was now just Gordon. *Gordon.*

Daphne put her mug down, then picked it back up, deciding a still-warm comfort blanket might not be a bad thing even if it was empty. She opened the door and stepped into the room amongst the slow-moving, silent women as she walked towards the Detective Inspector. Gordon. Just Gordon.

Gordon didn't look up, leaving Daphne standing opposite him at his table, looking down at him, heart pounding.

Finally, Bright looked up. The look of recognition was tiny and fleeting, but there.

'Hello again,' said Daphne with a quiver. 'Can I sit?'

Gordon Bright gestured for her to sit as he started to scan the room as if for danger, but with half a look of excitement in his eyes too.

'Is he back? Has he come back for me?'

'Thank you for remembering me,' said Daphne.

'I remember you well, little ant,' he said. 'No mushroom popping out of your head, I see. Lucky you. Not yet.'

Perhaps his sanity had been completely ripped out of him by the demon inside his mind. That would be no surprise at all.

The silent women continued their slow, circular march around the room. Daphne became silent too. She had no idea what to say. It was a situation so completely alien to her. But then Gordon Bright made it easy.

'What do you want, Daphne Locke?'

The name surprised her a little, even though it was her own, and she quickly worked through the anxious fog in her brain but came up with nothing, her brain freezing. It was easier just to continue the lie, even though it didn't make sense anymore.

'I'm looking for my friend, Olivia. I was hoping she might be here.'

'Well, is she?'

'No.'

'Or is she?'

'No.'

'Look closer.'

Daphne looked around at the face of every woman in the room. None were Olivia. 'No.'

Bright looked at Daphne and gave a big, bright, knowing smile. 'The mushrooms pop out the top of the heads.' He placed the tip of a forefinger on the top of his head. 'Pop.'

'I need help, Mr Bright.'

'He is here,' Bright said with a creeping smile that terrified Daphne, who looked over her shoulder so fast she startled two of the women.

She saw nothing.

'He is not,' said Bright, bringing relief. 'He is near.'

This was just more nonsense. Daphne fought the block in her stomach and mind, something refusing her entry to the question she wanted to ask. But she fought it, felt the warmth of the tea mug in her hands, and won.

'What happened two years ago. Is it happening again now?'

'Dot,' he replied, and rested his forehead on the table and closed his eyes.

'Dot?'

Bright didn't open his eyes or move his head at all. While his head looked peaceful as it lay face down on the surface, his voice sounded agitated. 'Dot. I know you wish to connect the dots. If it's back, what does it want? Is it me again? Dot.' He rolled his head to the side and smiled softly as if the tabletop was the most comfortable surface in the world. Then he opened his eyes quickly, giving Daphne a little jump. 'Okay, Miss Locke. Make yourself at home.

Home amongst the ultra-sane and the crazies. Be comfortable.'

Daphne was sitting on a hard plastic chair in a room full of silent, weirdly-moving women in front of a man who had almost destroyed her. There was no way she would be making herself comfortable.

Bright sat up and back before he started, and wiped his finger through the grease mark his hair had left on the table. 'Somewhere, living in an underground labyrinth of roots and fungus is a nematode worm. Understand?'

She understood the words but not the relevance.

'What do you know about roots, fungi, and nematode worms, Daphne?'

'Not much.'

'As good as nothing. There is an entire world underground as above, vast networks of roots all controlled by the fungus. Picture that, the roots of plants and trees are controlled by the fungus and not the plant. So much of your life, so much of the world, is controlled by the fungus. More than you will ever know. And somewhere underground, right now, a nematode worm is being crushed by the fungus to be devoured. Do you care about that tiny, inconsequential nematode worm, Daphne?'

Her mind pulled a blank.

'It's a very straightforward question.'

'No.'

'Why? Don't answer, I'll tell you. Because it's tiny and irrelevant to your life and before right now, you didn't even know anything about it. So you don't care. Now, take that huge network you knew nothing about, and make it greater by a factor of a number too big for your tiny, tiny little stupid mind to comprehend, and then take something worthy of living in that greater, superior network. Would they care about that pathetic nematode worm?'

'No?' she guessed.

'Quite right. And would they care about a single human? No. In the same way you don't care about that nematode worm. Unless, of course, the worm was a delicacy.'

'They want to eat us?'

'No no no no no no no no!' Bright raged with quiet venom, his wattle swinging under his chin as he shook his head. Then he stopped and smiled. 'Because when you say *us,* you mean *them.* Worms. You are not a human. I know that. I saw everything. You are not human. You are not nematode. You, little Daphne, are ant.'

'Ant?'

'Keep on track, Daphne. Fungus! Do you not watch nature? There is a fungus that will inhabit an ant and control its movement from inside. The ant becomes a zombie ant. A fungi-ant, and it does what the fungus wants it to do, just like the roots of the plants do. And what is that? I don't hear you ask. It wants it to climb up above the colony. And what happens then? It sits on a leaf and dies painfully, and then a mushroom pops out from its head and drops spores onto the other ants below so they can all die and spread death too. You not worm. You ant.' He looked embarrassed for a half second. 'Me worm.'

'I don't understand.'

'Because you have a tiny mind that has not seen.' He put his fingertip back on the top of his head. 'Pop. See?'

'How do we stop the demons?'

'Ah, that's easy. There is an easy way. I will tell you because you will not understand. As I say, it all comes down to your patheticness.'

'What is it?'

'Those who sniffle and snuffle the truffles.'

'What's a truffle?' asked Daphne.

'Are you next going to ask me what a truffle pig is?'

Daphne was getting nowhere. She'd hoped for some information on what on earth was going on, perhaps a lead to find Olivia, and was getting a lesson, if indeed any of it was grounded in reality, in fungus and insects. She was getting frustrated.

'Any questions, tiny ant?'

'Why are you being so cryptic?' Daphne asked, annoyance rising inside her and making her hand tremble.

A soft and shaky female voice from somewhere in the room poked out above the murmur. 'Hair.'

Again, from a different corner, 'Hair.'

'I think I've been very helpful,' continued Bright. 'Anyway. They've sniffed you.'

'Who?' Daphne looked around the room.

A woman was creeping towards her. She was young but haggard, moving slowly and stiffly. She broke her silence with an elongated whisper. 'Haaaair.'

Daphne self-consciously ran her hand through her hair, wondering what was wrong with it.

'An ant did this, I assume,' smiled Bright.

Daphne looked around. Some of the silent women were staring at her.

Another one spoke softly but straight at her. 'Hair.'

Then another. The women from the boat were all staring at her, and more were starting to speak, their voices breaking from whisper to voice, getting louder. 'Hair. Hair.'

'You should go, now.' That was the first direct thing Bright had said the whole conversation, and it didn't get much clearer than that.

More of the women were staring at her. Then all. Every last one.

'Hair.'

'Hair.'

One voice sounded closer than the rest and she whipped her head around to see the glare of a woman with a curly blonde bob and freckled face, the vacuum behind her eyes now replaced with hatred. 'Hair,' she hissed.

Daphne stood from her seat and backed away from the freckled woman.

'Hair.'

'Why are they saying that?' asked Daphne.

'They smell ant,' said Bright. 'Worms can smell too. And while worms fear fungus, perhaps today you should fear the nematode, little ant.'

The room was full of monotone female voices. 'Hair. Hair.'

Daphne's hands trembled with fear. 'Where's Olivia?'

Bright put up his open palms. 'Who?'

'Tell me.'

'Hair. Hair.' The women were getting closer. Confused nurses tried to guide some back to seats but they did not move their glares from Daphne. 'Hair, hair,' as Daphne hastened towards the double doors.

Gordon Bright stood and, somehow looking more human, called out to Daphne. 'Question the bean-nighe,' he shouted over more chants. 'She can tell you what you need to know. Ask her anything, and she will tell. Is that clear enough for you?'

'What?' replied Daphne, struggling to hear over the women, one hand on the double door as the women inched closer, glaring at her with anger, the chant getting louder.

'Hair. Hair. Hair.'

'The bean-nighe,' shouted Bright, now with a look of genuine concern. 'Find her, find the washerwoman. Go, go now!'

Daphne bolted from the room and down the corridor, turning through the next set of double doors. She looked back down the corridor to see the women marching slowly after her, their shock and fear now fury as they continued their monosyllabic chant.

'Hair.'

Daphne ran on to the final set of double doors. The huge picture of the cock and balls next to her wasn't so funny this time. She pulled on the doors but they didn't open. She pulled harder and they just rattled, locked firmly shut.

'Hair, hair,' grew louder and nearer. Behind her, the slow-marching women approached, slowly, step by step. 'Hair, hair,' their faces contorting with rage, glaring right at her. The doors rattled harder, the handles firmly in Daphne's fists.

'Hair, hair, hair.'

The women came close. And they all walked with death in their eyes. Closer. The door rattled louder and the chants grew fiercer. 'Hair, hair.' The women, metres away now. And a buzz. The door light flashed on, and Daphne burst through, closing the doors hard behind her. They locked with a click. The woman at reception looked at her as if she was stupid.

'You have to touch your pass to get out,' she said. 'It's not difficult.'

Daphne threw back her lanyard and ran out of the entrance of the Gwydhenn Centre hospital, across the car park, and out into the road, where normal life suddenly looked surprisingly jarring.

A motorbike roared in the distance.

A squirrel stopped and stared.

A leaf gently fell from the trees.

# Chapter Fifteen

It took Daphne fifteen minutes to walk back to Hanging Hill Lane at a pace that left her feeling breathless and unfit, trying to process what had just happened with every step. Bright had spoken in riddles yet sounded so convincing. The women had singled her out. They knew she was different.

The instinctive thought fell into her mind to message Paulie and seek the feeling of safety he brought. But then the horrible memory hit her: she'd ruined everything with him. She checked her phone to see if he had messaged, but there was nothing. More than anything, she just wanted to know he was safe.

As soon as her mind could spare a moment, she would message him and ask to meet and fix things. She hated what she had done. It had felt like it was someone else doing it – she watched the incident in her memory as if she were watching a stranger push him to the floor, and she hated that stranger. It had felt weirdly like that at the time, too, as if she were watching from above as she assaulted the first man she thought she might love. She didn't recognise herself.

She reached the curve at the top of Hanging Hill Lane as a dark cloud passed across the sun and a cold breeze brushed her face as the light quickly dipped. As she rounded the bend, she stopped, her way blocked by a short figure dressed in green. It was the young girl. Now closer, Daphne had a clear look. The girl stood, staring back at Daphne, almost bulging out of her green school dress. The top parts of the dress were held together by raw vines and thin tree branches, and the thorns on one side cut into her skin. She was filthy. One eye looked in awful condition, bloodshot and weeping gunk and pus. Her toes poked through the front of her shoes, her black toenails so long they curled. She stood and stared back at Daphne, holding a short black metal stick as though ready to defend herself.

'Are you okay?' asked Daphne with genuine concern.

The girl looked at her and slowly and cautiously walked towards her, studying her through her one good eye. Daphne looked around for an adult, perhaps a parent or just anyone who could help, but the child was alone. When the young girl got close enough, her face turned. No longer scared or timid, she grimaced and grinned and whacked Daphne hard on the side of the calf with the stick with such speed she heard the *whoosh* through the air. A split-second later it hit with a hard thwack that stung like hell and left Daphne hopping backwards. The girl followed her and cracked her other shin, and pain shot through Daphne's legs. She quickly hopped away, not wanting to abandon the child but mostly wanting to get far enough away not to be hit again. The young girl accelerated and hit Daphne once, twice, three times more, stinging her calves and knees, and she accelerated around and past the girl and away down the road.

The girl chased, her evil grin not subsiding for a second. As Daphne slowed down, she got another whack from the hard metal stick right on the ankle bone, causing her to hop once before accelerating again. When Daphne neared her house, she slowed down to get her keys from her bag and got a hard rap on the back of the knuckles as she fumbled for the zip.

'Stop it!' she shouted, and ran to her door. As she put her key in the lock, she felt three more stinging blows to her legs. And though the urge hit her to turn around and boot the little shite, instead, the door opened and she jumped in and pushed it firmly closed behind her. Daphne turned and looked through the spyhole. She couldn't see anyone out there. Nothing. Until the child backed away from the door and stared back towards her. A large black crow flew down and landed on her shoulder, and appeared to lean into the girl's face as if kissing her on the cheek, then flew away over the trees. The girl's grin dropped as she turned around and, as though following the bird, skipped joyfully down the road into Hanging Hill Woods.

'What the hell?' Daphne said to herself as she sat on her sofa and pulled away her clothes to see the array of red marks that had almost drawn blood.

And then it twigged. Where she'd seen the girl. Her face had been on the news a lot two years before, and occasionally since, but it had changed. She had gone missing from a nearby street at the same time as the murders on her road and become a high-profile case. She looked different from her photos in a very sad way, a little older as if aged by stress, bigger, dirtier and in a horrible state. Could it be? Daphne grabbed her phone and searched for the name she had in her mind.

Penelope Pengilly.

It was definitely her, even if the evil grin hadn't matched the online photos of the sweet girl who had gone missing from just a few streets away two years before, right at the time the demons had been here last.

Dot.

Daphne hated that dot. She hated how they may be joining up. As the anxiety rose through her chest and dried her mouth, it felt like the dots were joining around her neck and starting to constrict.

Somehow, this dot pulled harder than the rest and she felt it in the front of her throat.

Daphne picked up the card with the number for the missing persons police team. She was just about to dial when she realised she would rather not get drawn into a police visit right now. She had something else to discover. She anonymously called the standard police line, very quickly told them she had seen Penelope Pengilly on Hanging Hill Lane, and hung up.

She knew exactly who the washerwoman was.

Minutes later, she walked out the front door.

Chapter Sixteen

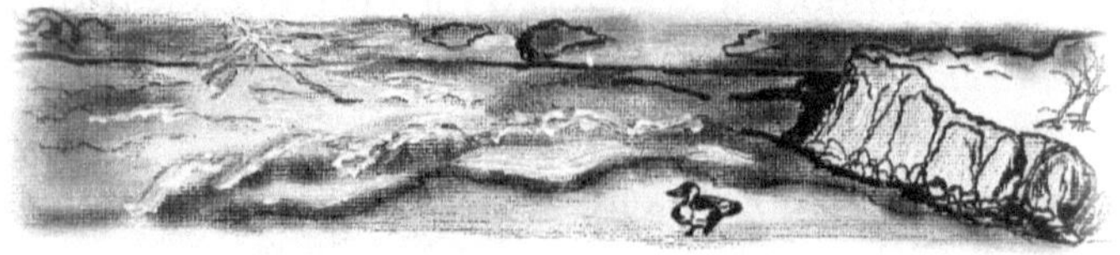

Darkness and the faint smell of salt. A thin sheet of sunlight pierced the cracks between the wooden slats, illuminating sparse particles of dust into a subtle, peaceful glow as they wafted softly on the salty air in the small, dim space. It was quiet, save for the gentle sound of the not-so-distant sea, and a gently stifled sob that somehow blended with the wind and water as if in harmony, and gently punctuated the otherwise peaceful rhythm of the nearby waves, crunching in over the sand and shells, the pebbles clacking as each wave's *whoosh* faded.

Olivia lay naked on the floor.

She'd never ever felt so scared before.

Chapter Seventeen

THE NEW MISPER OFFICE was quiet, aside from the occasional flurry of fingers on keys. There had been no news on Mattey nor the missing father with the baby and little progress anywhere – apart from one thing. Olivia Merrigan's laptop had been obtained by a response officer, with family permission granted to crack her passwords and check her social media messages and feeds. It would take a couple more hours for the tech team to get in, and then they hoped for progress. This felt like a key moment. Without it, they still had nothing.

When the phone rang, Detective Ovary answered. Joanne Bach listened.

Ovary sighed and said, 'Anonymous? Hoax? We'll check it out. Where was the sighting?'

The room went even more quiet.

'Yeah, that sounds pretty hoaxy but we'll get someone there. Thanks.'

He put down the phone, looked up to the room, and said, 'We need someone to run back down to the countryside for us.'

'Sure,' replied Jim. 'Where?'

'Hanging Hill Lane.' Everything stopped. The room somehow went quieter. 'The bottom end, down by the woods. Probably another hoax but we've got to check it. It's Penelope Pengilly.'

'Bloody hell, not again,' said Tim.

'I'll go.' Joanne Bach felt tiny, judged by every man in the room. But it had to be her. 'We're waiting on Merrigan's access here. I can go.'

The Sergeant looked back blank-faced and said simply, gently, 'Okay.'

Tim walked over with a mouth full of cake. 'No luck with the blonde yet?'

'She's not going to be your girlfriend. See you in an hour,' said Beverly Trevithick, standing.

Joanne Bach picked up her jacket and felt an unexpected fear cascade through her body. Something about getting in a car suddenly terrified her, the image of the crashed driver flashing up in her mind. The schoolchildren in the window. The tree with the heart in the bark. When she looked up, the whole room was looking at her, and Bach wondered if they could somehow see her fear, or the images that had flooded through her mind. Of course not.

'Alright then,' croaked Beverly Trevithick, placing her untouched slice of cake back on the table.

Joanne Bach had never found getting into a car so difficult before. But she had to go to Hanging Hill Lane. She had to get into the car and breathe. She had to pretend she was okay.

Chapter Eighteen

DAPHNE WALKED OUT OF her front door, and immediately pretended not to see the police car coming down the road, and hurried into the woods. *Find the washerwoman*, rang through Daphne's mind in the voice of Gordon Bright. She knew exactly who that might be. Her stick-whipped legs stung as she accelerated into the thickening undergrowth.

For as long as she could remember, an old homeless woman had lived in these woods. Every time she recalled seeing her, she had always been down by the stone bridge over the stream washing her clothes. It made sense before. A homeless person needs somewhere to wash clothes. But all the time? She never did anything else. She'd always had a feeling of unease at seeing her but had put that down to the guilt of living in a cosy old house so close to an elderly homeless woman. But now she realised that feeling hadn't been guilt at all. It was pure dark unease. That had to be the washerwoman, the bean-nighe as Bright had called her. Daphne rushed into the woods, then slowed as she approached the old bridge.

Sure enough, there she was. She must have been well over seventy years old, hunched over the stream, washing a dirty stained garment. A small gap in the thorny undergrowth ahead would allow Daphne to get through to the clearing where the washerwoman crouched, and Daphne watched for a while as the old bean-nighe went about her endless and now unsettling laundry routine. Something felt very wrong about the whole thing. The uneasy feeling flooded in. The old anxiety that had nailed her feet to the floor returned. Only this time, it felt like it had good reason. Daphne managed a shaky step towards the gap in the bushes, but no more, fear holding her back from stepping further. She looked back over her shoulder, back up the path through the undergrowth. That path led to failure. That way led to the near-certain loss of Olivia, if she wasn't gone already. So she stepped another two steps towards the clearing, and again, her legs decided to stop moving. As her thoughts turned to her old friend, her memory took her to the time on the beach when she struggled to make her first approach. That time, she had lost her battle against the nails of anxiety until Olivia had invited her forward. That time, she had promised next time she would not fail. That next time was now, and it was terrifying. As she felt like she was about to lose that fight again, a picture of Olivia filled her mind, sitting on the beach, raising her sunglasses up onto her forehead.

You coming or what?

Daphne stepped carefully towards the gap, legs feeling weak as she approached.

An old line of dirty twine stretched from the disused stone bridge to a tree with a few bits of cloth and clothing draped from it. Shirts. A suit jacket. A small dress weird enough for a pop star. On the ground beside her was a pile of clothing, all stained with blotches of a dark colour. She'd never got this close to her before. Her mother had always subtly moved to keep her distance, and Daphne had learned subconsciously to do the same, something deep inside her trying to pull her away by filling her with the unease that was now filling every corner of her mind.

The gap through the undergrowth looked anything but inviting. The ground at the bottom was thick with roots, one looping up ankle-high as though designed to trip anyone trying to pass through. Insects buzzed and clicked in the bushes on either side. The large thorns of the undergrowth were somehow highlighted by the beams of light that seeped through the trees above. Stepping through that gap between the bushes, something felt deeply wrong. But Daphne knew she needed this strange old lady. Or at least needed to know what Bright had meant. If anyone could make sense of what was going on, if anyone knew how to help Olivia, it would be her. While Daphne stepped over the looped root and avoided the thorns quietly, her last step into the small clearing was onto a stick that cracked so loudly it echoed through the woodland, causing birds to flap away and Daphne to stop suddenly, her heart beating so fast she could feel it pounding against her ribs. The washerwoman did not look up or even seem to notice.

As Daphne walked closer, the washerwoman's face became clearer, and as it did, fear welled up further in Daphne's gut. And though she hadn't used the word to describe anyone since she'd been a young teen, there was only one word to describe her.

She was ugly.

She had a hooked nose with some kind of growth on it. Her skin was dirty and cracked. One eye must have been half an inch higher than the other. As Daphne moved close enough to speak, she noticed the woman's biggest, weirdest abnormality.

She only had one nostril.

The washerwoman squeezed the garment and red-tinged water poured into the stream as something with a tail scuttled through the undergrowth in the woodland behind her.

The adrenaline in Daphne's gut and the mounting stress in her brain did not make for a powerful voice when she spoke.

'Excuse me.' The washerwoman showed no sign of noticing. Daphne took another step closer and stopped. 'Are you the bean-nighe?'

The old woman turned her head slowly and looked up at Daphne. She really was the most diabolically ugly woman Daphne had ever seen in her life. Somehow her expression made her features even more repulsive. She was positively disgusting. Daphne was a little surprised when the washerwoman's voice came out in a broad Scottish accent.

'A question for a question.'

'You're the bean-nighe, right? The washerwoman?'

'Aye, yes.' The bean-nighe smiled creepily, revealing how few teeth she had left. 'Now here is my question to you.'

Daphne hadn't come for games. She'd come for answers. Olivia was missing, Daphne felt her own world was about to fall apart, and this one person may have been able to give her an answer.

'My question is,' the washerwoman said, then paused, looking at Daphne while chewing on God-knows-what before spitting it out into the stream. The thing she spat out moved, crawled for a second, and died. Then she snapped her question right at Daphne's face. 'Do you know that you are just a stupid cunt?'

Daphne was stunned.

'Answer me, stupid witch.'

The bean-nighe knew. Of course she knew. She was part of all this. The old woman she'd seen in the woods her whole life had always been part of this, part of the supernatural that Daphne had barely begun to find her way through. And now here she was, as unpleasant as she was ugly.

'I don't think I am. I mean, I'm not.' Somehow, of those two words, it was 'stupid' that had stung the most.

The bean-nighe looked her up and down and smirked an ugly smirk. 'Time will tell, time will tell. Next question. Next question for a question.'

Daphne was confused. Of course this was never going to be easy. But this was just weird. All she wanted was an answer from anybody, be it Gordon Bright or the washerwoman, and all she was getting was weird lectures about fungus and ants and getting called a cunt.

'My friend Olivia is missing. Olivia Merrigan. Do you know where she is?'

The bean-nighe looked back at her and pushed a finger into her single nostril. 'Aye.'

'Where?'

'A question for a question.' The elongated vowel sounds usually so charming in the accent of Scotland somehow managed to sound thin and sharp, and as if each microsecond of elongation was deliberately holding Daphne up further.

Daphne's fear was fast turning to anger. This woman had answers and was playing with her. And yet through it all, she was really struggling not to keep noticing how ugly she was. The bean-nighe spoke through her ugly mouth and flaking lips, and something crunched the leaves behind her as it crept through the undergrowth. She took her finger from her nostril and wiped it on the ground.

'Do you know you are a killer?'

This was easier. 'No. Where is Olivia?'

The bean-nighe laughed a disgusting laugh and dribble stretched and slid from the corner of her mouth. 'She is exactly where she needs to be. Hidden in the dark.'

Daphne was about to snap with rage.

'But,' the washerwoman continued, 'she will find you when she is ready. Until then, she is in the dark, hidden, where she needs to be. Now. A question for a question.'

Daphne had had enough. 'You don't know anything. It's just a stupid game. If you know something, tell me!'

The washerwoman took another garment off the pile and plunged it into the stream with an ugly snigger. 'You will soon find out,' she said, and then held eye contact with Daphne as she squeezed a deep red liquid from the clothes into the muddy stream. 'I think you will find the answer quite, let's say, involving.'

It hit Daphne that she wasn't going to get answers here. Only torment. And if the washerwoman was tormenting her, deliberately getting under her skin, then she was likely in league with the demons, another tool to break her. Daphne had nothing else to say. She glared at the bean-nighe for just long enough to project that she wasn't running away, then turned and stepped towards the path.

'Locke,' the washerwoman called, and Daphne turned around. 'The moment the stupid in you blossomed, you lost.' The washerwoman turned back to the water and pushed some cloth deep under, and mumbled to herself just loud enough for Daphne to hear, 'And blossom wildly, it did, aye.'

Daphne's anger drove her back through the gap in the undergrowth with less care than when she entered. The thorn she brushed past drew an unusual amount of blood, and it flowed down over the stick-whipped bruises now growing on her shins and calves as she hurried towards home.

Chapter Nineteen

THE MISPER ROOM WENT quiet when Joanne Bach and Beverly Trevithick stepped in. Their trip back to Hanging Hill Lane had turned up nothing as expected.

Stupid hoaxsters.

No one on the quiet old street had even answered their doors. Most of the houses seemed vacant now. A Penelope Pengilly sighting, on Hanging Hill Lane of all places, was almost certainly a hoax, but Joanne Bach still took any excuse to get down there and scope it out. She could recognise she might appear akin to a kid fascinated by the Bermuda Triangle, but the feeling was so strong. She was still learning to ignore it. The weird events of recent days had made the urge stronger again. The opportunity to glance at number six and see her final memory of her fiancé was a pull, too, even if it hurt.

A civilian was stripping the wall of the photographs of all the women who were now safe, physically at least, in the psychiatric hospital. Another civvy boiled the kettle. Jim and Tim tapped away on their computers.

'Any news on Mattey?' asked Joanne Bach.

'Nothing,' replied Tim and Jim in unison.

Joanne and Beverly sat. Photos of Olivia scrolled by on Trevithick's computer.

The door burst open. An angry man stormed in, stocky in build but haggard in face as though he'd been through several years of psychological torture. A flustered, very young uniformed constable followed.

'Sorry,' said the young man.

'That's okay,' said Sergeant Cox. 'Mr Pengilly. How can we help?'

Joanne Bach had been unofficially briefed on Peter Pengilly. The father of a missing child who was now long lost and very unlikely to ever return, he wasn't giving up. No one could blame him for wanting his daughter back, but he was a frustration to the small local police force, demanding money and resources be poured into this long-lost cause, kicking up a stink if he didn't get his way. It really didn't help that he was an editor at a local newspaper, the cheapest shitrag of them all, and pushed his agenda by making the police look incompetent whenever he felt progress wasn't being made. His daughter had received more press coverage than any other missing person in the history of the small town, possibly in the whole history of Cornwall. Of course, internet armchair detectives were convinced he was guilty of murdering his own daughter, and that his behaviour was just a front to deflect the police. As far as the police were concerned, he'd been scrubbed off the suspect list the same afternoon he was put on it.

'What's going on then?' demanded a flustered Peter Pengilly. 'And tell your new copper kid to get some bloody manners.'

'I'll have a word,' replied Cox.

'So there's a whole team looking for my daughter now? Looks like they've finally put some bloody money into it. About time.' Peter Pengilly's attention was taken by the photograph of Olivia Merrigan on the wall. Briefly captivated by it, he pulled his mind back to what he came for. 'What you got then? Anything? You've got something new, right? I can feel it in my piss. Just tell me it's not the nonces.'

Sergeant Cox, ever calm, said, 'We're still working on it, Mr Pengilly. Still checking any lead that comes in.'

'You've had leads? What leads?' He paused and looked thoughtful, then worried. 'Not the nonces, right?' His voice cracked a little and his eyes glistened with tears, which he tried to cover with some extra bluster. 'I'll find her myself at this rate.'

'There is no reason to suspect that, Mr Pengilly, no. I'm sorry we can't tell you more.'

'It's been two years. What have you been doing?'

A message flashed up on all the computer screens. Jim looked up. 'Sarge.' He looked to Peter Pengilly. 'Sorry, one moment.'

All the officers read the message on their screens in silence. Two phone masts had pinged, set off by a text message from Mattey's phone, sent moments ago.

Ovary said, 'That's the south coast masts.'

Cox followed, 'The clifftop. He might be on that stretch of cliffs. Jim, get in the car right now and get down there. Grab that photo and get eyes on Mattey. Go, now.'

Jim stood.

'Tim. You need a mental health worker, a negotiator if that's all there is, someone who's trained to talk. Jim, why are you still here? Go!'

Jim sped out the door and Tim gathered a few things.

'By the time you get there hopefully Jim will have eyes on Mattey. Go, now.'

Tim sped out the door past an irritated Peter Pengilly, who shook his head in disbelief.

'So, one man decides to top himself, his own free choice to end his own shitty life, and you lot scramble like the Jerry are flying in over the channel. But my little daughter, not her fault, a sweet, sweet girl who just wanted to play, and after two years you're still sitting here with your thumbs up each other's arses. What the bloody hell are you playing at? For fuck's sake.'

'Mr Pengilly,' said sergeant Cox, 'language, please.'

'I don't give a shiny shit about language. My daughter is missing, you lot are doing fuck all about it, and you're complaining about the sounds that come out of my fucking mouth?'

Sergeant Cox maintained his calm as he said, 'I'm sorry, Mr Pengilly. We have rules about that and we have to follow them too. We are looking for her, we promise. But for now, I have to ask you to leave because that's the rules all of us have to adhere to regarding language. But Detective Ovary here can certainly have a chat with you outside the room.'

'Language.' Pengilly shook his head.

'We have your number,' said Cox.

Pengilly turned and left. 'Language,' he scoffed one more time as he slammed the door behind him. By the time Ovary had reopened the door to follow, he was at the far end of the corridor being shown out by the young officer. 'Fucking language,' came the echoed shout down the hallway and into the misper room.

Sergeant Cox turned and walked back through the room towards his office. 'What a shit,' he muttered, almost quietly enough to have been to himself.

'Poor guy,' said Joanne Bach after Cox had left. 'Must be hard for him.'

'She's gone,' said Beverly Trevithick. 'It's sad but he needs to accept it now. She's nothing but a regular news story and hoax calls now. Poor girl. He needs to learn to let go. Then he'll have a life to live again.'

'He's had no closure,' said Joanne Bach. 'He's in an endless loop of hell. We need to make it make sense for him.'

Beverly Trevithick looked back softly.

'So, Mattey's phone ping,' said Joanne Bach. 'That's the last place Miss Merrigan's phone pinged too, right? Are we sure she's not at the bottom of the cliffs?'

Beverly Trevithick smiled and said, 'Closure. It's a wonderful thing when you can get it.'

Chapter Twenty

DAPHNE HAD BARELY SLEPT. She was worrying about the killings on the beach, and not knowing what happened was inducing more anxiety than if she knew for sure whatever it was that had done it. She was worrying about all the things that might happen. Worrying about Olivia, who she might never see again, coming to the same brutal fate. Every time the thought of going to her mother for help appeared – and the thought still appeared even two years after her passing almost as much as it always had done – she worried that she might never be able to bring her back.

For much of the night, she had been worrying about what she'd done to Paulie. She hated herself for doing that, and yet, it didn't feel like it was her who had done it. Explaining to him that she had been previously violated by a demon and his kisses had reminded her of that just wasn't possible. He would have thought she was crazy. It was at that moment that Daphne partly understood why Sara hadn't told her anything the last time the demons had come. People just don't believe that kind of thing. It's just not from their world.

Now the darkness of two years before was back, and innocent people were dying again. The fact that Olivia, her onetime best friend, had also gone assured her that demon trouble was coming her way very soon. The vagueness of the facts made it somehow more terrifying. It was just dots that were connecting around her, closing in on her. She would be the final dot.

When the doorbell chimed through the house, it felt like further confirmation. It had been much quieter for the last two years, and now, at least, chimed a new sound that would not remind her of those events. But somehow, lying in bed tired and scared, the doorbell filled her body with adrenaline and her brain with cortisol once again. She had no choice but to answer it, and her stomach felt heavier with each step towards the door.

She felt her breath shudder as she slowly peered through the spyhole. There was nothing there. Nothing but the distant house opposite and the trees, which looked browner than the day before, as if they were dying quickly, just like they had the last time the demons had infested Hanging Hill Lane. Daphne studied the outside for a while and saw no one. No movement aside from the trees in a gentle breeze. Whoever it was had gone. It was then that something metallic quietly creaked from below.

She looked down to see the letterbox flap slowly open. She looked back through the spyhole to check no one was there, and, still, her doorstep was empty. Whoever was out there was either invisible or very short. The fear that shot through her stomach was fast joined by a sharp physical pain that hit her right beneath her navel. She looked down to see a thin black metal stick poking through the letterbox, sticking into her gut. It retracted and the letterbox closed. Then it popped open again, and the stick jutted back in, poking hard into Daphne's gut just above her groin, causing a spiking pain as if she'd been stabbed, and she clutched at it with her hands as she stumbled back. She crouched down slowly to look back through the wide-open letterbox. Two young eyes, one bloodshot and the other pus-filled, peered back at her, with two small fingers holding the flap open, the fingernails long and dirty. The young girl stared. Daphne stared back. The girl's infected eye twitched weirdly. Something was moving under the bottom eyelid. A huge maggot poked out from under the skin and clung to the eyelashes before rolling down them and falling. The young girl stared right at Daphne and whispered more loudly than any girl that size should be able to whisper, the words whistling and echoing through the house.

'Three days.'

The flap dropped shut with a click, and everything fell silent and still.

Daphne walked into her lounge, where she pulled up her top to see her painful stomach, her hands shaking. The pointed stick had broken the skin and there was some blood, but nothing serious. She grabbed the first aid kit from the kitchen and disinfected the bloodied skin while she thought about what on earth was going on.

Why was Penelope Pengilly doing this? Daphne had tipped off the police that she'd seen her, but obviously they hadn't come and picked her up. Something very strange was going on, but if this girl – who had gone missing the very time when the demons had last struck – had singled Daphne out, then she knew that this wasn't a matter for the police. It was a matter for her – and Sara – so she headed for the front door to visit her friend for advice. Sara somehow always knew more than her. She'd been brought up with the ways of the witch while Daphne had been sheltered from it.

Daphne opened the front door and felt a crack of pain whip through her shin. There she was again, Penelope Pengilly, swinging the small metal stick into Daphne's legs with a strength that belied a girl of that size, and Daphne darted back inside and slammed the door. She was getting angry with the pain. It wasn't the kind of pain that felt like a genuine injury or that really mattered – except it was really bloody annoying and Daphne felt her anger rise. That Penelope Pengilly kid, it turned out, was a real bitch.

Daphne opened her laptop and searched the name she'd seen countless times on the news. Firstly, with anger to see this stupid child she was up against. A child who was clearly not a normal human. But then, as the anger subsided and rational thought returned, she found herself gathering information on what the hell might really be going on. It wasn't hard to find more information than she could possibly need.

Penelope Pengilly had been seven when she had disappeared, on the day the murders on her street had ended. She'd now be nine. She was said to be a kind child, doing well at school and popular with her friends. There was nothing to suggest any kind of mental illness or psychological condition that might turn her into a little lunatic wielding a stick and whacking strangers. She'd just been a very normal kid. This was terrible news. She was now working under the influence of something else, and Daphne knew exactly what that would be. The first dots finally connected and fused. Penelope Pengilly was under the control of the third demon.

Daphne called the anonymous police number again and told them that Penelope Pengilly was on hanging Hill Lane. Again. And again, the woman on the phone sounded utterly disinterested, even rude. The human police would be of no use, but the demon would likely hide from them and buy her some time if they sent a few officers down to search.

Sara answered her phone within a couple of rings.

'Sara, I need to talk to you. We've got another problem.'

'Come on round.'

'That's just it,' said Daphne. 'I'm trapped in. There's a little girl that keeps hitting me with a stick on my doorstep. It's back, Sara. The demon is back.'

Silence. Then footsteps and the sound of the wind came through Daphne's phone.

'I'm outside, there's nothing on your doorstep.'

'Stay there. I'm coming right now.'

Daphne opened the front door carefully, protecting her legs as she did. There was no one there. She closed the door and walked quickly to Sara, who beckoned her into her house with a concerned smile.

Chapter Twenty-one

OCTOBER, 1647. AN HOUR before noon. Three rough ropes waited at the gallows, a hungry noose tied at the ends, as three trembling women stepped forward. All had been accused of witchcraft. None had admitted guilt.

In the middle stood Iris Carter, staring lovingly into the crowd. To her right, twenty-six-year-old Mavis Love, crying. She didn't want to die.

She had been caught walking through some woodland admiring the bugs and beetles with her young son, Jack. When she picked a mushroom, she saw something under the earth from where it came, so she reached in and picked it up too. As she did, it gave a slight glow, as some mushrooms naturally do. It had looked so magical that the pair had gasped. When she turned around, she was confronted by the witchfinder, who manhandled her away while young Jack cried all the way home alone.

She'd been pricked and hadn't bled. The witchfinder, a confident, qualified professional, immediately deemed her a witch and claimed his twenty shillings. Some more good work of the Lord done, and another fine payday.

The executioner stood proud. A good, strong man doing God's work and living a pure life.

Little Jack stood at the front of the crowd, his father's hands on his shoulders, crying. Mavis Love didn't even look up. The pain of seeing her son who she knew she would never see again was just too great. She looked down and cried as a rotten apple flew from the crowd and struck her on the crown of her head. It made her angry but there was nothing she could do. If only she really had been a witch, there may have been some way to escape. But this scared human just waited out the last few moments of her life, crying, in too much shock to move. What a waste of the last few moments of life.

Crack.

A cute little swing.

Little Jack cried harder. He'd been a lovely kid.

Little Jack became big angry Jack and, fuelled by the pain of the moment he had seen his mother hang, became the biggest bully of them all. He got his teenage sweetheart pregnant and the bullying continued until he died of a painful liver disease in his early forties, broke and alone. The visual memory of his mother's execution hadn't stayed with him, but the effect it had was passed to his son, and from his son to his grandkids, to his great-grandkids, and beyond.

Generations of alcoholism and violence. Child and partner abuse. Mental illness. False accusations against good and gentle people.

One son in the family line hadn't got violent at all despite his brutally angry parents. Instead, from a very early age, he'd learned to become absolutely adorable. That trait, which had served him well to avoid getting hurt as a child, morphed into charisma as he grew older. He never laid a hand on anyone and became incredibly popular. But the generational trauma hadn't let him go. He started a cult and fathered many children from within. After the cult's mass suicide, only one child remained. She went on to harm her own children awfully, undetected behind the charisma she had inherited from her father and a society that didn't think a woman was capable of such evil. Ironic, considering society had caused it by deeming a good woman evil and acting evilly towards her all those years before.

For fifteen generations, the chain of trauma remained strong. It's hard to become strong enough to beat it when you're the product of an abusive family. It's hard to do much else but just continue the chain.

In 1890, one abused link gave birth to yet another. This one almost managed it. He almost beat it. He married a lovely woman, so gentle and kind, and working together, the family trauma chain began to finally dissolve, the string of trauma finally breaking under true and gentle love. In 1917, he was shelled on the front line in France and watched several of his friends blown to pieces. Humans are not supposed to see anyone's intestines, let alone their friends'. Humans aren't supposed to see what is under the skull of another. Humans aren't supposed to see feet not attached to legs and legs not attached to hips. Humans aren't supposed to expect certain death and then not receive it when all their friends do. Humans aren't built for that. It breaks them. And then, sometimes, they break others.

When he returned home, he was not so gentle on himself or the couple's young child, a daughter, who grew up self-loathing and subconsciously sought out a man who would help her keep up her self-loathing by loathing her too, and subconsciously made sure to find one who would demonstrate it physically.

Her embedded trauma pushed her to taunt him mercilessly, asking for the punishment that she deep down believed she deserved, pushing him to use his fists.

After every beating, he truly felt bad. One part of his mind said how sorry he was and it was never going to happen again. That part of him truly meant it. A more powerful part remained in the background and waited for the time to emerge again: the next inevitable taunting which would unleash the anger. Whatever surface excuses they made for their behaviour, it was a darkly symbiotic relationship of horror they never got out of until he died. She found herself another abuser and the children saw everything. With a history like hers, it wasn't her fault, but she blamed herself every second until she died.

When their grandchild was born, she was as shy and anxious as they come. She, out of desperation for company, married a man who hurt her in front of their only daughter, Joanne, and then, eventually, hit Joanne too.

One night, at fourteen years old, after a firm right open palm, Joanne had a dream. She was cowering on the floor under the dinner table, waiting to be struck by her father again. When she opened her eyes and looked up, she didn't see her father. He was, instead, cowering alongside her, head under his hands, hiding behind the thin white tablecloth right next to her. Looking up, she saw her grandfather standing over them both, his father over his shoulder, another angry man over the shoulder of him, who she knew to be the father of her own great-grandfather. She saw the familial chain of trauma and abuse link by link and understood her mission. She woke up with a deep feeling of fear but also strength, knowing she wasn't ever going to join this chain. She would be the one to break it. She would fight back, not fight forward. After that, for some reason, her father no longer hit her and the couple broke up shortly after.

Joanne was special. She was a fighter, but a fighter for good. Her title of Police Constable Joanne Bach became official a few weeks before she was the youngest officer at the scene of the six-eight-ten killings. One of the toughest, too.

If she could have travelled in time, she could have arrested an awful lot of her gene pool.

Now, she sat in the misper room as a notification flashed up on all the screens in the team. Bach and Trevithick read together.

'Oh no,' said Joanne Bach.

'Shame,' said Beverly Trevithick. 'Be gentle with the boys when they get back.'

Sergeant Cox entered the room quietly. 'Mr Mattey had a long history with psychosis. His demons are no longer with him. No names to the press, please, till I say. Mr Mattey's mother's address is on his report. I'll have a word with the boys before they go, it'll be their first time.'

The officers and civilian workers in the room quietly nodded and Cox left the room.

Beverly Trevithick closed the message box on the screen. 'The beach under that cliff is rocky as hell. I feel for the recovery team on that one. Those two masts are the ones you never want to hear ping on a misper case. They make a real mess down there.'

'But not important for Olivia Merrigan, right?'

'She'd pinged those two masts about ninety times a day for months. I don't think we can read too much into it.'

'Or write it off.'

'I wish we could,' croaked Trevithick with a cough. 'I guess we can scroll through some low-riskers while we wait for the laptop. Looks like a couple of new ones have come in.'

'People go missing a lot round here, right?'

'Humans don't make sense. Stay in this job as long as me and you'll learn that. No sense at all.'

The thought of Olivia Merrigan splashed across a rocky beach filled Joanne Bach with dread. She'd feel terrible if they couldn't find her in time.

One of the civilians entered holding a laptop and a charging cable and put them in front of Bach and Trevithick. 'Olivia Merrigan's laptop. It's unlocked, and we're into her messages.'

'Fuck yes,' said Trevithick.

'Language,' said Ovary with a grin as he walked over. 'Let me know if there's anything useful. Progress at last.'

Joanne looked at Beverly, who offered a smiley high five. Joanne laughed and their hands slapped together.

'Just as I was finally going to eat that damn cake,' said Beverly Trevithick. The officers swung their chairs around with energy and purpose to look at the laptop. 'Alright, cake in twenty minutes, and I'm having two slices, and if this leads to us finding Merrigan, it's pint time tonight.' The pair smiled, some good news at last.

A message box popped up on the police monitor screens.

REGINALD H MATTEY. CASE CLOSED.

Chapter Twenty-two

SARA LOOKED STRANGELY CALM as she stood at her washing line in her back garden, unpegging her clothes one by one. Daphne helped.

'It's not drying,' said Sara, 'it's that new cold wind.'

'You know who Penelope Pengilly is, right?' asked Daphne.

'Of course.'

'That's the girl who keeps hitting me.'

Sara stopped, holding a damp blouse, and looked back at Daphne. 'She's alive?'

'She's alive and being a little shit. But I checked her out. She was a normal girl, and now she's not. And her eye, Sara, it's disgusting. She should be crying in pain and she's not.'

'Well we've found our third demon then, Daphne. Jesus, he's been living in Penelope Pengilly for two years now. That poor girl.'

Daphne was determined not to show Sara she wanted to instantly break into tears. Sara looked so calm and the last thing Daphne wanted was to look the fool in front of her old friend and closest ally.

'I guess this is a rescue mission now,' said Sara, while Daphne felt the kind of fear that she hadn't felt for two years. She was still suffering, still having sleepless nights, was now getting flashbacks and being struck with an anger she'd never felt before, and Sara didn't seem fazed at all. It just didn't make sense. But Sara's calmness somehow helped Daphne feel a little better.

'Aren't you worried?'

'Of course. He was a right handful last time. He'll have been watching us too. Finding out what gets under our skin. Getting stronger while he waited, while that poor child will have suffered every day. I can't even imagine what she's been through.' She looked at Daphne seriously. 'Same thing applies, Daphne. You can't let him get inside of you. That would be unimaginable.'

'Help me, Sara,' said Daphne, her eyes wetting.

'It's not you and me against the evil world, Daphne,' said Sara warmly as she stopped with a frilly white blouse in her hand. 'There are forces on our side. There's just one demon left of the three and two of us. I'll tell Mum, maybe she'll head back. Come inside.'

The thought of Agatha Hunter returning was scary in itself, and Daphne still felt like a child in trouble just thinking about her. Still, she wouldn't mind an ally like that around when the demons were back.

Sara walked through her house to the front garden. Daphne followed, scouring the street for any sign of Penelope Pengilly. Another sting from that stick was the last thing she needed.

Daphne followed Sara into the garage, where she struggled to get a big box down from the shelf. Daphne hurried in to help and almost tripped over another fishing rod that fell from the wall in front of her.

'Sorry,' Sara said. 'He was supposed to collect it years ago. Never does. Never visits Alfie. Probably for the best, mind.'

'Cock.'

'That's about as mild as I'd go. I hate that one day Alfie will refer to him as "Dad".'

Daphne picked up the rod and pushed it back up against the wall. It had knocked a box down, too, and some of the contents had spilled out onto the concrete floor. Daphne grabbed it clumsily, more preoccupied with keeping an eye on the street outside.

'Ouch!' Blood oozed from Daphne's fingertip.

'Those damned fishhooks,' said Sara. 'Leave them there, I'll chuck 'em out when I get a minute. You okay?'

The sight of the barbed hooks and the blood and the pain of the cut combined and shot their way down Daphne's neural pathways starting a chain reaction she couldn't stop, and she fell into a terrifying panic attack, feeding her snippet by snippet of vivid flashback memory.

She breathed faster and faster until she hyperventilated. She fell.

✳ ✳ ✳ ✳ ✳

Daphne, lying in bed unable to move, eyes wide open in the dark, sweating, shaking.

Daphne, lying in bed unable to move, as the cover slowly slides off her.

Daphne, lying in bed unable to move, as a voice whispers in her ear.

And then we hooked and pulped the two at four.

Daphne, lying in bed, crying, with visions of Sara and Alfie killed in horrific ways by the demon. Hooked.

Pulped.

You stupid little single girl, alone.

Stupid. Stupid.

STUPID.

The word on which the whisper turned.

✳ ✳ ✳ ✳ ✳

When Daphne came back around, she was breathing into a paper bag, firmly pushed against her mouth by Sara's calm hand. Slowly, she gained control of herself.

'What's happening to me, Sara? I'm so scared. I'm so scared all the time.'

'I'm here for you, Daph.'

'How can I stop this happening? I thought you were dead, Sara. They said they'd hooked and pulped you, and I believed it.' Daphne broke down in tears, helpless.

'I don't know, Daph. I don't know. I'm okay. We're both okay.'

Sara slowly led Daphne to the couch in the lounge, where eventually, once the adrenaline was gone, she remembered why she was there. There wasn't time to waste crying. While the rest of the world finally started making a bit more space for people to despair in peace, the demons moved in on her own despair, circling, ready to pounce. Crying would have to wait. Daphne composed herself and got back to business.

'Do you know anything about the bean-nighe? The washerwoman?'

'Old woman in the woods. Stay away from her, Daphne. Please, promise me you will stay away from her.'

'Too late. I went to see her. Remember that policeman in charge? Detective Inspector Bright? I bumped into him. He's in the mental hospital now.' Daphne breathed deeply and helped herself calm down further.

'You spoke to the bean-nighe?' Sara looked deadly serious, ignoring the mention of DI Bright.

'Yeah. He told me she would be able to help with whatever is going on. She's so fucking rude though.'

'What did you say, Daph?' Sara now looked terrified and Daphne couldn't help but feel it with her. The calmness was gone.

'It's okay, Sara,' said Daphne as she tried to convince herself. 'Not a lot. I just asked her where Olivia might be but she didn't tell me.'

'You just asked her that one question?'

'Yeah.'

Alfie started to cry. It was the first time Daphne had seen Sara ignore that.

'Just one? Tell me it was just the one question, please.'

'Yeah, just one. But she said it was three.' Sara's horrified look wasn't helping Daphne to calm herself.

'You asked her three questions? Tell me you didn't ask her three questions.' Sara hadn't blinked for what seemed like an eternity. 'Be very, very clear. What happened?'

'She said I asked three questions, yeah. She didn't answer any of them and she was rude as hell, then I just left.'

'Shit, Daph,' Sara said with feigned strength failing to cover the look of shock and horror. Daphne could see the blood drain from Sara's face. She'd never seen her so pale as she burst into tears. It was the first time Daphne had seen Sara cry.

Daphne sat looking back at her distraught friend, fidgeting, waiting for Sara to say more to somehow stop the worry that was building inside her. But Sara's bottom lip just trembled every time she looked like she was going to speak. Eventually, she mustered up two words.

'I'm sorry.'

'What's going on? Tell me this time, please.'

'She tricked you.' Sara fought to speak through her tears. 'She's given you three days.'

'Three days for what?'

Sara stared back and didn't say a word. Daphne looked back and a new kind of worry hit her. The silent seconds that followed felt like an eternity, so she asked again.

'Three days for what?'

'I'm so sorry, Daphne.'

'For what?'

'Until you die.'

Chapter Twenty-three

DAPHNE SAT STUNNED. IT didn't make sense. A few days ago, she'd been as happy as could be, playing with her boyfriend and putting her past behind her. Now, her world had descended back into terror. She was twenty years old and being told she had three days to live. As Daphne felt the dread in her gut, one single, quiet word slipped from her mouth.

'What?'

Sara stared at the floor for a moment. 'That's the rules, Daphne,' she said at barely a whisper before looking up. 'The third question is the trigger. You ask three questions, you get three days. That pile of clothes she's washing, all people who fell for her tricks. Three days later, she'll wash their clothes and soon after the sun goes down that night, they'll be dead.'

Daphne sat completely still, aside from blinking to clear the tears that had built up in her eyes. 'You can stop it, right? We can stop it? We can do magic.'

'If it can be stopped, I don't know how. I fucking hate that bean-nighe. I hate her.'

'So what do I do, Sara? I read about the bean-nighe, I couldn't find anything that says they kill. They don't make the future, they just prophesy, right?'

'Daphne, where are the mnathan-nighe from? Did you read that?'

'Scotland.'

'And where are we?'

'Cornwall.'

'We don't get any further from Scotland on this whole island. That's why she's here. The mnathan-nighe are horrible, evil creatures, and this particular bean-nighe is an outcast even amongst them. She's hated by everyone. A trickster and a killer. I really wish you had come to me first.' Sara softened. 'I'm so sorry.'

'So what do I do?'

'I'll ask Mum. Get some rest. If I can find something out, you might need your strength.'

As Daphne left Sara's house and walked the few metres to her own front door, she clenched at the sight of a short figure standing on the road opposite. It was Penelope Pengilly, stick in one hand and a crow on the shoulder of her other arm. The child walked forward towards Daphne, who hastened towards her own front door. But as Daphne turned her key and looked over her shoulder, Penelope Pengilly wasn't attacking her. Instead, she stood a few metres away, looking Daphne right in the eye, smiling with an evil grin. The young girl's grin didn't even flinch as the crow flapped and jumped on top of her head, then dropped its head down and pushed the tip of its beak under her infected eyelid. Daphne watched in horror as it pulled a live worm slowly from her pus-filled eye. The worm stretched as it slid out and pulled free with a bounce and swing from the bird's shining beak. It gave a final wriggle and twist before it was gone in a single gulp. The girl hadn't stopped grinning the whole time. Hadn't stopped staring at Daphne.

Daphne jumped into her house, closed the door behind her, fell to the floor, and cried.

Chapter Twenty-four

JOANNE BACH AND BEVERLY Trevithick scrolled through Olivia's social media messages. Bach gently shook her head as she spoke. 'Look at all these men. Daphne Locke wasn't wrong about the creeps, was she?'

'All unopened. She wasn't entertaining them.'

Between the unread messages from man after man were a few read messages from friends. Bach opened a few and read. 'No sign of any plans. No arguments. No engagement with weirdos. It's just all so normal.'

'Apart from all the men.'

Joanne Bach laughed. 'That's not that unusual. I get too many, and I'm a copper and not half as pretty as this one. The key is not to open them if they've got images attached.'

'I've never had a dick pic in my life,' said Trevithick. 'But then again, it wasn't so much of a thing when you had to get the pictures developed in a shop. Still, I might have appreciated an occasional seven-inch Polaroid or two.'

Joanne laughed. 'Jesus, Bev.' She opened another message. 'See anything? I'm getting nothing helpful here.'

'Nope. Let's list these men and run them through the database, see if any have a history of stalking or violence to women.'

'There must be hundreds.'

Beverly Trevithick grabbed a pen and noted down name after name. Eventually, 'There.' She passed the paper to a civvy and asked for a name check for stalkers and violent offenders. The civvy waddled off, list in hand.

'Wait, got something,' said Joanne Bach, causing Beverly Trevithick to lean in slightly, less sluggishly than usual. 'Message from the Blue Horizon Agency, whoever they are.'

'That's models and actors,' said Beverly Trevithick. 'They came up a couple of times when we were researching the yacht girls.

'So there is a connection?'

'No. One of the women on the boat looked like a model from the agency. Not her. What does it say?'

Joanne Bach scrolled to the top of the text conversation. 'It's an invitation for a sample photoshoot, see if Merrigan wanted to join the books. They headhunted her.'

'Well, she looks the part. Did she go?'

The constables read through the messages as quickly as they could.

'She accepted,' said Joanne Bach. 'Shit. The meeting was the day she disappeared. Four o'clock.'

'Keep scrolling.'

'And there we are,' said Bach. 'Midday, final message says she'll text their phone number when she's on the way. What time was her last phone ping from the coast masts?'

'Two thirty. Saying she's on the way, I suspect.'

'So if she got to that meeting, they will have been the last people to see her. We need to get down to Blue Horizon. Where are they based?'

'I'm just looking. Oh, there look, above the Blue Horizon Venue and Bar. That's not far from the coast either. It's all very localised.'

'That's near where the murders happened. Which is definitely not good.'

'Let's get down to the – what was it called? – the Blue Horizon Bar?' croaked Beverly Trevithick, with a little more energy than usual.

'Yeah. It's karaoke. Weird.'

'We'd better let the murder lot know Olivia Merrigan might be moving to their department. It's all a little too close. You do that, then we'll get down to Blue Horizon. I'm gonna piss myself if I don't use the loo first. See you at the car.'

✳ ✳ ✳ ✳ ✳

The Blue Horizon Bar and Venue car park was empty except for a few cars, but there was movement inside. Police Constables Joanne Bach and Beverly Trevithick simultaneously closed their car doors, donned their hats, and approached the door of the club, the crunch of gravel underfoot poking up above the sound of the sea. Bach stepped inside first, noticing the smell of stale beer was partly masked by a distinctive smell, something quite floral and pretty mixed with the salt and seaweed of a sea breeze.

A fruit machine flashed away by the wall, and a middle-aged man in a sleeveless vest sat alone at a table, the only drinker in the whole bar. He did a quick double take at the arriving policewomen, sipped his pint of ale, leaving a foam moustache, and got back to his newspaper. The front page's picture was William Head, although the top bar had a different story. A photo of Penelope Pengilly with a caption that simply read 'Jokers'.

The police officers walked to the bar just as a woman arrived from the other side of the tall drink fridges. She was around forty years old with a friendly face that wasn't fazed at all by the arrival of two law enforcers.

'Hi,' she said in a voice that Joanne Bach found noticeably pleasing. 'Can I help?'

'I hope so,' said Constable Trevithick. 'Just a few questions, if that's okay?'

'One second.' She thumbed her phone for a few seconds and looked back to the police officers. 'Just messaging the partner to come down.'

'No problem,' said Joanne Bach.

'We had a call already, mind. The cameras don't show anything beyond the bar and the car park.'

'Cameras?' asked Joanne Bach.

'The boat. The murders. Burger and that lot. We were asked if our cameras saw anything but we're too far away really. We sent the files but there wasn't anything useful on them.'

Another woman arrived behind the bar. She was also in her forties with a charismatic smile. 'Hi,' she said. 'I'm Nina. How can I help?'

'I'm Heidi, by the way,' said the first woman. 'We're partners here at the bar.'

'We're actually looking for an agency,' said Joanne Bach. 'Blue Horizon?'

'Oh,' said Nina with a smile. 'That's us too. We already spoke to someone about that though. One of the girls on the boat matched the description of one of our clients but it wasn't her.'

'We're here about someone called Olivia Merrigan,' said Joanne Bach, producing a photograph and showing the women who leaned across the bar for a closer look. 'Do you know her?'

'I don't think so,' said Heidi.

'No,' said Nina. 'She's not one of ours, but she's kind of familiar.'

'You've not met?' asked Trevithick.

'Ah, I know where I've seen her,' said Nina. 'On the news. That's the missing woman, right?'

'Ah yes, I think that's her,' said Heidi.

'But you haven't seen her? Never met her?' asked Trevithick.

'Not to my knowledge,' came Heidi's smooth and pleasing voice.

'Okay,' croaked Trevithick. 'You invited her for an audition or a trial for your agency last Thursday. Last thing we know we believe she was leaving to see you here. You're saying she never showed up?'

'Oh, the no-show? That was our no-show, Heidi,' said Nina.

'I knew I'd seen that face. Oh no. So where is she?'

'That's why we're here asking you,' said Trevithick.

'She didn't show. We were all set up ready to go. Photographer was here, you can check his invoice, he charged us anyway. Typical tog.'

'Did you message her to see where she was or check if she was running late?' asked Bach. Perhaps they'd drop themselves in something if they were lying.

'We don't contact no-shows. In our experience, once a no-show, always trouble. Shame. She would have been very popular with our clients, I'm sure.'

'Did you receive a message from her around two-thirty?'

'Perhaps,' said Nina.

'Could you check, please?'

'Of course.' Nina tapped on her phone. 'Yes, two-thirty-seven on Thursday, it just says "On my way."' Nina held out the phone for the officers to read, and they both leaned in.

Joanne noted down the number and looked up. 'You didn't find it odd she messaged to confirm she was en route but never made it? Didn't think to check in on her?'

'They get nervous. No-shows are normal for newbies. She never made it. One second, please.' Nina checked through her phone. 'See, due here at four. Never showed up.'

Joanne Bach looked up and said, 'She was due at four and left at half past two. She lives, what, thirty minutes away by foot, if that?'

'I don't know where she lives,' said Heidi.

'Sure?' asked Trevithick.

'Sure. You've got our car park footage. It covers both entrances. She was a no-show. I'm really sorry we can't help.'

'I hope you're okay for us to check that then.'

'Sure. Anything else we can help you with?'

Beverly Trevithick dropped a card on the bar. 'This is us. Call that number and ask for PC Trevithick or Bach if you hear anything or see anything or whatever. You must meet a lot of people here. If you hear anyone chatting and think you have something, even if it's tiny or you're unsure, please, please call.'

'Even any gossip,' said Bach.

'Of course,' said Nina, dropping the card into the till drawer and smiling pleasantly over her shoulder at the officers.

'Thank you, then,' said Beverly Trevithick.

'Our pleasure,' said Nina as the pair walked away around the bar and out of sight, one humming a tune as she walked away. The man at the table quickly stood and scampered over to the bar to catch them as the pair of officers exited and crunched back over the gravel. They sank back into their car seats and let out a communal sigh.

'What now?' asked Bach. 'Check this camera?'

'Let's take the drive back to her house on the obvious walk route. Keep your eye out for cameras or anyone who looks like a regular fixture who might have been a witness. Then we'll get back and check these cameras. Then if there's no Little Miss Merrigan coming in here on the footage, we'll get back to the drawing board. We can get an appeal out too. We know where she left from, when she disappeared, and where she was going. Someone's got to know something.'

'You've done this before, haven't you?' Joanne smiled.

'Once or twice.'

'It's weird, though, right? They recognised Olivia Merrigan from the news reports but didn't recognise her as the girl they were expecting and didn't turn up. That's definitely off.'

'Could be. You'd think if they headhunted her they'd know what she looked like. And they saw her on the news reports but didn't say anything.'

'Something's up with those two.' Joanne Bach compared the phone number from the text to the number in her file. 'Yup. That text was sent from Olivia Merrigan's phone. She was coming here.'

'And never made it.'

Joanne Bach stared out over the clifftop to the sea and the distant horizon and said, 'Perhaps. I don't trust them at all.'

Anxiety hit her out of nowhere. She felt her stomach churn. And then her brain made that stupid connection. Somehow this was linked to Hanging Hill Lane. She closed her eyes, trying to block out that thought. Up flashed the image of the dead man in the car. She shook her head, opened her eyes, slowed her breathing, and focused on the sea.

Then she noticed Beverly Trevithick looking back at her, concern in every wrinkle of her face.

Perhaps she should see the psychologist after all.

Chapter Twenty-five

Two thirty-seven. Plenty of time before the photoshoot appointment at the Blue Horizon Bar. It was a beautiful day for a walk.

Olivia did her final checks in the mirror. Basic makeup touch-ups but no heavy styling had been her instructions, and then she sent a final message to the people she hoped might start her modelling career. On my way, it said.

She walked past her little car, preferring to shed some nerves on a short walk through the countryside to the venue. The road wound through leafy trees and the sun warmed her face. She slowed her walk a little, not wanting to sweat too much and risk her look. A cool sea breeze helped, and swayed the branches above her head as she walked.

It was a quiet day in a quiet suburb, and there wasn't a car on the road. After thirty or so minutes, as she rounded another tree-lined corner, the bar's car park came into view. She stopped to compose herself, her nerves barging forward as they would at any job interview. She wasn't going to get any work if she looked nervous in the photos.

As she approached the car park, a big black four-by-four crept out from a small side street and pulled up alongside her, making her speed up her pace. A tinted electric window slid down, revealing two people in their forties.

The relief that the car contained women washed over her, and she stopped.

'Olivia?' asked one.

'Yes,' she said, caught a little off guard.

'Hello. I'm Nina, we were chatting on messages. This is Heidi from the agency. Hop in, we're going for some outdoor shots today.'

Olivia was a little surprised but felt safe with the women, both looking completely relaxed and as charismatic as you'd expect modelling agency owners to be. It hadn't occurred to her that her photos wouldn't be taken in a karaoke bar, but it made sense. A black strap hung over Nina's neck and the large camera dangled onto her lap. Olivia looked at the expensive four-by-four car, door shining in the sunlight with a thick handle. It pulled open easily and lightly even though the vehicle seemed to be built like a tank, and as she pulled it open, her excitement and feeling of being special grew. She felt safe as she got into the soft and comfortable back seat of the huge vehicle. She was about to reach for her seatbelt but, seeing that the other ladies were not wearing theirs, made the split-second decision to go with the crowd and not wear hers.

The drive was short and pleasant and Olivia's nerves waned quickly. These were two wonderful ladies and she was thrilled about the possibility of working with them. She sat in the back of the car and smiled all the way to their destination. Within minutes, a clifftop came into view.

Below the cliffs, jagged-sharp rocks towered above the shallows, a luxury yacht glistening on the horizon.

Chapter Twenty-six

THREE DAYS RANG THROUGH Daphne's head. It didn't take long until the next phase of coming to terms with death kicked in. Fear turned to fury. With barely a thought, she walked out the front door and slammed it shut.

She made the short walk into Hanging Hill Woods, passed the ancient stack of stones, and angrily stalked up the dirt path, making a beeline for the bridge where the bean-nighe still crouched.

There she was. The old ugly washerwoman, washing some garment from another poor, tricked victim. Daphne approached cautiously through the gap in the bushes, barely registering another scratch from a sharp thorn. Dread built up in her stomach with every step until she felt sick with nerves and anger. She stopped a few small paces from the bean-nighe, who didn't even look up from the stream.

'You tricked me,' said Daphne, spitting anger with her words.

'I did not.'

'You made me ask questions.'

'I did not. But ask you did.'

'You're not going to kill me.'

The washerwoman looked at Daphne and smiled. The half of her face that housed her only nostril also displayed lips that curved up plenty more than the other side. 'I am not. But aye, you will die. On the evening of the third day, twenty minutes beyond nightfall, and I cannot be the one to stop it. I am powerless, witch, such is the agreement. It was you who set it in motion.'

A thick bush that lined the clearing moved and crunched.

'Who can stop it? If you can't be the one, then that means someone can.'

The bean-nighe almost laughed and somehow looked even more ugly. 'Four questions? You are a wee stupid one, aren't you? I wonder, do you now realise that you are truly stupid?'

Daphne looked at the pile of clothes next to the washerwoman. A rogue sleeve dangled out, a few garments down from the top. It was familiar. Hers. The white blouse with the neck frills she had worn when she had first met Paulie. A gift from her mother. It was like confirmation that everything Sara had told her was true.

She would be dead in three days. *Three days*. That's what Penelope Pengilly had hissed through the letterbox.

'Tell me how it can be stopped,' Daphne demanded.

'Answer the question. A question for a question.'

'Oh fuck off you ugly bitch.' Daphne shook as much in anger as fear. Crouched as the bean-nighe was, Daphne could probably take a run up and boot her ugly head right off her shoulders and up into the trees and bushes. It was tempting.

The bean-nighe creaked her head up slowly to look Daphne in the eye. 'I'll repeat the question: Do you now know that you are stupid?'

Daphne wanted to lash out. Wanted to punch her in her ugly face, wanted to grab the back of her head and plunge it in the mud at the bottom of the stream and drown her, or find a rock and smash in her skull. Maybe then she might survive. She can't wash that blouse and complete the agreement if she's floating dead in the stream or her head is sitting solo in a bush. But this woman was not just an ordinary old woman. God only knew, and perhaps the demons knew too, what kind of unnatural strength she might have. Time was running out. Three days remained until the bean-nighe would wash her blouse in the stream, and then the laws of the unnatural world would take her. She had to do something now, or she would die.

Daphne crept forward. She bent down and snatched her blouse out from the pile of washing and ran as fast as she could.

The bean-nighe wailed a shriek that likely could have been heard as far away as the clifftops a few miles to the south. The bushes around her shook and shivered, and small, child-sized figures scurried alongside Daphne as she ran, some appearing from behind the trees, others hanging by their spindly arms then dropping from the branches and giggling as they chased. One creature sprang out of a hole as Daphne ran past, and grabbed at her bruised ankles as it sneered a razor-toothed grin. She got a better look at that one. Child-sized perhaps, but its face was aged like an old man's, the skin grey and leathery, mischievous eyes that shone brightly in the moonlight. At a glance, its ears looked pointed.

As Daphne rounded the dirt path, one of the figures dived out in front of her, tripping her into a bush of sharp thorns that scratched her arms and face, drawing blood. The long thorns scratched and dug deeper into her arms and legs as she yanked herself from the bush and onto her feet. By the time she was upright, she was bleeding all over. Blood oozed from cuts on her arms, legs and torso. She was surrounded by the creatures, all around three feet tall and dressed in green. Most wore rough, hessian tunics, gathered at the waist with a rope or old leather belt. Some wore weathered and torn branded t-shirts, the bottoms ripped off to fit their small stature. One of them stepped forward and grinned up at her, looking her right in the eye. It was a strange little thing, humanoid but with the shape of pointy ears pushing through a dirty hat on its oversized head, with a mischievous smile on its face that revealed its pointy teeth.

Daphne held the blouse tight, and blood from the deep scratches on her arm seeped into the fabric as she looked around at the creatures that stared back at her silently. The one that stood barely two feet away barely reached her waist in height, but did not seem intimidated at all. Then in a flash, it stamped on Daphne's foot, and the circle of creatures broke into cackling laughter before it snatched away the blood-stained blouse from her hand and disappeared through the circle, back towards the bridge where the bean-nighe worked her wicked ways.

The stamp hadn't hurt, but the taking of her blouse had. Once the bean-nighe washed that frilly fabric, Daphne would die in whatever way death chose to come for her. Whatever the agreement was that the bean-nighe had with whatever power was in charge, there was nothing Daphne could do. Now, she stood surrounded by creatures she had only ever read about in books and occasionally laughed about in local jokes. Daphne had heard stories of the piskies but never thought they were real. *No one* thought they were real. But here they were, upholding the bean-nighe's rules in their tiny but terrifying ways. Daphne was scared, but these things were so small, just like in the stories. So she ran, breaking through the piskie circle, and the creatures gave a giggling chase.

Down the dirt path she ran. She was quicker than them but well outnumbered. Up ahead, more piskies appeared on the path, forcing Daphne into the undergrowth. Sticks cracked under her feet as she sped through the woods and into some stiff bushes, pursued by dozens of horrible, cackling little creatures. Obscured by the undergrowth, she took a sharp turn to try to throw them off and silently crouched down and peered through the foliage. Three piskies searched nearby, laughing and playing all the while.

A small hand reached around from behind Daphne and covered her mouth. She froze in fear. Then, right in her earhole, *'Shhhhh.'*

The tiny hand loosened its grip, and a small figure moved to crouch alongside her. It was a piskie, but was somehow different from the rest. The way its eyes were slightly bigger and rounder, and its slow blink made it look not nearly as vicious. It wasn't quite so ugly. It seemed anxious rather than amused. A pair of piskies approached and the small hand pushed Daphne's head down. The anxious piskie jumped out of the bush to meet the approaching giggling pair. Daphne listened.

'Not, not over here,' stammered a thin voice, metres away.

'She's getting away,' said another.

'She'll be trying to get home. By the stack, stack, stack of stones,' said the first, and two pairs of little footsteps scampered off into the distance with a giggle.

The small piskie returned to Daphne's hiding place in the undergrowth. Daphne looked at the creature. It was dressed differently from the others too. A small male. Perhaps a leader of sorts. Perhaps an outcast. Probably an outcast, judging by the stammer. She didn't have time to ask.

'Help me,' she said.

'They will all be moving towards the stones now. They know where you live. Just. Just wait here, catch your breath, and then you will go the other way.'

'They took my shirt,' said Daphne.

'They will do that,' replied the piskie. 'You're Daph, Daphne, aren't you?'

'Yes.'

'A very special witch,' said the piskie before grinning nervously.

A stick cracked nearby, and Daphne and the piskie looked out through the bush, hiding their faces behind the thick leaves. In a small opening was Penelope Pengilly, moving unnaturally, creeping quietly, holding her metal stick like a short spear or javelin. She looked, quite weirdly, like she was creeping up on a tree, as if not to spook it. Daphne watched the young girl as she got close to the thick trunk. She slammed the pointy end into the bark, and the stick seemed to go straight into the tree's thick old trunk. When she stepped back, a squirrel squirmed and died on the end of the stick, now several inches shorter. The girl then plucked the animal off the point of her stick and took a bite out of its furry body, the stringy flesh stretching as she pulled a chunk off its back. She chewed, took the squirrel in one hand and the stick in the other, and ran back off into the undergrowth away from where Daphne and the piskie crouched.

'Your mother was a wonderful lady to me,' said the piskie. 'I will help you where I can, I promise, but we don't have much time.' Piskies' voices chittered louder and closer and the friendly creature put his tiny hand on the back of Daphne's. It was shaking. 'I am Charl. I will help, but now, now you have to run. Run. Get to the animal shelter, then call for a vehicle. They won't let the humans see them, so they'll hide. But go, now. Run and don't, don't stop. I will find you when the time comes.'

'Thank you, Charl.' Daphne ran as fast as she could, speeding past the bean-nighe, who shrieked again. The bushes and trees remained still, aside from a few disturbances from fleeing animals or birds. Daphne registered every little movement as a possible threat, but nothing emerged. She was faster than the piskies and just kept running until she reached the edge of the woods, where the animal shelter came into view. As she felt herself reach safety and slow with exhaustion, a small foot slid out of a bush and sent Daphne crashing to the dirt face-first. A piskie stepped out towards her, laughing. Daphne looked at the shelter, so close to safety, but the piskie moved to block her path as she stood. Her strength surprised her when she placed her palm on the side of its stupid head and launched it forcefully to the ground. Sticks on the woodland floor cracked behind her under the weight of more small feet, and she ran again.

She bolted across the car park and into the shelter entrance, where she doubled over, fighting to catch her breath, panting in and out heavily, until she heard a voice.

'You okay?'

'No,' she panted. 'I need a taxi.'

The man stared back, a worried look on his stubbly face. 'Your arms.'

Daphne looked at her arms. They were bleeding more than she'd realised. She raised one up for a closer look, then looked around for a bathroom to find some tissue. There wasn't one. The man had disappeared, somehow, and then returned holding some bandages.

'These are for dogs, really, but it'll do to get you home. What I can't really get you is animal disinfectant. But use something, okay?'

Daphne stared back, then at the door into the main sanctuary, hoping Paulie might step through at any time and make everything better. She always said she'd visit him at work but never thought it would be quite like this.

'What happened?' the man asked, wrapping the bandage around her arm. It was a question she could not answer. It was a reminder that she had to distance herself from Paulie, as desperately as she didn't want to.

'I fell over,' she said. 'Is Paulie in today?'

The man smiled gently. 'Ah, you're the girlfriend aren't you? He didn't show up today, didn't call. Don't worry. He's not in trouble. Kid's got demons, we have to cut him some slack for that.'

Daphne felt stunned. Demons.

The man continued, 'Lovely, lovely kid, you'll look after him, right?'

Daphne cried inside and hid it as she spoke. 'I'll try. Could you call me that taxi?' She had no idea what he meant by 'Kid's got demons'. She didn't know of any issues he had, and the man certainly wasn't talking about the actual kind of demons that she was now dealing with.

Demons. Always fucking demons.

* * * * *

When Daphne got home, she cleaned up her painful cuts, shut herself in her room, checked herself in the mirror, and rested her phone on a book. When she hit the call button, her stomach filled with dread.

The ringtone continued for what seemed like an eternity. And then he answered, looking typically awkward as he always did on a video call.

'Paulie!' Daphne almost cried. 'Are you okay?'

'I'm fine, just been sleeping a lot.'

'I'm sorry, Paulie. I'm sorry for what I did. I'm sorry I pushed you, I'm sorry I upset you, I think the world of you. Honestly.'

Paulie just stared back as if nothing unusual was going on. 'That's okay.'

'I tried to visit you at work. They said you didn't show up.'

Paulie smiled, and it almost looked genuine. 'I got the rota mixed up. I'm okay.'

She could tell he wasn't. And even though she wasn't used to seeing him in this kind of state, she was really, really happy to see him. 'I'll make this up to you, I promise. If you'll let me.'

A smile flashed over Paulie's face for a split second and then disappeared. 'Okay.'

'I've just got some stuff to deal with first.'

'I know.'

The two stared at each other's tiny screen faces for several seconds, enjoying a mutual understanding that no more needed to be said but wanting to enjoy the pictures of each other for a little longer nonetheless.

And then Paulie's awkwardness took over. 'I have to go.'

'Me too. See you soon.'

'Yes, please. I love that you called me,' said Paulie, and a second later, the call ended and the rest of Daphne's terrifying reality flooded back into her mind.

Chapter Twenty-seven

DAPHNE'S THUMBS THUMPED INTO her phone screen keyboard: IT'S NO GOOD.

She sat alone in her lounge, both arms bandaged and stinging, safe from the piskies but anything but safe from the agreement she had set in motion, whatever that was. In three days, if what Sara and the bean-nighe had both said was true, she would be dead. A sharp memory of Penelope Pengilly's unnatural letterbox whispering filled her mind as vividly as the flashbacks she had been suffering. *Three days*. It felt like confirmation of the fact she was fast slipping towards her end.

Sara's text reply didn't do much to make her feel any better. WORKING ON IT, PROMISE, was all the message said. Another pinged through seconds later: LOVE YOU, SIS, STAY STRONG.

Daphne desperately wanted to ask Sara if she could stay with her so she wasn't alone. But she now knew that couldn't happen. She needed to be in that house. An unattended house on Hanging Hill Lane with all the secrets it held could lead to terrible things, especially as there was a demon lurking nearby, watching. She knew that terrible things could happen and she had been warned starkly by her mother and by Sara, though she didn't know exactly what those things were. If she were to die in two days, then the world would soon find out.

She was tempted to ask anyway. But the thought of dragging that darkness closer to little Alfie stopped that thought in its tracks.

Then her jaw dropped and her vision softened and her attention landed somewhere inside her mind on a realisation that made her feel utterly stupid.

She'd been tricked.

Fury rose inside her the moment she worked it out. The feeling of stupidity was engulfed by rage, and her fingernails pushed deeply into her palms.

The bean-nighe wasn't the first one to trick her. Gordon Bright had sent her to the woods for answers, literally telling her to ask the old washerwoman questions. A trap. Why would Bright do that? He was still under the instructions of the demon, even if the demon had long since left his head. The rage brought in some hatred.

Things started to make sense as Daphne pieced the parts together, the dots finally coherently connecting, the pieces dropping into place, and the puzzle forming a horrifying picture.

The demon killed celebrities on the beach to announce its presence and introduce Daphne to her greatest fear: Itself. Dot.

The demon used a possessed child to hurt and scare her from a vessel – an innocent child – that her morals wouldn't let her fight back against. To mock her and scare her, to start breaking her down. Dot.

Daphne was tricked into thinking she was going to die, and that the death was coming from a higher power greater than any human, witch, or demon, leaving her feeling completely hopeless. Dot.

It had stolen away a good friend too to bring guilt back into her life. Dot.

It felt like the dots were joining up around her neck and starting to pull tighter, tighter, crushing her throat. Constricting anxiety built fast, reaching her lungs and chest and squeezing her windpipe. She looked at her phone, desperate for some kind of release. Nothing more from Sara.

But this rope of dark dots somehow brought a little hope. She had to be right. If she was right, then she wasn't going to die. It was a ploy to break her down, and though it felt like it was working, she'd fight till the end. Killing her was not in the demon's interest. They needed a witch to possess and use her to gain power amongst the other witches, or perhaps destroy them, like the fungus that took control of the zombie ants that would then drop the fungus spores all over the other ants. Then it dawned on her as further dots connected in her mind.

Bright had called her an ant. Why? Because she *was* an ant. The demons were the fungus, the mushrooms that sprouted from the heads.

Demons needed to possess witches to kill more witches. Maybe *all* the witches.

Bright wasn't speaking pure gibberish, after all. As for the truffle pigs he spoke of, she had no idea. As things felt like they became clearer in some ways yet murkier in others, she started to feel like she was somehow in reach of a little bit of control, and that made her feel a little better. The tiniest slither of hope. A loosening noose. She grabbed her phone and searched for what a truffle was. It was a word she hadn't heard used outside of chocolates. When the answer flashed up on her screen, another dot connected.

Truffles are fungus.

And like the fungus that connected everything under the ground, as Bright had said, the dots were connecting somewhere invisibly in the peripherals of her mind, slowly working things out. She could feel it. It felt like hope.

And then that hope seemed to disappear as quickly as it had arrived. Some things just didn't fit. Why had Olivia not been found horrifically mutilated? That's how the demons played their games. They literally nailed her neighbours to their front door. Killing someone with no fanfare was not in their playbook. It was always for effect.

And who were the women on the clifftop? What had happened to them to make them that way? And why had they gone for her? And why were they chanting about her hair? Whatever had happened to them, it definitely felt like a huge dot in the web of what was happening, though she had no idea how to connect it. She grabbed her phone and texted Sara: Do you know anything about truffle pigs?

Her phone pinged back a second later: Please, just give me some time to get this sorted.

But do you? Daphne tapped into her phone and waited a few seconds, which felt like hours, for the reply.

Really sorry, no.

Just as Daphne thought she was making progress and working something out, she'd hit a brick wall. So much still didn't make sense. There was no time to sit and wait for news. She had to make a breakthrough herself, and fast. So she went into a room she rarely went into and asked a group of women for help. A group of women who would definitely know what to do. If only they weren't made of plastic.

* * * * *

The old floorboards creaked as Daphne stepped gently into her mother's bedroom. Four mannequins stood along the front of the bed. How she wished these ladies could be around to help her now. They had saved her last time, and she had hoped to bring them back, but not even Sara had worked out how to do that yet. The textbooks were so vague on the matter.

'I'm going to need to borrow this,' Daphne said to the mannequin wearing her old friend Gugwana's colourful clothes, and slid the beautiful knife from her embellished belt. She looked at the other mannequins, which seemed to still somehow have a faint glimmer of life in their eyes. Morwenna Rowe's mannequin was beginning to grow some tufts of red hair. Deanna Tamblyn's eyes occasionally seemed to follow her around the room, though it would have been imperceptible to any human onlooker. Only Gugwana's darkening mannequin gave any real movement, especially when it smiled. These changes had given Daphne hope for the last two years that there was a chance for these old witches to come back into the world as they once were. At the current rate, it would take years or more. For a woman possibly in her final days, it would be too late.

The mannequin dressed in Daphne's mother's clothes looked as plastic as it would in any clothing store in the world. There was no sign of life returning to that one. That fact hit Daphne with pain and grief every time she looked at it. But she kept her hopes alive. It was too painful not to.

Daphne approached Morwenna Rowe's mannequin and picked up the old broomstick that leaned against it. The end of the handle was still snapped off, a reminder of the moment she had dispatched the last demon against all the odds. She sat on the bed and turned it in her hands.

Two years before, she had slayed a real demon with this very broom handle. She had always hoped she wouldn't have to do it again, but now it was looking horribly likely. She placed the wooden pole across her lap and started to sharpen the end with Gugwana's knife. Shavings gathered on the floor by her feet, and fear welled up inside of her. She'd had two years to prepare for this moment. She had shelves of thick books to learn from. Yet all her trying had failed. She loved Sara, but watching her make so much progress had made her feel utterly inadequate, even stupid, so she'd put practising aside. It always led to failure, but with the books, at least the page count made her feel something akin to progress. Now she really wished she hadn't. The very fact that her hands were in front of her, working hard to sharpen a weapon to fight a demon again, terrified her. She was reverting to what had worked two years ago. It hit her how she had really made no progress at all.

If she was right, and if the bean-nighe's three-day lead-up to death was a demon-instigated bluff to break her down, she would need to fight a demon again. The sharpened broom handle gave her little hope, but it was all she had. So she shaved more and more wood from the end until the sharp point felt painful when pressed to the palm of her hand.

She stood and gripped it in front of the four mannequins and looked at them. 'Help me. Please.'

Silence.

Stillness.

Plastic.

If her old friends couldn't help her, then who could she turn to? Sara was already doing her best. Olivia briefly flashed to mind as the person she could always rely on. At the shared house by the college, she truly had been the most reliable friend anyone could dream of. But Olivia wasn't exactly the first person who would come to mind to slay demons, and even if they were still friends, she was missing and probably dead. Daphne suddenly felt more alone than ever. She was panicking and needed answers. Even if Sara was thin on the replies to her messages, it was a very short walk to visit.

She leaned the spiked broomstick back on the plastic Morwenna Rowe, walked down the stairs, dropped her keys in her pocket, grabbed her phone, and opened the front door.

A sharp pain shot through her shin and she clutched it in both hands as the child rushed past her into the house, gripping its stick and laughing as it swung it again, cracking Daphne on the knuckles as her hands defended herself.

The child stepped back into the hallway, twirled the stick in her fingers, and smiled.

Chapter Twenty-eight

DAPHNE STOOD STUNNED BY her front door and a feeling of dread built inside her, the feeling that she'd just really fucked up, as she looked back down her hallway at Penelope Pengilly. She stood barely a metre away, telescopic black stick in hand, a grin on her face that didn't match the terrible mess of her eye. At this range, it was finally clear what the stick was: a police baton, even if it was a little dirty and the end beaten and scraped into a point. Daphne reached forward, grabbing at her, ready to throw the child back out of the house, but ended up with a sharp *thwack* on the fingertip from the stick, forcing her phone onto the floor. As Daphne lurched down to get it, she ended up with a hard whack on the nose, forcing her back as Penelope Pengilly stamped hard on the phone, once, twice, three times, smashing it into pieces, then skipped down the hallway into the kitchen. Daphne wiped her wet upper lip. A steady drip of blood fell from her stinging nose.

Daphne was angry. She'd had enough. And now, with the clock counting down, she had nothing to lose. So instead of running out the door away from the demon or hiding in the house she knew so well, she hurried back up the stairs and grabbed the broomstick she had sharpened just a few moments before. She'd done it before and she'd do it again. It was time to end this. Now.

She stood in front of the four mannequins, holding the sharpened wood, knowing very well that the demon was downstairs in her house. 'I guess you're not coming to help this time, ladies,' she said. The four mannequins looked as plastic and lifeless as ever.

'Come on then, demon,' she whispered to herself, dragging her finger over the sharp point of the broom handle before yelling so loud it would have been heard by the piskies in the woods, 'Let's do this, you little fucker.'

* * * * *

As much as it sometimes felt like it, Daphne hadn't wasted the previous two years. She had worked hard and learned all she could. It was just her progress always seemed so slow, like there was some kind of invisible brick wall somehow stopping her from moving forward.

There must have been hundreds of old books on the shelves and in boxes left by her mother, and she hadn't known where to start. She felt a little embarrassed to discover that she'd even been tricked when she believed that witch magic revolved around rhyming spells. After searching the books for it for days and finding nothing, she asked Sara. It turned out that those old witches had been doing magic and hunting demons for so many centuries that they were simply making things more interesting, having their own little competition. Daphne knew it wasn't quite as simple as that though. Gugwana's little winks had conveyed extra information, and Daphne knew that she'd been quite deliberately fed the illusion of confidence. It had worked. Gugwana had fed Daphne a placebo to get her through the night, a reason to believe in herself. How she would have loved Gugwana to join her now. She wondered if there had been any other lesson in her performance that she had missed.

But that had all meant that the only thing Daphne knew is she still knew nothing at all. Even what she thought she knew was wrong. Just a game. As soon as she'd worked that out, any hint of magic she had just stopped working. She'd lost the belief and that was enough to lose the magic. Just a game. Why did everything in the non-human world always feel like a game? A game she always felt like she was losing.

Sara, meanwhile, confidently progressed in huge leaps. By eighteen, Sara could turn into a hare like most witches could, apparently. Daphne couldn't at twenty. Sara could control the undergrowth, walk around on the ceiling for fun, and open and close doors with her mind. Daphne couldn't do anything like that.

She had spent a lot of time trying to revive the old witches in mannequin form, especially her mother. She had no idea if the progress on the mannequins was her doing or if the old witches were doing it themselves through some kind of afterlife magic or from within the plastic.

She had read so many books yet made so little progress. Sara didn't read much. She'd read a chapter and then implement it until it would work, even if it took weeks. Perhaps having her mother as some kind of remote mentor was the difference. Daphne's mother couldn't be a mentor anymore from anywhere except the past.

Aside from the books, there was one more piece of essential reading that Daphne could turn to. Inside the box of possessions left by her mother that she had opened after the last time the demons came, was a letter. On the old envelope was written *Daphne*, followed by a single *X*.

Daphne had read it probably a thousand times now. It still hit her as hard as the first time.

❋ ❋ ❋ ❋ ❋

Dear Daphne dear,

There are things I have not told you. I did not tell you out of love. Out of protection. Because you are special, and the special needs protecting. But now the protected must become the protector, as I am no longer here to protect.

There are things on this Earth, dear Daphne, that are not of the human world, and this includes you. Excuse my brevity, but longwindedness will not serve you. The magick, however, will.

You are, as am I, and many of our friends and neighbours, for want of a better term; a witch. We witches reside on the street, and have done for as long as it has existed, for a doorway exists in the adjacent woodland where monsters will emerge from other realms. We sisters are the first line of protection from this doorway. If you are reading this; I am sorry. I will not be able to be your mentor in magick as I had dearly hoped. Instead; I refer you to the women who will make themselves known to you, as was planned for this eventuality; once you let them in.

Just remember; always, that you are not alone. Others will come to help. The first line of defence is not the last. The people you least expect will be your greatest allies. Lovers and friendships lost come back stronger. As, if the magick allows, shall I.

Most importantly; do not ever leave this house post-night-fall. For your protection, there are secrets held here that will be revealed to you only when the time is right. And when you find the demons, or the demons find you, do not let them win. For that, you simply need to be strong. And while I have been weak in teaching you the ways of the magick, in the art of being strong; I seem to have excelled. However weak you feel, your strength will always be there. Nourished with gentleness and warmth, it is a seed that will grow beyond the sky, I promise. But should you ever need me desperately to help find that strength as only a mother can help, look to where the moon should be in the sky, and should you see stars in its place, you will know I am with you.

With all the love and strength from another world to yours,

Mum x

PS Watch out for Morwenna; she dallies.

✳ ✳ ✳ ✳ ✳

Daphne had read the letter most nights. Whenever she got down with herself for failing to learn witch magic, she would read it and feel its warmth. She loved her old-world spelling of *magic*, and her typical overuse of semicolons despite admitting she had no idea how to use them. She'd always done that, and Daphne loved that that little piece of her still lived on paper. The content still concerned her, but she always felt better for reading it. The last line always left her with a smile.

Always.

Now was not the time for dallying. She had a demon to slay, and it was in her house.

And she was furious.

✳ ✳ ✳ ✳ ✳

Daphne clutched the sharpened broomstick as she turned at the bottom of the stairs and walked into the kitchen, where she had seen the possessed child run. 'Come on, you little shit,' she shouted, gripping the broomstick until her knuckles turned red.

The kitchen door sprung open as if by magic, Daphne not knowing if she was the one to have done it or not. Her anger pushed her forward, feeling strong.

'I'm not scared of you,' she said, stepping into the kitchen, ready to stab. At the other end of the kitchen stood Penelope Pengilly. The girl flicked her wrist and the baton extended. Daphne stared at the girl as the child's eyes sank deeper into her face and a red glow started softly and intensified.

Then Daphne charged.

The girl sidestepped her, jumping with an unnatural quickness onto the kitchen work surface. When Daphne turned around, the girl was at the far end of the room, standing, upside down, on the ceiling. She hung down like a bat, but her hair and clothes remained hanging upwards, gravity be damned.

A tapping came from outside, making Daphne jump. She looked to the window, where a crow stood outside on the window ledge, pecking at the glass. When she looked back to the ceiling, the girl was gone.

A firm whack on the back of her right knee hit with such force it bent and her kneecap hit the ground. She immediately pushed herself back up with the broom handle and turned around. The girl wasn't there. *Whack!* Another crack to the side of the knee left her reeling. She turned around to see the girl skipping whimsically away from her down the hallway and into the lounge. The tapping on the window stopped and the crow flew away.

Daphne limped towards the hallway, surprised that such a thin stick could pack such a whack. She got to the open lounge door and stepped in, sharp broomstick ready to stab.

Sitting on the floor in the lounge opposite the door, against the wall, was Penelope Pengilly, crying, her small, dirty hands covering her face. Daphne stepped forward, watching the girl carefully, moving slowly and carefully closer, poised and ready to strike. This was her chance, and yet it felt too easy. This was just another demon game. And yet she stepped forward, scanning every detail of the scene, waiting for the girl to act, ready to stab her, whatever trickery was coming, and end this demon once and for all. She towered over the girl, broomstick raised and ready. The ease of it all made her hesitate. And though it would have been incredibly satisfying just to spike the little shit, something was wrong. The girl in front of her looked, for the first time, like a truly distressed little girl and nothing like the possessed child that had been attacking her. And yet she still, for a split second, considered just ending it there and then.

A slivery slip slid up Daphne's spine, sending her into a shiver. Then a thick, guttural voice spoke from behind.

'You wouldn't kill a child, would you, Daphne Locke?'

Daphne spun around. There was nothing behind her. Nothing visible. She looked back at the young girl, clutching her eye in pain, her cries turning to screams. Daphne looked around the room again and saw nothing. She listened as all her senses spiked. Nothing but the sounds of a distressed child. When a pan clattered loudly, she ran back into the kitchen, point poised to stab. But Daphne was fighting blind, and she knew it. She'd been tricked, drawn to almost attack an innocent child by anger masquerading as strength. She couldn't win.

And then the kitchen door flung itself shut with a *bang*. Daphne was trapped. Every one of her senses was dialled up to maximum as she scoured the kitchen, clutching the sharpened stick now through fear rather than anger. She stabbed into the air fruitlessly, moves of desperation.

Yet, nothing came for her. Nothing struck her, nothing whispered nor stirred. It was as if there was nothing there. Nothing at all. As if she were alone.

She scoured the kitchen for clues of an invisible presence. Everything was still. She picked up a large pot of parsley, took off the lid, and flung the dry herbs from the pot into the air, spraying them across the room, expecting a space to be left where the demon was. Instead, the herbs landed evenly. She was alone. And the child in the lounge had stopped crying.

Daphne moved towards the kitchen door. It was thick wood and she couldn't know what was on the other side. Perhaps an invisible demon ready to strike. Perhaps a possessed child with an extremely painful whippy stick. Perhaps a poor child going through something that no child should ever endure. But *something* was waiting behind that door.

She opened the door slowly. It was silent. The only sound was the soft wind and murmur of the outside world coming through the hallway, the front door wide open leading to the calm and quiet dimness outside. The sound of a duck quack rattled down the walls from outside. Even in the circumstances and Daphne's adrenaline high, it still struck her as unusual.

Daphne moved quickly to the door and looked outside. In the middle of the road, two birds fought viciously. A duck and a crow, flapping around and at each other, pecking and slashing with their beaks, gouging at each other's eyes and ripping out feathers. The crow squawked and retreated, ran a few steps down the hill with the duck speed-waddling in pursuit. The crow flapped a damaged wing but still managed to take off and flew into the woods. The duck watched for a few seconds, glanced back at Daphne, then took off and flew in the other direction.

Daphne closed the door, a little confused about the strange sight, but with something more urgent to think about. She crept back down the hallway, quiet as a mouse, ready to check the whole house, room by room, to check that the child had gone. She looked upstairs first, starting with her mother's room. As she opened the door and peered in, sharp broom handle in hand, readied, she was hit with an awful dread that made her feel utterly sick. It wasn't what was in there that shook her. It was what was not.

The mannequins were gone.

Chapter Twenty-nine

POLICE US

JOANNE BACH SAT IN the toilet cubicle at the police station and waited until the bathroom door thudded shut and the room fell quiet and empty. And then she let herself cry.

The visions of the man in the wreckage were getting stronger and more frequent, and sometimes when she closed her eyes just to get a break from her work, up flashed the pictures, clear as the day she saw it all happen. The kids in the window. The steam seeping from the car. The heart on the tree bark. The dog-collar spine. It meant she could never rest.

That tiredness led to her other mental faculties weakening, and she knew it. The strength she thought she was regaining after the loss of her fiancé was waning, getting swallowed up by the image of the man in the car. The grip on her crazy thoughts about Hanging Hill Lane was slipping.

Her poor fiancé. Did Daz look as peaceful in death as the man in the car?

The bathroom lights switched off, the timer on the motion sensor deciding that the room must now be long-vacated. Joanne sat in the dark, trousers round her ankles, head in her hands, eyes peering through the dark to see something in the dim light, anything, just so the mental pictures wouldn't reappear to torture her.

She was just a human doing her best, and her best was not feeling enough. Tears dropped onto her black combat trousers as she forced her mind away from the horrible memory, away from the grief, and back onto what she was there to do. To make a difference. People were missing and they needed to be found.

The strong young lady who joined the police force to make a difference was sitting on the toilet in the dark, hiding, crying, alone.

She had to put an end to this. She needed some closure. She needed the pain to go.

Closure would have to come from the place where it had all begun. It just made sense. She was going to go back to Hanging Hill Lane and say goodbye to the place forever. Just as soon as she felt ready. Then she would be able to move on.

And then she was going to find Olivia Merrigan and get back to being a 'bad-ass cop', as an American friend had once called her.

But first, she would try to stop crying.

Chapter Thirty

Daphne silently searched her whole house and found nothing. No possessed child. No demon. No mannequins in witches' clothing. Until she peered into her lounge.

The four plastic figures stood near one corner of the room, each facing outwards from the perfect square they formed. Daphne's head darted around, looking for any sign of the demon or the young girl. The demon seemed to love to play games with her, and messing with those mannequins had really pissed her off, as if it had affronted her own mother. And yet, it appeared to now be gone.

She would put the mannequins back in their place upstairs before the night was over. But first, she needed to search the house for the demon or child. Jut to be sure. To feel safe.

Three hours later, and she'd found nothing.

Nothing at all.

* * * * *

That night, as she lay in bed and tried to sleep, Daphne heard the flap of the letterbox squeak open, the eerie creak penetrating the silence of the night. She pulled the cover firmly up towards her chin and gripped it tightly.

Then an unnaturally loud whisper echoed through the house from below, filling the whole house with sound.

'Three days turn to two.'

Chapter Thirty-one

Daphne chewed her breakfast slowly. She wasn't hungry at all. She had barely slept and her nerves and tiredness made the thought of food completely unappealing and the toast taste dry. She ate only because she knew that she may need her strength for what was coming. Without a phone to send messages, she waited for sunlight to return before she would go next door. She needed to tell Sara what had happened and seek help and advice. But she also desperately wanted to know if she had found anything new. If her worries were true, death would be coming the following night, with nothing in the world that could stop it.

Daphne stretched her leg out from her dressing gown and looked at the growing brown and black marks on her shin and knee, and the large scabs that looked like they would bleed again with the slightest touch. The bruises from the whacks of the demon-possessed child's stupid hitty-stick were protruding and darkening, and while it hadn't done any real damage, it added to the discomfort of everything, and the sting from the hits made her wary to leave the house for fear of receiving more. She found herself getting furious with the child, and having to remind herself that it was not the fault of the child at all. That poor kid was another victim in all of this. Another victim of the demons, another life ruined because of her. The only way to save the child would be to defeat the demon. But as long as the demon was inside the child, that was impossible.

Her mind had raced for most of the night, desperately seeking answers, but the dots she had connected still had some missing threads. If she was really going to die, why would the demon bother still trying to break her? What was the agreement the bean-nighe had spoken of? The textbooks spoke of a certain lore but mentioned no agreement. The bean-nighe would wash Daphne's clothes at sundown, and minutes later, she would be dead. And that, according to lore, was that. She was beginning to doubt Sara was even looking for an answer, rather, just telling her she was to give her some comfort in her final days. Sara. She really needed to see Sara.

She found herself standing quickly, the idea of a second attempt to grab her blouse back suddenly feeling like the only option. She sat down again when the memory of the piskies flashed into her mind. She needed help. Really needed help.

And then the doorbell chimed. It was early for a visitor, but maybe this wasn't a bad thing. Perhaps if Sara had been messaging and had no response, she'd be there to check up on her. She might be there to bring news. Daphne had never walked to the front door so quickly, yet still stopped to check the spyhole. She wasn't going to risk another whack or poke from the stick, and definitely would not be letting the demon girl in again.

She leant in quietly and peered through, breathing silently, fingers pushing against the letterbox to stop it opening and a stick coming stabbing through.

A head of messy blonde hair stood facing away from the door, waiting. It was a woman, but it wasn't Sara. Then the woman turned to face the door, looking panicked.

The face on the other side of the small round piece of glass was familiar. Distressed. Beautiful.

The woman staring blankly at her front door was Olivia.

Daphne still scoured the street through the spyhole for Penelope Pengilly before she opened the door, and when she did, prioritised a scan for the girl before she looked at her old friend. Daphne couldn't believe it. Not long ago, she had been worried sick for the safety of the woman who stared back at her, fighting tears and losing. But in the last day or more, she had almost completely forgotten about her, sidelined in her mind by the fear for her own life instead. Barely a thought entered Daphne's head as she stared in shock. This just didn't make sense. When she could finally find a word to speak, it was only the obvious one.

'Olivia.'

'Can I come in? Quickly?' said Olivia. And then she cried.

Chapter Thirty-two

Sitting on Daphne's sofa and faintly smelling of the salty sea, Olivia looked a shell of her former self. She had bags around her usually sparkling eyes and her hair looked as though it hadn't been brushed for days. The happy glow was dulled. The mischief and cheeky twinkle were gone. She looked like she'd given up on life. Her face may have been on the news every day and was probably on the front page of the local papers, but it was likely she wouldn't be recognised from her photos. The terrified woman who sat in front of Daphne was not the same woman she remembered. She looked as bad as Daphne felt.

The last time the pair had been together, Olivia had let Daphne down in her greatest time of need. When Daphne needed to run and hide, Olivia had refused to help, far too scared by the events going on around them. Daphne had forgiven Olivia. Olivia looked like she had not forgiven herself. Daphne didn't know where to start. And while she would have loved to help her old friend, she had more pressing things going on in her life, which may very soon be heavily truncated. And yet, Olivia was here now and may be able to connect some dots. If only she wasn't so distressed she could barely speak.

'Daph,' Olivia said, her breath pulsating quickly, unable to make eye contact with her old friend.

Daphne felt an apology was coming and prepared herself to console her old friend. She genuinely understood now.

'I did something bad, Daph,' Olivia said in a shaky whisper, as if she didn't trust her voice anymore. Daphne had never seen her like this before.

'It's okay, we were all scared,' Daphne said, assuring her friend that she was forgiven for abandoning her in her hour of terrifying need.

Olivia looked confused. It took a moment for the penny to drop. But then, as another tear started to roll from her eye, she balled up her fists as if ready to punch something and hit herself in the chest. Then again, and again, the third time likely hard enough to leave a bruise. Daphne grabbed her hands before she hit herself a fourth time, and Olivia cried harder, her breaths quickening.

'No, Daph. I did something so bad.' Olivia's eyes streamed, completely inconsolable.

It was the first time Daphne had thought about something other than the demon and the bean-nighe's agreement of her death for some time.

It wasn't until several minutes later that Olivia could speak again, mumbling, 'Shit,' leaving Daphne more curious about what Olivia had done with each passing minute. Eventually, she had to ask.

'What, Liv? What did you do?'

Chapter Thirty-three

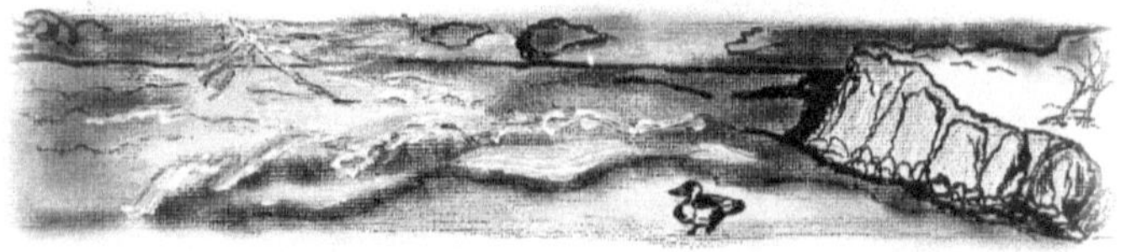

THE OLD WOODEN BENCH on the clifftop overlooked a small, grassy island and a beautiful beach below where waves lapped gently around a set of towering, jagged-sharp rocks. Olivia sat nestled between Nina and Heidi as they looked out over the calm Cornish sea, the black four-by-four shining behind them.

A sleek luxury yacht, partying women on deck, sailed by. Dance music wafted in over the waves and the steady beat climbed up onto the clifftop in the sea breeze, gently shaking the moment's tranquillity. Such a beautiful yacht. It glistened. It must have cost millions. There wasn't a cloud in the sky.

The whole thing had an air of perfection. The women sitting on the bench were the most perfectly beautiful women in the world. The sunset was perfect. The moment was perfect. As they talked, their voices blended musically, occasionally punctuated by the sound of the rolling sea.

Perfection was interrupted.

'I am truly sorry,' said Heidi.

'What for?' asked Olivia.

'Just go with it,' Nina said with a beautiful smile. 'No need to be afraid.'

'Afraid of what?' giggled Olivia, a little awkwardness unusually poking through.

'The sunset,' replied Nina.

Heidi quietly began to hum and gently raised her volume as it twirled into a pretty tune that somehow blended with the sound of the sea. She had a truly beautiful voice, the perfect soundtrack to the perfect view. Nina joined her in pitch-perfect soft and bright tones, quickly building power and breathing life into the melody. Their musical lines harmonised and intertwined, spinning up and around each other like the double helix of a strand of perfectly formed baby DNA, long to be touched by pain and darkness. When Heidi went up, Nina went down, and a cloud formed just over the sea. It was the most beautiful sound Olivia had ever heard, and the distant cloud turned grey.

Heidi placed her hand on Olivia's knee with a look that gently said, 'join us'.

Olivia knew now. *Don't be scared*. They were so damn good though, anyone would be scared of singing with them. She'd stand out like a sore thumb, a comparative cat-scream. But she felt compelled to try, and an intoxicating confidence hit her as soon as she hit the first note and felt her harmony blend in, bringing a pulling power to the sound.

Olivia had never known that three singers could tune into each other so quickly and produce such a spine-tingling, beautiful arrangement without a minute of preparation or practice. As Olivia and Heidi sang in perfect harmony, Nina punctuated it with a syncopated gentleness that seemed to pull the blackening clouds closer. As Olivia pulled a note into perfect pitch, everything suddenly felt so right, something profound in her life finally aligning.

The glistening yacht began a sharp turn towards the jagged rocks and beach below, the women onboard disappearing below deck as a cold wind blew up, and the waves grew taller as they crept in further.

The distant dance music stopped dead. The blood-red sun touched the top of the sea.

Nina briefly borrowed her voice from the music and smiled at Olivia. 'What a wonderful singer you are,' she said. 'What a wonderful singer you are,' before seamlessly returning her voice to the harmony as the temperature fell quicker than a witch dropping from the gallows.

A distant crack of thunder rumbled in over the sea and the wind blew stronger. The waves rolled harder and the yacht drew nearer. Nina whooshed, Olivia howled and Heidi's voice rolled as if up through magical scales, up, up, always somehow up, yet never reaching real highs nor crashing like the sound of the sea.

The sun sliced down through the horizon and darkness fell hard and fast, bringing with it a thick, black cloud which lined the sky. The lights of the yacht shone bright and near, bouncing violently on the roughening waves, dangerously close, and yet it kept coming. Closer. Closer, pointing towards the sharp tower of rock as the engines strained louder.

The waves crashed in and the women sang out, and the storm intensified. The boat raced in, dangerously close to the rocky beach, lights flickering, homing in at the knife-edge of the rock.

Nina stood and the others took her lead, heading towards an old wooden gate that led to a pathway down the cliffs to the beach. Olivia followed gladly and grinning, holding a soft, low note as she passed through. They walked lightly down the path towards the sand and rock, never missing a beat. Never missing a single beautiful note. The perfect arrangement of beauty, visual and aural. The perfect contrast to the ugly darkness that had formed above their heads as the rain began to fall and the boat accelerated towards the shore and the singing women who approached through the dark. Screams from the boat cut through their song.

Sparks flew through the darkness as the yacht smashed into the rocks, the stern yanked around onto the sand by the heightening waves, and all the boat lights flickered and fell. The moon shone through an opening eye in the cloud as the rain came down harder.

Small lights flicked on and shook inside the yacht. One, two, five, seven. The humans on the beached boat climbed down nervously, just crabs on a line. They were women. Young, beautiful women.

Olivia couldn't help but notice a familiar face: pop star Boddy stepped down rigidly. She stood by the boat and stared back at the three singing women. As Olivia looked at Boddy, once a musical favourite of hers, hate filled her chest and her breath quivered and her sung note filled with vibrato. She had never hated like that before. And yet, it still felt so right. She confidently loosened her tongue and trilled as she heard Heidi hit notes of new highs. And now they sang it with hate in their eyes.

More famous faces appeared from the boat. Deputy prime minister William Head jumped down in his tailored suit. Fat Brendan Burger followed. They'd been photographed together by the paparazzi just that morning, and the memes had been making the whole country laugh. But now, there was no humour. Just anger. And the anger was pure and right.

The sky roared and flashed, the wind forcing lashes of water across the beach and drenching the shivering, scared women who gathered under the cliffs. The three singing women followed the thunder's yell with a mischievous roar of their own, countering the brutality of the crack from the sky with a harmony so subtle and sweet that some of the young women holding their phone lights started to cry as they looked back from below the steep cliff face.

Three men in boatman's uniforms climbed down from the yacht and walked onward, drawn toward the three singing women. The crew had deep love in their eyes, somehow bringing Olivia a new level of fury, of rage, of an anger that could finally reveal itself.

The three crewmen marched towards the singing women. The three singing women stepped gracefully towards the three men.

And behind: Boddy. Burger. Head. All their eyes glowed red.

That was the moment Olivia felt herself split in two. The Olivia she knew herself always to be was aghast. She could do nothing but watch from the sidelines as her own body, singing more beautifully than she ever knew she could, marched on towards the three famous faces, her mind and body filling with bloodlust and hate.

The three crewmen had nearly reached the singing women, with looks of uncontrollable love on their faces. As they met, the men were thrust to the ground, each downed by one of the singing women, whose notes did not falter even as they struck. One man's leg cracked with a pop that matched the loudness of thunder. It bent at a right angle at the shin and a sharp break of bone poked out, the blood washing off quickly in the driving rain. His face betrayed he loved his attacker just the same.

Lightning flashed brightly. Three famous faces shone clear for barely a second under the sky's firebolt.

Boddy. Twenty-two. Red hair slicked back, purple lipstick smudged on her chin, thick makeup running down and across her face from the force of the pounding rain. Eyes glowing red and vicious.

Deputy Prime Minister William Head. Mid-fifties. Wig attached only to one side of his weird, bald head, flapping violently in the wind. Soaking suit. His red eyes glowed through his thick-rimmed glasses.

Brendan Burger. Forties. Topless and pot-bellied. Thin blood flowed from his unusually big nose into his mouth. His eyes glowed red as the thunder from the strike rumbled in across the rough sea.

The three women sang and walked and walked and sang, getting closer to those with the eyes that glowed, and their song matched the roar of the thunder.

Two of the red-eyed three started their approach to the women, love somehow glowing through their red eyes. But Boddy was stuck, her foot caught under the sea as another huge wave crashed in and a lightning bolt spat down onto the rocks.

Olivia glanced up at the horrors in the sky. It made her feel powerful. Then on the clifftop, silhouetted by a flash from the clouds, stood a woman. When the next flash came half a second later, she was gone.

As the two red-eyed men approached the singing women, pop star Boddy did not, her leg stuck to the sea bed, caught under the boat now beached in the shallows. Yet a creature from within Boddy was being drawn out of her, its horned head moving towards the singing women with demonic love in its eyes, discarding the trapped human shell behind it to reach the targets of its affection.

The three lovely singing creatures stepped within reach of the two besotted red-eyed men. Nina sang pretty and high, a soft and gentle trill, as she slammed her fist through the pigeon chest of William Head, ripped out his heart, and dropped it onto the sand where it gave its final beats. With the sharp point of her red right shoe, she toed it up in a gentle arc, and down it splashed into a small rock pool where a crab scampered across for dinner. Olivia watched as William Head's wig finally lifted off and blew up and away, dropped with the wind, and cartwheeled up the wet sand towards the cliffs. It amused part of her and horrified another. William Head crumpled and fell with a splash.

The horned creature had half left Boddy's body, inching forward out of her and towards the women. Heidi sang a beautiful counterpoint harmony as she double-palmed the creature hard, forcing it back into the human woman behind it, who fell into the sea, her leg snapping under the boat as she landed. Heidi put one foot on Boddy's back and dug in her shiny heel. She rolled her over in the shallow water and Boddy's eyes glowed again. Heidi knelt, wailed a wonderful coo just as Olivia and Nina beautifully traded haunting harmonics, and sliced through the pop star's chest with the fingertips of an open palm before pushing the hand inside. The wind howled and the red eyes sunk away, and the moon shone red through a smile in the clouds. It made a haunting reflection on the sea.

Olivia watched on from the passenger seat inside her brain as her feet stopped in front of fat billionaire Brendan Burger, and felt her anger reach new heights. She knew what she was going to watch herself do. She was powerless to stop it.

So she just smiled. And she sang. She took him over one knee. The blood from the moon was devoured by a hellish flash from the sky. Olivia coiled up a rock in her fist, and everything felt so horrible and right.

And then she paused.

She stopped singing. And she listened to the sound of the sea. It sounded loud, but not as loud as the rain that pounded all around. Not as loud as the anger. Such rage. A storm in her stomach and chest and head.

Brendan Burger, that fucking cunt.

She forced him to the sand on his back, and knelt.

Her voice came back on the perfect note as her hand smashed through Burger's chest. Something inside wriggled and clawed until she instinctively grabbed whatever it was and squeezed the life out of it, and the red eyes on Burger's fat face faded away. When she stood, she saw Nina at the shoreline, thirty yards away, holding high William Head's bald severed skull in one hand, spine hanging and dripping with synovial fluid, rain and blood, silhouetted against the soft, pretty moonlight reflected from the sea.

Then from behind that spine still steaming, there flew a duck, duck duckbill gleaming, and when it landed on the shore, it pecked and pulled and slurped the gore. *Something's not right*, Olivia thought, *ducks don't eat gore*. And then it pecked and slurped some more.

Olivia watched on from deep inside her head, in disbelief of what her hands had done, in disbelief of what she was seeing, in utter terror of what she was learning she was capable of. And yet, the anger still reigned. Her hands trembled. In fear, in anger, in coldness, it didn't matter. She still had more to do.

When she turned, the three boatmen were walking back towards them, one with a heavy limp and a shin flapping at a right angle, all totally entranced with heavy love in their eyes.

No red. Just love.

The wind howled louder, the sky cracked again, and the singers had lust in their eyes.

They didn't miss a beat as they slaughtered them all.

Olivia watched Heidi pull off every limb from the captain's body. She was singing an F-sharp note as the final leg tore off. Nina drowned one in a rock pool between two nonchalant crabs, then snapped his body in two. She sang a D note as she lifted the torso and poured the sloppy long guts into the pool. Olivia smashed the last man's head, smash after smash, hit after hit, crack after crack, with a glint in her eye and a rock in her fist until his face caved in and a chunk came off and the rain made small dimples in his brain. She smashed and she sang and she smiled and the flash – that cataclysmic lightning flash that felt like it would never fade – lit up the bloody sight and burnt a permanent picture into Olivia's consciousness like a photoflash.

The heavy rain pocked holes in his brain.

She'd finished on a cracking top A. It was a beautiful chord, a perfect A-major. And they sang it with lust in their eyes.

The poor young party women shivered and watched on in terror from under the cliff face, cowering. But as the breath drained away from the last male on the beach, the singing faded away with a last roll of tongue and thunder, and the anger retreated with it. The waves calmed and the sea sounded soft. It sounded like breathing. Like taking a breath. The peaceful, kind rhythm of the sea.

William Head's wig blew between the group of shivering women and wrapped around the bare leg of a pretty, young freckled girl with a soggy blonde bob. When the wind died suddenly, the wig dropped onto the wet sand.

'Go,' said Heidi, and the three singers marched silently off up the path.

'Well, that was dramatic,' said Nina with a conspiratorial knowing grin, as if giving a little wink to all those watching from other places well beyond the sky.

Olivia sank into her own head, starting to question reality, panicking, her trembles intensifying. She was distracted only by the strangeness of a hare hopping along the path the other way, heading down towards the beach, stopping right in front of her. It looked up. She looked down. Then the hare hopped past her towards the beach, and Olivia walked on.

Nina looked to Olivia as they accelerated back up the cliff path towards the wooden gate and smiled. 'What a good little piggy you are,' she said, 'what a good little piggy you are.'

The stricken party women remained down on the beach.

Those poor women.

One sobbed to the sound of the sea.

Chapter Thirty-four

'Shit, Liv.'

Olivia looked at Daphne as if some of the weight had been lifted from her shoulders, perhaps working in the same way as a confession.

'Wait, Liv. Just to be clear, there were three demons?'

'Demons?' replied Olivia, confused.

'Three people with the glowing eyes?'

Olivia stared back at her old friend, confused at the response. 'Why don't you care? This isn't just some story, this really happened.'

'I believe you, Liv. But listen, please answer my questions, then I promise I will explain.' The thought of asking questions briefly took Daphne's mind back to the bean-nighe's evil trickery, and a reminder hit her that she was likely now approaching her final day. Dots in

Daphne's brain tried to connect. Olivia just stared back blankly through her tears.

'Please, Liv. Three demons, right? Three people with the red eyes?'

'Yes.'

'And you killed them all?'

'Yes. The people and the things inside. I felt it. I was drawn to do it. I couldn't stop myself. Please don't hate me.'

'It wasn't my demon,' Daphne said softly.

'What?'

'Wait. She called you a piggy?'

'Yes. Fucking bitch. I ran away as soon as they tried to get me back in the car. It was like I woke up.'

'Truffle pig. You're a truffle pig.' One of those who sniffle and snuffle the truffles, one who can stop the demons now sat in her lounge beside her.

'Please, Daphne, don't be weird on me. Not now.'

'Truffle pig. Hunter of the fungus. You're a fucking demon hunter, Liv. Fucking hell, where have you been?'

'In a beach hut, hiding. I washed the blood out of my clothes in the sea that night and have just been hiding ever since. I had nowhere else to go. I don't know what to do, Daphne. Help me, please. I hate myself.'

'Olivia, listen to me, please.'

Daphne filled Olivia in about the world she was also a part of that she hadn't known existed. She told her about what had happened two years before, and about how the witches guarded the demon entrance at the bottom of Hanging Hill Lane. About Morwenna Rowe, Deanna

Tamblyn and Gugwana. About her mother, and the mannequins that stood in her mother's room upstairs.

'So,' said Olivia. 'So what am I?'

Daphne smiled. 'A truffle pig.'

'Why do you keep saying that?' asked Olivia. 'I'm a murderer. The whole thing feels like a dream.'

'You keep the evil from this world, Liv. It just seems you ladies do it with a little more... I don't know, collateral damage.'

That phrase didn't sit well with either of them, and Daphne regretted it as soon as she said it. She continued, trying to soften it. 'It's the way the demons work, Liv. Take control of influential people and bring terrible evil into the world. I dread to think what might have happened if you hadn't been there to stop them.'

'Those people died,' Olivia cried again.

'That's not on you. That's on the demons. Whenever the demons are around, people die. That's not any of our fault. We're the protectors.' Daphne half realised she was alleviating her own guilt as much as Olivia's. She now had fifteen fewer live neighbours than she had two years before, and she knew it was because of her. 'Demons bring evil. We stop them, Liv. And you do it better than me.'

'I enjoyed it though, Daph. I've been over and over it again for days. I've been torturing myself, trying to work out what happened and what I am. I thought I knew. I thought I was a...'

'A what?'

'Doesn't matter. But now you're telling me I'm a stupid truffle pig. And that's what she called me. A piggy. What the hell is going on?'

'Call it what you want, Liv. I call you a demon hunter. And that's pretty fucking cool.' Daphne smiled, trying to bring Olivia out of her slump. It didn't work.

'People died, Daph. I took innocent lives. A week ago, I was a fashion graduate getting pissed off trying to build my website. Now apparently I'm a demon hunter. I'm a murderer.'

'No. I'm glad you're here, Liv.'

'What?'

'Liv,' Daphne said, suddenly looking serious and a little down. 'I've got something to tell you. I think you might end up going it alone on this one. I can introduce to you my friend Sara. She can look after you. She knows more about all this than me.'

'Where are you going? You can't leave me now.'

Daphne looked sad. 'They tricked me. I don't have much time.'

Olivia's face dropped on the realisation of what Daphne had meant. 'The demons?'

'I don't know.'

Sadness bubbled up behind Olivia's face. 'But we killed them all.'

'There's one more. And even if I beat it, I don't know if that will save me.'

'Can I help?' Olivia asked, a little unsure.

Daphne thought back to the images of what Olivia had said. Slaughtering the people who housed the demons without thought or hesitation. It would be a death sentence for Penelope Pengilly. She might as well have just stabbed her herself.

'You can't, Liv. I'm sorry.'

'Well, then I don't know what to do. I can't go home, they'll find me and I'll definitely go to prison.'

Daphne looked at her old friend and what a state she was in. 'You could start by having a shower,' she said with a gentle smile.

'I'd love that.' Olivia smiled back. 'But I've got no clean clothes.'

'You can borrow mine?'

Both of them knew that the full foot of height difference meant that wasn't going to work. It was the first time either had even considered a smile.

'Get in the shower,' Daphne said. 'I'll have something for you when you're ready.'

* * * * *

Daphne knocked on Sara's door, Sara looking a little surprised to see her as she answered.

'Any news?' asked Daphne.

'I'm sorry.'

'Can I borrow some clothes? I have a friend in my shower and mine won't fit her. Just for a few days.'

Sara looked back, a confused expression on her face. 'Sure. Come in.'

Daphne pushed the front door closed behind her and stepped in as Sara rushed upstairs. She reappeared a minute later with a couple of tops and some loose trousers and handed them over to Daphne.

'Thanks. So you've got nothing for me? I'm really running out of time.'

'That's why I'm a little confused about you popping around for clothes.'

Daphne thought about how she should start the story of what she'd just heard. But then Sara spoke again.

'I'm so sorry, Daphne, I'm in the middle of something important. I don't mean to kick you out, but I've got to do this. It might be some light for you, if I can manage it.'

'Oh, thank you,' Daphne said. 'Thanks for the clothes. I better go then.' She turned.

'Wait.'

Daphne turned back. Sara was looking back at her.

'You must be hungry, Daph. Have you eaten? Or got enough food? You must eat.'

Daphne thought more about Olivia than herself. She probably hadn't eaten for days.

'You want a pizza?' Sara asked.

If there was anything that would get Olivia eating, it would be a pizza. The thought even appealed to Daphne, who hadn't realised she was hungry until now. 'You got one I could warm up?'

'One second.' Sara disappeared inside her lounge and returned three seconds later with a small smile and two steaming hot cardboard takeaway boxes and handed them over. 'Just something else I recently learned. Enjoy.'

Magic pizzas. Any other day that would have been cool as hell.

'Wait,' said Sara, as Daphne stood with the hot pizza boxes, and Sara's expression fell to sadness. 'Can I have a hug?'

'Of course,' replied Daphne. The hug was physically awkward with the square boxes in between them, but even in the seriousness of the situation, Daphne realised she was grateful for that little bit of distance.

'Sorry,' said Sara as she released her arms and backed away. 'That was selfish of me. I'm just worried.'

'That wasn't selfish, Sara. I'm here for you too. Especially if you're going to give me magic pizzas.' Daphne felt her eyes start to water, matching Sara's.

'I need to get on, I don't have much time.' Sara backed away and smiled through her sadness.

Daphne made her way across the front of the houses, keeping a firm eye out for Penelope Pengilly and her whippy-stick, clothes and warm pizzas in her arms, and safely made it into her house. Sara had given her some jogging bottoms and a couple of tops, one white with some frills and one blue. Blue had always been Olivia's colour. This would probably please her and make her feel a little more like herself, if she noticed. A bulge in the pocket of the frilly white top made Daphne check inside. It was just some of Alfie's mittens. She dropped that top on the sofa, walked to the bathroom where the sound of running water had stopped, and passed the clothes through the door.

* * * * *

Daphne was awoken on her sofa when Olivia emerged in Sara's clothes, looking halfway back to her old self. She must have been incredibly tired to have dropped off like that. Of course she was. The pizzas smelled good.

'Thank you so much,' Olivia said with a smile. 'You want to sleep, don't you? I'm going to sneak back to the beach hut and have a think. Work out what to do. Because right now, I have no idea.'

'You want to stay here tonight?' Daphne realised too late she shouldn't have said that. As much as she would have loved someone on her side to fight the demon that tormented her, she knew that it would mean death for poor Penelope Pengilly.

'Thank you. But I just want to be alone. Is it okay if I come back if I change my mind?'

'Of course. Always.' Daphne picked up Olivia's freshly charged phone, unplugged the power cable, and passed it over. 'I don't have a phone right now, so don't text. I'll check for messages on the laptop though.'

'Perfect. Things will be alright then, I'm sure.' She didn't look sure.

'Want to take a pizza?'

Olivia looked at the box and silently shook her head.

'Stay safe,' said Daphne, kind of pleased to be left alone so she might get a little bit of sleep. But instead, her mind just raced. She should have told Sara about Olivia. She felt bad for not mentioning it. She took a bite of a slice of cooling pizza, and then, out of nowhere, Paulie jumped into her mind. The thought that she would likely never see him again felt like a punch to the gut, and panic rose and overwhelmed her.

Paulie. She had started a lovely new chapter in the story of her life with Paulie. And then the demons had come back and snuffed it out. That was now over.

The pizza slice fell to the floor.

Chapter Thirty-Five

DAPHNE SHIVERED HERSELF TO sleep that night in the house that felt so cold. She was so, so tired from the sleepless nights and the fear and anxiety that filled her days. From the stress and worry. From the huge spikes of adrenaline that would subside and leave fatigue in its place, deeper each time. The worry would have kept her up almost any other day of her life. But tonight, she was so tired that the idea of being dead the following nightfall somehow felt like it had some kind of peaceful finality to it, like she was finally free to give up and rest, and it helped her finally drift off. Weirdly, she had a happy sleep.

She could almost tell she was smiling as she slept, dreaming of her mother and her quirky silliness. It was like, even in death, this wonderful lady would return to comfort her in her dreams. Daphne dreamed she was a child once more, her mother sitting on the side of the bed, reading her a bedtime story. But the words she spoke weren't from the *Three Billy Goats Gruff* or *The Very Hungry Caterpillar*, but the letter Daphne had read so many times that, even in her dreams, it was word-perfect.

But then her dream changed.

Her mother dissolved into the bedsheets as Daphne found herself running through Hanging Hill Woods, away from creatures that could not be seen. Next, her body stopped moving, even though her legs kept running. As her lovely dream turned to nightmare, her running legs felt themselves stop moving at all, her arms pulled into and against her sides by the undergrowth of the woods reaching out from the bushes, constricting her body, limbs unable to move, a great weight on top of her as a piskie moved right up against her face. Daphne tried desperately to punch it but her arms wouldn't move, and the piskie smiled, revealing long, sharp teeth. She was terrified enough to be jolted awake.

It wasn't a piskie a few inches from her nose.

It was the face of Penelope Pengilly, one eye dripping with pus, the lower lid twitching, the child grinning through the dark.

Daphne instinctively tried to pull her arms up to push the girl away, but even awake, they still did not move. She tried to kick her legs in panic, but they, too, were stuck. Stuck against the mattress and stuck together. She bounced and wriggled but she was somehow bound to her bed, completely unable to move, trapped with this evil young girl right on top of her, staring at her out of an infested eye. The child sat up, and in the light of the moon that shone through the window, Daphne almost threw up when she saw what had bound her so tightly.

The bottom half of the girl was no longer human, rather, a series of long slimy tentacles like an octopus or deep-sea squid. The tentacles wrapped tightly under the bed and around again, squeezing her down, while others stretched and bound her feet and knees together and her arms to her sides. There were so many tentacles, all wound together like a tangle of thick string, that she didn't know where one tentacle started and another one finished. And on top of them all sat the torso and head of Penelope Pengilly, smiling, something moving under an infected eyelid.

Her chest felt constricted and breathing felt heavy and slow, her knees pushed outward but this thing was so tough she might as well have been pushing against two brick walls.

One slippery tentacle tip brushed Daphne's face, leaving a stinking slime across her cheek, and then rose above her, a few inches from her eyes. Then from the soft wet underside of the tip of the tentacle, a small slit opened revealing cat-like teeth and what looked very much like a human tongue, which slid out and lapped around the air right in front of her eyes. Daphne instinctively jerked to roll across the bed to grab the sharp broomstick she had left on the floor next to her, ready if she needed it. Her body didn't budge. She was trapped. She had lost. She looked up at the face of Penelope Pengilly, the humanity of her face gone, and evil stared back through the eyes. Two more tentacle ends moved towards her face, the toothy slits opened, and tongues slipped out. It was the most disgusting thing she had ever seen, in waking or in her night terrors, and the three tongue-tipped tentacles descended on her face, licking her cheeks, chin, and forehead, leaving thick trails of slime as another tentacle slowly slithered forward, its tongue pushing into her left ear while another worked its way through her hair.

Daphne squeezed her eyes closed, helpless and trapped. All the textbooks she had read, all the hours and weeks she had studied them, every note she had made, now all revealed as utterly useless.

But, as nightmares can persist into the hours of the waking day, her beautiful dream persisted into this nightmare, and her thoughts turned to her mother's letter, as if she had been visited in her dream to remind her of these exact instructions. *Do not let them win*. It was starting to feel too late for that.

'Your last day will not be a pleasant one,' hissed the demon voice and a tongue forced itself partway into her mouth. Daphne felt the tongue tip dance around in her mouth, and when it hit her tongue, she couldn't help but notice the taste. And while her tongue did the unavoidable tasting, her nose felt like it was going to explode, as if the juice from the bottom of an abattoir's bin on a hot summer's day had been thickened and shat in and poured into her mouth and nostrils.

Daphne lay silent but for her squirming, forcing her lips together, and did not let the tongue in further. She squeezed her eyes tighter and pictured her mother. She pictured the letter she had read every single night, trying desperately to gain strength from somewhere. She could feel her breath quickening through her nose, faster and faster, out of control. She felt the tingling in her fingers and toes and her head went light and she found thinking too difficult. She had nothing left but the capacity to panic, a last evolutionary attempt at survival like a fish flapping around on the ground in the hopes it might randomly land in water.

The flapping never lasts for long.

As her head lightened with hyperventilation, so too did the grip of her lips against each other, and the tongue slipped deep into her mouth as her strength turned to limpness.

'I can stop,' hissed the demon through the little girl's mouth. 'I can stop and make life so much fun.'

Daphne's breath now sounded like shivering and she retched on the tongue that made its way back towards her throat, almost bringing up a wave of vomit.

It was then she felt it again. Just like in her flashbacks to her first horrible demon encounter, it was almost like she left her own body and detached herself and watched on from outside her physical self. That was the only way the pain was not too great. Though the anguish she felt was gone, she knew she wasn't confronting the demon like she was supposed to do. She was running away from her own head. And if she wasn't in her own head, then perhaps there was room for the demon to get in, and that was something she wasn't prepared to let happen. Not ever. She opened her eyes and watched as the demon appeared to be entering her head, leading with its front tentacle, sliding in through her mouth.

She turned her eyes and looked outside through a slit in the curtains to the moon, desperate to see the stars her mother had promised her, and the full moon shone bright. Daphne would have to rely on her own self, and she fought herself all the way from the depths of her mind to bring her attention back to what was really happening right there on her bed: the demon squeezing her to the bed with horrible, slippery tentacles, determined to break her. To get in. Just knowing that she wasn't going to run away from her mind brought her a little strength, even if her body had none that could compare to the evil demon that slid up her stomach, as if ridden by a young girl with glowing red eyes.

The full moon shone brighter.

Daphne had to act fast or lose. She looked straight at the possessed girl's face. The tentacles gripped so tight that Daphne feared that even if her mind would not break, her body felt ready to crack and split. The hangover from Daphne's dream was not one of fear, however, despite the scary chase through the woods. It remained one of strength, given to her by the image of her mother sitting on the bed with her. It was with that strength that she bit down hard on the intruding tentacle, the demon screaming and yanking it from her mouth, its human-like tongue retracting into the tip and the toothy slit closing up.

She screamed as she felt a wet tentacle slide under the covers up over her left ankle and onto her calf. But Daphne still felt strength. And now she felt anger. It was a combination she knew she could use well, so she smiled back at the demon inside the child.

'Why do you want a cuddle so much, demon? Is it because I killed your stupid bitch wife?'

The demon slid a tentacle up to the back of her knee and Daphne held back the urge to scream with dread. Her strength was starting to diminish with the returning feeling of helplessness as the tentacle made wet circles in the back of Daphne's naked knee. Instead of trying to push apart against the constricting tentacles, her leg muscles reversed and instinctively forced her knees together.

'I have already won, Daphne ant,' hissed the demon. 'You would have killed this little girl if I was not there to stop you, and you know it. You have changed, because you have broken, and now I merely await space to enter. You cling on by a breaking thread and you do not know it because you are stupid.'

'Fuck you,' Daphne said, doubt flooding into her mind and body.

'You would have stuck that stick right through her sweet little head. You were about to strike. I stopped you.' The slippery tentacle whipped up under Daphne's body to the small of her back, and inched up her spine, repeating the feeling she'd had while she had towered over the young girl with the spiked stick.

'You're wrong,' Daphne said. But in her mind, doubt was pushing her to remember. Would she have done it? She was angry. She had the demon where she needed it. She had the chance to end things and win. She could easily have struck. She had been inches away from killing a little girl. Perhaps she really would have done it. Part of her had wanted to. But she had hesitated. Of course she wouldn't have done it. Except she didn't really know that.

The young girl looked at Daphne and spoke in the sad, sweet voice of a human child. 'You were you going to kill me, Daphne. Why do you want to hurt me? I didn't do anything wrong.'

'I would never hurt her,' cried Daphne with sympathy, tears growing in her eyes. The girl waited until her eyes filled with water and a tear fell down her cheek, then gave a huge whack from her stick right across the side of Daphne's face before speaking again in a cute little voice that, under any normal circumstances, would have given Daphne a huge smile.

'Will you be my friend?' it said, then brought the stick down hard on Daphne's forehead before hissing like the demon it was. 'Get out. Let me in and your suffering will stop.' The tentacles squeezed harder and the air wheezed from Daphne's lungs.

'I'm not going anywhere.'

The young girl gave another almighty whack of the stick across Daphne's face, stinging her cheek and leaving her ear ringing and wailing, before the tentacles untwined and moved back off the bed across the bedroom, the tongues retracting back into the tips of the long tentacles. Daphne breathed again as she watched the girl who was once Penelope Pengilly sit atop a walking nest of smooth-moving tentacles, which crabbed across the floor and then up the wall, where the girl sat perfectly perpendicular, her hair falling sideways towards the wall rather than the floor, looking directly at Daphne, tapping her stick in the palm of her hand.

A tiny worm dropped from her eye and bounced then wriggled on the carpet.

Daphne inched towards the edge of the bed where she had left the spiked broom handle, as the demon girl watched on. When Daphne jolted to grab it, the demon yanked it from the floor before she had a chance, the broom quickly becoming entwined in a long, disgusting limb.

'Want this?' it asked with a surprisingly nurturing voice, passing the broom handle from its tentacles to the little girl's human hands. She dropped her baton to the floor and inspected the sharp wooden spike as a tentacle gently caressed her cheek.

Daphne felt another drop of hope disappear. She had lost the physical battle from the very first moment and she knew it. But this was a battle of minds. She sat up, then stood.

The girl pulled off the straw end of the broom and dropped it on the floor. Then she turned it around and looked at the spike. 'Stabby stabby,' said a cute young girl's voice.

Daphne stood tall and stepped towards the demon by her door, stepping forward with little to lose. 'I've still got two days left, you fucking moron,' she said as she opened her bedroom door. 'Two days that you gave me, right? Two days that you cannot reverse because you made an agreement that you cannot change. You're not going to do shit and you know it.' The demon looked back. For the first time ever, it somehow looked lost for words. Daphne stepped away from the door. 'Now fuck off out of my house.'

The demon beast climbed down the wall to the floor, gently placing the young girl on her human feet, and the tentacles disappeared mysteriously back inside her. The young girl moved quicker than Daphne could see, let alone react to, and she felt the end of the broomstick strike deep into her stomach like an enormous punch in the gut. Then the little girl stepped back and Daphne realised that she hadn't been stabbed. She'd been hit with the blunt end and winded, but not cut.

'You forget something crucial, as the stupid do,' said the demon girl.

'What?'

'You're out of date, Daphne ant. Out of date and out of time.'

'I won't let you win.'

'Oh, but I have won,' grinned the demon child. 'I'm sure even one as stupid as you will work it out. Or you would if you had time. Now, go to bed like a good little girl.'

Then the girl dropped the broom handle, picked up her little black baton, and walked on her own two feet to Daphne's bookshelf. She dragged the baton's tip along her selection of horror books. 'Stories for children,' said the child, which pissed Daphne off more than she expected. 'Stupid books for stupid people, written by the stupidest of them all.' It carried on running its finger along the spines of the books. '*The Exorcist*?' It laughed. 'It doesn't work like that.'

Daphne watched, scared and confused. What was it doing? It stopped on *The Suffering* and pulled it out. Then it walked back to the corner of the room, pulled out the chair from under the desk, sat down, and started reading. It looked up at Daphne and whispered, 'Sweet dreams.' Then the child looked back at the book. Daphne could see her one good eye moving side to side. The demon really appeared to be reading.

Daphne stood, poised and ready to fight. But the demon in the girl just sat there, reading. It turned a page quietly. Daphne backed away. She thought she'd beaten it, for the night at least. She hadn't let it win. And now it was just reading. Just sitting, reading, with one eye scanning the page, left to right, left to right, and the eye weeping with pus fixed directly onto her, glaring with a horrible, unblinking stare. When the weeping eye blinked, it would have looked like the girl had winked at her, except a wink wasn't fitting with a glower like that from the fixed, gunk-filled eye that crawled with another tiny worm. It was horrible. And then she realised its simple plan.

It wasn't going to let her sleep.

After barely any sleep for a few nights now, that simple plan might be enough to break Daphne. She sat on her bed, still ready to move if the child did, her nervous system on high alert. But the most the demon moved was its fingers, simply to turn the page.

Daphne sat on her bed for what felt like hours as the adrenaline spike made way for tiredness. She felt her eyelids falling and forced them back up a second later, expecting the demon to have seized the moment of blindness.

The demon just turned another page. Then it looked at Daphne's clock. 'Midnight. And there's sand in your book.'

Daphne looked at the clock. It spoke the truth. It was only midnight. It had felt like she had been fighting sleep for the whole night.

Then the demon spoke again, calm and matter of fact. 'Two days turn to one.' Then it returned to its reading with its good eye, the other never straying from her.

Eventually, Daphne gave in to closing her eyes. It felt like just for a second. And then realising she was falling asleep with the demon in her room, she threw them open again, her body jolting, hands ready, preparing to defend itself. But the demon had gone.

Daphne searched the whole house. There was no sign of the demon or the young girl it inhabited. She was so tired she couldn't tell for sure, but she really did believe it had gone.

Returning to bed, Daphne couldn't sleep despite her extreme tiredness. After the demon had left, she found herself alone with something that was becoming much more terrifying.

The thoughts she could not stop.

Chapter Thirty-six

SOMEHOW, AS TERRIFYING AS the demon in the girl was, Daphne had still found the strength to survive its games. Strength to fight back and refuse to let it win. And now it was gone. That strength, still bubbling and punching, had nowhere to go. She'd been poised to fight for hours, but the demon had just sat down reading, protected by the shell of a young child and Daphne's morals that ensured she would never strike. And with that strength still desperate to fight, now she was alone, that strength had found a target.

That's when, full of fear and tiredness and worry, Daphne got to work torturing herself.

This might be her last day, alone in her bed, a failed witch. She'd never had a real boyfriend and had so few close friends. She'd never achieved anything. And now it was too late. Her whole life suddenly felt like a failure. And she had no time left to fix it.

As thoughts of Paulie rushed into her mind, she found herself gasping in despair. They were starting something. She knew he really liked her. He would be devastated when she was dead. She pictured him receiving the news of her death and breaking down, then alone and grieving painfully after she was gone. The pain that the image inflicted on her was more painful than any hit from the child's baton. Her beautiful time with Paulie was over before it had even begun, and it would be Paulie left to suffer and wonder. That was her fault. She'd done that. If she didn't cause him to die, she would cause him more pain than anyone could ever deserve. So selfish. So stupid.

And poor Olivia. She had been such a good friend at college. The perfect friend. She'd messed up once because she was scared, and Daphne had just let her go. Dumped her as a friend for being scared of demons. What kind of a stupid, nasty bitch would do that?

And Sara. Why hadn't she listened to Sara? She'd hidden in the pages of her mother's old textbooks instead of practising her only way to fight, it was so clear now, and she was paying the price of her own stupidity. She had been hiding behind the illusion of progress, page after page of the dusty old books, pretending to herself that she was learning while Sara was off doing great things. Creating magic, not reading textbooks. It was so clear. She'd been scared of herself and learned nothing. That was her fault too. And now Sara would be left alone, the last witch on Hanging Hill Lane. That could be the end of her. That was

Daphne's fault too. Perhaps that was partly Sara's fault. Perhaps she should have given her more warning about the demons last time. Sara and her mother clearly thought she was too stupid to know. Turns out they were right. Daphne deserved it.

She had never felt so intensely alone. For a brief second, she considered falling on her own spiked broomstick. But she was quick to dispense with that thought.

Why hadn't she spent more time with her mother? Sure, she didn't know their special bond was going to be severed in an instant without a goodbye, but now she missed her more than anything. That unassailable grief had never left her, only been buried under the textbooks and the illusion of progress and distractions of talk of an incoming war. And yet, that was the lesson all along. People can go forever without a goodbye. Her mother's final lesson had been to value people because one day they won't be there, perhaps quite suddenly. She hadn't listened and, instead, hid in bloody textbooks.

So stupid.

Now, she'd completely messed up everything and destroyed the lives of the people she cared about the most. She was distraught. If she were to die, she deserved it anyway. It wouldn't be long. Perhaps the demon was just dishing out justice based on what people deserve. Maybe she should just let it happen. Or maybe – fuck it, maybe she should just let the demon have its way with her. It's not like she could mess up any more than she already had. At least then the torture might stop.

In place of sleep, the memories regressed further. At nine years old, she'd called her best friend fat to impress the cool new kid. Stupid. She wished she hadn't done that. She'd tripped up the geeky girl during a netball game just because she could. Stupid. She wished she hadn't done that. It felt like all the bad things she'd done were coming back to haunt her, and trivial as they had always seemed, they now felt like the most important things in the world. And the time she said something embarrassing at a party and cringed every time she thought about it ten years later. She was a kid, but she must have always been stupid. These things were back to punish her. And she deserved it. She didn't need a demon to beat her into despair. She was quite capable of doing that for herself.

But there were more parts than one at play in Daphne's tired mind. There was always a spark of light deep inside, watching on, ready to ignite her being with hope. And when the dark thoughts had tired themselves out and the punches softened, the spark called from its cage.

What if she would live?

What if it really was all a bluff to break her? Then she would make something special of her life. Get away from the textbooks and get shit hot at being who she was. She would find Olivia and tell her everything, help her through her nightmare, and be the friend to her that she deserved. And Paulie. She would squeeze him so tight his eyes would bulge and make his silly face look even sillier. She would chase the special things now.

All the special things and more.

It would be beautiful.

If only she would live.

And then her train of thought crashed. The demon had left her alone not because it was bored or failing. It was a ploy to do just that, leave her alone in the dead of night with just her thoughts, waiting for her to break herself. But she hadn't. She had come close.

Now she was very aware that the real battle lay ahead in the next few hours, as the bean-nighe's agreement would come to pass. She told herself she would stay strong, just like her mother's letter had told her to. She would banish the evil thoughts for the rest of the night. She would find some strength. She would fight, she would live, and she would make her life awesome, with all the special things.

But first, she would sleep.

She didn't.

As she lay on her bed, she noticed the copy of *The Suffering* lying on the floor near the door where the demon had left it. Something was poking out of it. A bookmark. The demon had used a fucking bookmark.

She knew the demons well enough now to hear the message.

It was telling her it was coming back.

Chapter Thirty-seven

It was late at the police station and plenty of bodies bustled around the building. This time of night would normally feel almost dead, but teams were working day and night to catch the high-profile murderer.

The misper team had all gone home, with just Joanne Bach staying behind. She had a feeling in her gut she was missing something, and if she went home, she would only be alone with her thoughts anyway. With the pictures that flashed through her mind.

The checks on messages and potential perverts had shown up nothing. Nor had the footage from the bar's car park. There had been no cameras, shops or busy spots the whole way back from the bar to Olivia's house. Barely a car on the road. It would be a perfect spot for someone to abduct a lone walker – there'd be no one there to see it or stop it. Somewhere, in between Olivia Merrigan's house and the bar, she'd vanished into thin air. A roadside abduction seemed the most likely thing, unless she'd been distracted since leaving the house and gone somewhere else. It felt unlikely. There were two women who knew the area and knew this young, attractive woman would be out walking alone. This gave Joanne Bach the feeling that she was onto something. But aside from that, she had nothing at all.

There had been another hoax call about Penelope Pengilly too. Someone claiming to be a dog walker in Hanging Hill Woods called and said they had seen her earlier that evening. No one attended. Joanne had considered going, using it as the push to say her goodbyes to the street and get that damned closure, but the thought of it made her feel sick.

She promised herself she would go tomorrow. This had to end soon.

The hoaxes were coming in again now after the father had published an age-enhanced photo in the paper, which was supposed to help but it only brought back the jokers and trolls, and that in turn fuelled press interest nationally. This just fuelled the hoaxers some more in some kind of nutty feedback loop for weirdos.

The police dealt with the annoying press and hoaxing public as best they could while they concentrated on yet another influx of low-priority missing people, as seemed to happen at times of major incidents. There had been no progress from the other departments on the murders at all, even with the bigwigs and terrorism teams coming down from London to front the investigations. But Olivia Merrigan remained Bach's priority, and there was something she just wasn't getting. Tim and Jim had even finally done something useful and ruled out the trafficking gang. That had never felt right to her anyway.

She scrolled further and further through Olivia's social media, mindlessly watching her screen while her mind rested. As it rested, it wandered. When it wandered back to her fiancé and his odd suicide during the killings at Hanging Hill Lane, sadness and pain rose inside her. This was supposed to get easier. Right now, it didn't feel like it would ever end.

Then she saw something that brought her attention back to the room, snapping her attention forward and leaving her pain briefly sidelined. Olivia had posted about wild swimming. The evening she disappeared, there had been a short but unexpected and quite violent thunderstorm. Perhaps she had bottled the interview and gone for a swim instead, and then the storm came in. If she'd gone off a cliff she would have been found, but if she was caught swimming in the sea by the storm, she might roll back in with the tide weeks later or even never.

Perhaps, but doubtful. The following morning, the Olivia Merrigan case was to be bumped up to high-priority. Joanne Bach had no idea how that would help. There was nothing about her anywhere. Nothing. And if there were no facts for her brain to cling to and work with, her mind would continue to wander.

Her intrusive thoughts of Hanging Hill Lane kept washing in. The police psychologist had explained how the obsession was linked to the trauma of her fiancé's death, and that the strangeness of the situation and unexplained parts had opened a cognitive loop in her mind that hadn't been able to close. She had likened it to a cliffhanger on a TV soap opera. Loops are opened, and our minds obsess over things until the loops close. Because of the trauma, she was stuck in that loop, and her constant feeling that something was happening on Hanging Hill Lane was her brain's desperate attempt to go and find something to close the loop, which would ease the pain. That's why they call it closure, she'd said. Perhaps solving a crime around Hanging Hill Lane might somehow close that loop, the solved case acting as an ending her brain might accept. Until then, she was in loop limbo, desperately wanting to force something and get back there and say goodbye. And yet, the feeling felt so real. Intuition was normally praised. This particular intuition was looked upon with sympathy and, recently, frustration.

The Hanging Hill Lane mystery still felt very alive, and it taunted her. Poor Mr Pengilly's loop must have been raw and open too.

Even a confirmed death would close a loop. Like the case of Mr Mattey, which was upsetting but would not play on their minds for long. She had found his final words horrifically sad when they had been revealed to her when the guys had returned. "Demons are real," he'd said. "They fucking haunt me."

And then he'd just jumped.

Loop and case closed.

Tomorrow, she would say goodbye to Hanging Hill Lane.

Tomorrow, she would slip down there alone, quietly, and close the loop.

Tomorrow was a special day.

Chapter Thirty-eight

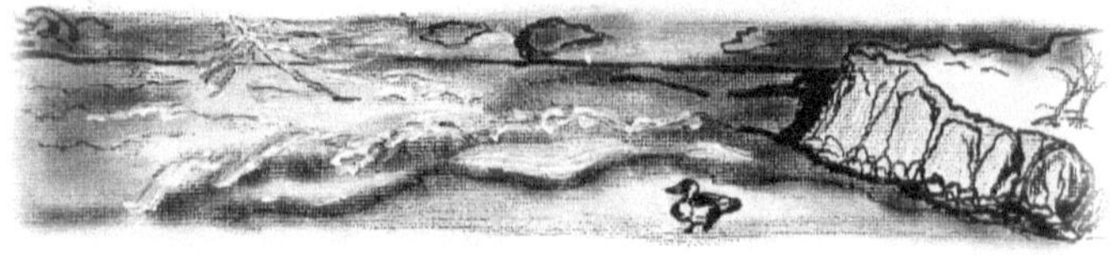

Olivia sat lonely at three a.m. She couldn't bear to sleep. Since the night on the beach she'd barely slept – she'd just lie in bed and weep.

She deeply scared herself.

It wasn't just the nights when her brain played tricks on her. It had been the mornings and the days. The evenings and the hours she spent with no idea what time it was. Her days and nights were filled with fear and guilt, bright and lively pictures in her mind of the terrible things she had done.

Every time she blinked her eyes, up flashed that rain-pocked brain. And every time she tried to sleep, there came that rain-splashed face, crumbling away. Over and over again. Always the rain. A bloody rock in her bloody fist lit by a bolt from the sky, blink after blink, dream after dream, skull crumbling away, and there, underneath, always there.

That rain-pocked brain.

All she wanted was for the pain to stop. It felt like it never would.

All she wanted was for the rain to stop.

Always pocking the holes in that brain.

Chapter Thirty-nine

OCTOBER, 1647. AN HOUR before noon. Three rough ropes waited at the gallows, a hungry noose tied at the ends, as three trembling women stepped forward. All had been accused of witchcraft. None had admitted guilt.

In the middle stood Iris Carter, staring lovingly into the crowd. To her right, twenty-six-year-old Mavis Love cried. To her left, Matilda Tamblyn, looking out over the stupid crowd of stupid humans to her daughter, a young Constance Tamblyn, watching from the treeline. When the witchfinder had pricked Matilda, she hadn't bled. *Guilty*.

The Guilty woman waited patiently.

Crack.

No swing for Matilda.

Constance Tamblyn lived to be three hundred years old and gave birth to Deanna Tamblyn in 1925. No father was ever named. The small road they lived on right next to the woods had been named Hanging Hill Lane in 1901.

Matilda's name was carved into one of the stones piled high at the wood's edge, metres away from where she was hanged, Matilda existing now only in moss-covered rock. Deanna, meanwhile, existed in plastic. A mass-produced mannequin.

Matilda Tamblyn could have bled if she'd wanted to.

Chapter Forty

DAPHNE LAY IN BED, watching the room slowly lighten with the rising sun, minute by minute. When the sun dropped down again, it would signal her final few minutes, unless she worked out a way to beat the demon and the bean-nighe before then. She was dragged out of bed by a knock on the door, which she answered with the normal trepidation and checks. Eye to the old spyhole, she saw what she dreaded to see the most.

Nothing.

Nothing out there.

Or potentially a child, too short to see.

She knelt, well back from the letterbox to avoid a poke in the eye, reached forward, and opened the flap to check for signs of a possessed child. Instead, she saw the top of a cardboard box.

She opened the door carefully, checking for signs of danger. When she stepped out, she scanned the street again. There was no one there. Just the box, addressed to her. She rocked it to check the weight. It was a little heavy, but not heavy enough to contain a possessed child. She dragged it inside and closed the door.

She opened it with Gugwana's knife, something she would now carry until the minute she stopped breathing, just in case she got a chance to use it. For now, it made a handy box opener, even though she dreaded what might be inside. She opened the lid carefully and peered inside, keeping her distance in case something struck at her from within.

The contents of the box were in no way dangerous or supernatural. They were entirely synthetic and safe.

It was plastic.

As she took it out, piece by piece, limb by limb, it became clear very quickly. It was a mannequin, ready to be assembled.

At the bottom of the box was a small rectangular box, perfectly wrapped in beautiful paper, finished with a pretty twine bow. Daphne unravelled the bow slowly, then peeled off the paper. The small box lid opened easily.

Inside, a long animal tongue lay still, dry and dead, a few words stitched into it in a thick thread: I hope this is your size.

An image flashed through Daphne's mind. A mannequin wearing her clothes.

She had only put the old witches' clothes on the mannequins out of instinct and a chance to smile. It just felt a little playful, perhaps a way to honour the women who had saved her. And then they had started to show signs of life. Now those signs were growing, and she wasn't sure it was a good thing. Especially as the demon was now promising to do the same thing to her.

What would it feel like, buried deep inside that plastic? Would she feel imprisoned for eternity? Is that what she had done to the other witches? Imprisoned them in plastic? And her mother? Had she jailed her mother?

She would likely find out twenty minutes after sundown when her own clothes would end up wrapped around this brand-new mannequin.

It was then she caught the slightest movement in her peripheral vision. It was just the mirror. The same mirror she had caught her mother playing peekaboo in after being fed the witches' love salt all those years before. Daphne approached it and stared at herself. She looked tired. Haggard. Distressed. Almost beaten.

But there was something else she saw in the face that looked back at her. For the first time, she noticed a family resemblance. In one subtle way, she looked like her mother.

It was the first time she had really smiled in what felt like forever.

It was a source of strength. And she needed it now more than ever. She raised her hands to her face and covered her eyes. Then released them to see herself again, and mimicked her mother in her favourite memory.

'Peekaboo.'

The young woman in the mirror stared back at Daphne through the gaps in her fingers, knuckles scabbed and bruised black from the strikes of the demon child's baton.

She studied the tired eyes in the mirror. There was something beyond the tiredness and the redness, beyond the bags and forming tears. Something deep inside that she hadn't expected to see, but it very definitely was there. It made her smile. It was strength. That strength came out in her voice as she spoke to her reflection.

'You're gonna have to kill that fucking demon.'

Daphne needed a plan, and fast. Her brain, addled with anxiety and tiredness, pushed hard to think straight. And then it came to her.

If there was one person who knew the way this demon thought, it was a man who had had closer contact with it than anyone else, and she knew exactly where to find him.

Chapter Forty-one

THE WOMAN BEHIND THE glass at the Gwydhenn Centre reception looked up at Daphne and dropped her phone down by her keyboard.

'Checking in?'

'I'm here to see a friend,' lied Daphne. 'Can I visit?'

'Oh,' said the receptionist. 'Thought you were here for help. Sure, sign in here.'

Daphne noticed her reflection in the glass. She looked terrible. The sleepless nights and constant thought of the coming of her death had taken its toll, and though the receptionist was clearly rude and unprofessional, she could kind of see her point. She probably looked exactly like someone who might attend this place for help. Dazed, she leaned in towards the glass for a closer look. It was the second time she had seen the resemblance to her mother. Her mother wasn't this haggard, was she? She definitely wasn't that way in her memories. Daphne raised her hands to her eyes and the reflection followed. And away again.

'Peekaboo.'

The receptionist stared back. 'Are you sure you're not here for help? There are people here who can see you.'

Daphne felt embarrassed for a moment. She really was out of it, so tired she was forgetting where she was, in her own little world. A world that felt safer and more comfortable. She yanked herself out of it. 'I'm here to see Gordon Bright,' she said. 'He's my friend.'

'Sign and go on in,' said the receptionist, sliding a lanyard pass through the gap under the glass.

Daphne walked down the corridor to where she had last seen Gordon Bright, turned at the sign that signalled the lounge, and approached the double doors. She looked through the glass. It was quieter than last time, save for a few people who looked to be a TV or film crew. And there, at the same table as before, sat Gordon Bright. Daphne pushed through and stepped into the lounge, doing her best to look invisible, hoping she wouldn't be recognised from the last time she was there.

It was then she saw another familiar face next to the door that led to the side room where she had awoken from her panic attack. Setting up for an interview was reporter Angela Shipman. A small, jittery woman brushed Shipman's face with a large makeup brush as a suited man stood alongside her. Perhaps they might know something useful. But then the pair walked through that door and it closed. Daphne wouldn't be able to hear a thing. She looked at the member of the film crew who guarded the door and thought fast.

She took off her visitor's lanyard and pushed it into her pocket, ruffled her already messy hair, and gave in a little to her tiredness, allowing it to guide her walk and movements. Then she walked to right next to where the guarding man stood, and listened. The voices from inside sounded quiet but clear.

'You can't come here, miss,' the man said. 'Just for a few minutes while they're filming.'

Daphne stared back for a moment. 'I always stand here,' she said, fully knowing she looked more like a patient than a visitor. 'If I can't stand here, I'll scream. Can I stand with you?' She pulled her hand up and gently rubbed it, drawing the man's attention to her bruised and scabbed knuckles.

The man looked back and smiled softly. 'Okay, miss, quiet as you can if that's okay.'

Daphne looked back, put her finger to her lips, and let out a quiet *'Shhhh,'* which the man playfully responded to by placing his own finger on his lip. They would both stand quietly. They would both be happy with that.

The talking inside the room carried on. 'And you're not going to release any of this until tomorrow, right? The police really won't be happy with us otherwise. I'm serious,' said a man.

'Yes, tomorrow is fine,' said Shipman's familiar voice.

'Okay, quiet please,' commanded another, and the other voices behind the door fell silent. It was then that Daphne noticed Gordon Bright staring at her. She would deal with that in a minute. From behind the door, the voice spoke again. 'Okay, and action.'

Daphne listened to Shipman's voice intently, looking away to put Bright out of sight.

'I'm here in the Gwydhenn Centre psychiatric hospital with one of the head psychiatrists here, Doctor Andy Haire.'

Haire. Perhaps it was Doctor Haire that the women had been calling for and not talking about her hair at all. She dragged her mind back to the conversation behind the door.

It must have been Doctor Haire speaking. 'We have released several women who were under our care, and while they will still make contact with our outpatient team, we have every reason to think that they will make a full recovery. They're doing surprisingly well.'

'And these were the women from Brendan Burger's boat, am I correct in saying? On the night that he and five others were killed?'

'I can't speak about details and specifics for patient confidentiality reasons, but the young women here all seem to have made excellent, and quite sudden, recoveries.'

'And is this normal? To have a group of people all suffering the same kind of, well, trauma, I suppose, and the same reaction to it, all at once?'

'Trauma reactions are normally very varied. What sends one person to self-destruction will send another on a path of seeking enlightenment or perhaps to simply withdraw from life. So this is a little unusual, yes, but we're very happy with how these women have done. They've done excellently.'

'And they still have a long, difficult path ahead of them as witnesses in one of the most high-profile murder cases in recent history, yes?'

A pause.

'I can't say what will happen next.'

'Doctor Haire, thank you very much.'

'And cut!'

Murmurs from the crew started alongside mechanical clunks, probably the gear being rushed down. But then the voice of the doctor spoke again. Daphne leaned in, struggling to hear.

'Please don't put this out in public. I could get into all sorts of trouble, but it was weird. It was like they all just woke up. Late last night. One after the other. Over about the course of three minutes. Right back to normal, as far as I can tell.'

'Really?'

'Yeah. Excuse me for not answering that last question. I'm sure you understand. But as things stand, they won't be useful witnesses. They can't remember a thing about it.'

'Huh?'

'They have no memories of anything in between boarding the boat and waking up here. It's quite fascinating. Sure, I've seen rare cases of selective amnesia, but collectively, never. I would have said it was impossible if I hadn't seen it.'

'Fascinating.'

'Please, please do not put that out. I'll let you know if things start going that way. Somebody will want to write a paper on it, and that will be public. Perhaps I will have something sooner. I don't know.'

The door flung open and Daphne darted back. A man stumbled through carrying a tripod. Other commotion followed, and finally, Angela Shipman walked out. She glanced at Daphne as she walked by, then, two paces later, stopped and turned back.

'I know you, right?'

Daphne shook her head.

'Oh. Never mind.'

Shipman and her crew left, and Doctor Haire followed. Doctor *Haire*. At least that one was answered.

And then it was time. Daphne's heart raced as she approached Gordon Bright and sat her sleepless, tired body in front of him. He hadn't taken his eyes off her from the moment she had stepped into the room.

'You look like *shit*,' he really spat that word out.

Daphne didn't argue. She didn't even feel insulted. He was right. 'Help me, Mr Bright.'

'Help you?' Bright looked back at her and smirked. 'Once upon a time, you would have called me Detective Inspector. Detective Inspector Bright. And you would have been right. A glorious title for a human. But it is still a worm title for a worm. I am more than that now. So much more.' Bright leaned in close and whispered, 'He came back to see me.'

Adrenaline shot through Daphne again. It was here.

'He comes sometimes,' Bright said, leaning back again and looking around the room. 'He visits a few people here.'

Daphne looked around too. It had been here. Recently. She had no idea of knowing if it still was. 'Is it here? Now?'

Bright looked back and considered his answer. When he finally spoke, he leaned over to Daphne and whispered fast and close into her ear, the words flowing out without pause. 'He is here, he is not, he is near, trip and drop.'

The hairs on Daphne's neck rose and stood firm. She hated that Bright was getting into her head like that. She thought and fought through the fog in her brain. The demon couldn't enter in its Penelope Pengilly suit, the whole world would see. 'And what about the girl? When he comes here. Where is she?'

'You make assumptions. The assumption that he works alone. Perhaps he does, perhaps he does not. But. All great things come in threes.'

'We got two. Sent them back. That's the last one.'

'All great things come in threes, including... threes. Anyway, if it will shut your little mind up, she has keepers. More than three because they are not great things.'

The piskies. The piskies were keeping the girl while that damned demon came and went into her mind and body as it pleased. Somehow, that made Daphne far more angry than anything it had done to her. That poor child.

'I need to know how to beat him.'

'You can't. He is superb.'

Daphne let the anger rise. 'You tricked me. If he needs the help of a worm, he is not that brilliant.'

Bright sat back and crossed his arms. He almost looked offended. 'Wrong.'

'He won't win,' said Daphne. 'I won't let him in.'

'Then you will die.'

'I would be happy to,' Daphne said, the words forced out more by anger than thought, surprising herself. She'd meant it in the second it took to say it. She was tired enough to be okay with that finality. But immediately after, she knew she didn't mean it at all. Still, it had appeared to have ruffled Bright.

'Let him in. It's so beautiful when you do, trust me.'

'And if I don't?'

Bright sat back and thought. 'Then you will need to kill the child, or die.'

'Why are you on his side? Are you actually an idiot?'

Bright just smiled back and whispered, 'He is near.'

'Well, then tell me how to stop the bean-nighe instead. Do something useful for once in your life.'

Bright leaned in and smiled, a sparkle in his eyes. He paused before he spoke. 'How to beat the washerwoman? By suckling on her long, long titties.' He leaned back and raised his eyebrows.

'Gordon Bright, you're a fucking idiot. A weak-minded human who deserves to be in here.' She was furious and no longer gave a flying fuck about being civil, especially to this moron. 'You're as fucking useless now as you were last time.' Bright put his thumb in his mouth and sucked it like a small child.

The anger had pushed Daphne's volume up enough to be heard by several of the hospital staff, and to them, it must have looked like this crazy young woman was bullying this poor, vulnerable man. She wasn't getting anywhere. She rushed out the door before she was asked to leave, leaving Bright feigning tears. What a waste of time. She shouldn't have come. Stupid idea.

She stormed back to the entrance, tapped her pass hard, shoved through the doors, and stepped into reception. She threw back her lanyard, avoiding her stupid reflection in the glass, and stepped out into the car park.

Outside, the sun shone brightly. The planet continued to spin, and ordinary people went about their ordinary days. The normality jarred.

The news crew were loading up their van. Shipman was gone. Three hospital cleaners stood smoking at the edge of the car park. For these people, it was the most ordinary of days. For Daphne, it may well be her last. *He is here, is not, he is near, trip and drop.* The phrase echoed around her tired head, creeping her out and pissing her off.

Gordon Bright. What a shit.

Then, as she set off quickly across the car park, she tripped and dropped. The cleaners all fell about laughing at her as she lay squirming on the ground. When she looked at the news crew, they stifled their laughs too. She felt so stupid as she stood. And that's when she realised. There was nothing to trip over. She had tripped over nothing. Again. She was being played with. Being made to look stupid. *He is here, he is not, he is near.*

He was here. She was going to destroy this fucker.

* * * * *

The walk home gave her a chance to clear the anger from her mind and think. She was consciously sure-footed, knowing she was likely being stalked by an invisible beast intent on making her look stupid. If she fell, so be it. She was too tired to care. The cold breeze somehow sharpened her mind.

But stalk as it might, there was one thing it could not do, and that was see into her mind. It was on this walk home that she hatched her plan, and it was ready before she reached Hanging Hill Lane.

As she walked past the boarded-up houses, she saw a small stationary car with a familiar woman sitting in the driver's seat, window down, looking towards the house at number six. It was the young policewoman who had visited, though she was in civilian clothes and the tiny car definitely wasn't a police vehicle. Daphne smiled as she sped up, ready to get home and put her plan into action.

But then the woman spoke. 'Hi, Daphne,' she said in a quiet voice that conveyed something important was happening, and Daphne stopped, hoping the conversation wouldn't be too long.

'PC Bach, right?' She looked smaller out of uniform.

'Just Joanne.'

There was a pause between them that would have been awkward if the two women weren't both focused on things far more important. The officer looked emotional.

'Did they look after you, after it all happened?' said PC Bach in a soft, flat voice. 'Did they give you the help you needed?'

'They made me see someone. Doctor Bohn. He was helpful.'

'Me too,' replied Joanne. 'A therapist at work. Was kind of helpful, kind of not.' Bach stared at the house at number six. There was a pause before the off-duty officer spoke again. 'How do you continue, after something like that? How do you do it?'

Daphne didn't know how to answer. She just stood silently.

Joanne continued softly, 'You've just got to do what you've got to do to survive, right? On the days that suck. The moments you think you can't do it anymore. We've got to make the choice to live. We've got to be survivors if we want to keep doing the good things, to keep making a difference. That's what I think I'm learning.'

Daphne wasn't sure if she was talking to her or herself, and would have loved to stop and talk, and maybe even help this clearly distressed woman, but she had urgent things going on. So she said nothing.

'Two years ago. We didn't handle it very well. I'm sorry, please forgive us.'

'It's fine. There's nothing to forgive.' Police aren't trained to fight demons. If only Daphne had been.

The pair just waited, silently, semi-connected.

'I have to go,' said Daphne.

'Yeah,' replied Joanne absently, and Daphne walked away and into her house.

She logged on to her laptop and opened her social media messages. Then she sent a message to her friend, asking her to come round quick. She could use the help of this old friend.

This old friend was a truffle pig.

A demon killer.

Chapter Forty-two

IT DIDN'T FEEL RIGHT.

Joanne Bach had fought herself hard to make the drive down to Hanging Hill Lane alone, fighting through the pain, determined to get down there and simply say goodbye. A chance for some kind of ending to the pain, some forced closure.

It didn't feel like it was working.

Just as she was about to give up and drive home, the young lady from number two had walked past and they'd had a short conversation. That hadn't helped either, though it kind of felt nice to see her.

Joanne looked at number six, picturing her fiancé going in that final time. 'Goodbye,' she said to the house and to the memory. It sounded as forced and fake as it felt.

Chapter Forty-three

THE TRAP WAS SET. Daphne would 'accidentally' let the possessed girl into the house, then pretend she was about to kill the girl and the demon. When the girl was free of the cowardly demon, which would leave her body to avoid her spike, Olivia would strike from behind. Neither really knew what they were doing. All they could do was trust who and what they were.

Olivia made herself comfortable in the storeroom opposite the lounge, where she sat quietly on a soft chair. The women had checked the room for creaks and anything that might make a noise, then oiled the door hinges so it would open silently. The lounge door had received the same treatment. All Daphne had to do was repeat previous events, get the dumb demon to leave the girl, and then call for Olivia to pounce. The pig would get its truffle.

It sounded so simple and easy. It was simple. They had no idea if it would be easy. They would both be flying completely on instinct and the bare minimum of knowledge. It was amazing how reading a hundred textbooks could still amount to knowing nothing.

Daphne set her sharpened broomstick hidden behind the lounge door. She could trick the demon into thinking it had sprung her trap, not knowing that the real trap waited behind it, ready to strike.

Then, if it worked, perhaps – just perhaps – her death would not come. If the agreement was between bean-nighe and demon, and the demon was gone, then she would have won. The demon wouldn't be around to kill her to complete the deal. She'd survive. It was her only chance at life.

Daphne and Olivia had talked enough. Evening was arriving. Olivia switched off the storeroom light and sat quietly.

Daphne checked through her spyhole one last time and saw nothing. Just the trees that blew gently in the wind, more leaves falling than should be for the time of year. She pulled the door wide open and stepped outside. She looked down the hill into the woods, where there was no sign of the child. She looked up the hill. Nothing. Nothing unusual at all.

Surely the demon would be there. If she was right, this was the last opportunity the demon had to take her. The last chance for the fungus to take control of the ant. If it didn't strike now, it would fail and be forced to kill her.

And without its ant, it would not be able to kill the other ants. It had to come.

It had to.

Then it did.

Walking out of the woods brandishing its stick came the child, eyes glowing red, accelerating towards Daphne.

Daphne turned to her house and started to run. She tripped and dropped, landing on her stomach.

The plan was working.

The demon child ran into the house. Into the trap. But then the front door slammed shut. This was not part of the plan. Why would it leave her outside?

Daphne's heart was in her mouth as she checked her pockets for her keys.

They weren't there. Being locked out was not part of the plan.

Daphne felt anger bubble inside her. She'd been tricked, made to look stupid, had her last hope taken from her. The soft empty lining of her pockets, the missing key – such angering things. Just as she thought she might win, she'd been outsmarted. And now she was angry. She looked at her door, locked firmly shut, and felt the rage boil up. And then she realised Olivia was in there, and the child was now in danger too.

The door shot open, and Daphne knew that it was she who had done it. Finally, the simplest of magic was working. Finally, it had for the first time done something useful, even if she hadn't known how she controlled it. She walked into her house and closed the door behind her, bolting it shut. In her heart and head, something felt different.

Perhaps she could do what she was destined to do. Perhaps she wasn't stupid. The feeling was fleeting, bobbing above the anger for a second or two before the anger stepped up to power her voice.

'Leave now, demon,' she said, 'you will not get inside me and you are out of time.'

The voice hissed back down the hallway. 'I have won, ant.' The voice came from the lounge. Perfect.

Daphne's view was obscured by the doorway as she slowly approached. It wasn't until she could peer around it that she saw the girl standing in the middle of the room, eyes glowing red, tentacles starting to leak from the bottom of her stomach. Daphne stepped into the lounge.

'Getting brave now, ant?' the child said. 'It's too late for that.'

'I'm going to kill you,' replied Daphne. She reached across, grabbed her spiked broomstick, and clutched it like a weapon, staring at the demon behind the child's eyes.

'I am a child,' said the demon through a smile, and stepped towards her.

Daphne started circling the demon, her weapon pointing at the girl's head. She didn't stop until the girl's back was to the door. Without any eye movement to give it away, Daphne watched Olivia emerge from the storeroom behind the girl. As soon as the demon left the child, Olivia would sing, and the demon would not be able to resist. It would be attracted to her like a fly to the sweetness of a Venus fly trap, and be gone. Then, perhaps, Daphne would be saved.

But the demon just stared back at her, smiling, eyes still glowing red. Daphne feigned stabbing as if readying herself.

'What are you waiting for, ant?' hissed the demon. 'It's what you're here for, what you're made for. To dispatch demons.'

This was not part of the plan. Daphne would not stab the girl and the demon knew it. It must have known that killing a child would be the thing that finally broke Daphne down, allowing another demon to swoop in and take the ant prize. Daphne knew it too.

If she was right, this meant just one horrifying thing. There could be more than one demon.

Then the child sniffed. For a moment, Daphne was sure it looked scared.

'Piggy,' the demon child hissed and spun around. There, right in the lounge doorway, it was confronted by Olivia. Olivia's eyes filled with anger, and one arm rose to strike at the girl. As the demon child ran, Daphne dived forward just in time to stop Olivia from hurting her. Penelope Pengilly ran out of the front door, and Olivia looked at Daphne as if returning from a trance.

'I can't do this,' Olivia cried. 'Something inside me takes over. I'll kill her.'

'I need you, Liv. Or I am going to die.'

Olivia looked back, terrified at herself. 'I'm not going out there.'

That was the moment that Daphne felt like she'd really lost, and she fell back into the lounge and allowed herself to collapse onto the carpet, beaten.

On the carpet, inches from her nose, was a slice of pizza, dirty and useless, a single bite taken from it. Nightfall was minutes away. Then twenty minutes later, the demon would fulfil its agreement.

Daphne would be dead.

Chapter Forty-four

DAPHNE MAY HAVE BEEN with her demon-killing friend, but she could hardly stay right next to Olivia every second of her life forever. As soon as Olivia slept, Daphne would be killed. All hope was gone. Kill the child, or accept death. Death was the only option Daphne would even consider.

She looked up at Olivia and saw what a terrible state she was in. She was no longer the twinkly-eyed, mischievous stunner. There was no gracefulness left in her movements. She was slumped, her skin was dry and her eyes looked exhausted. She could almost see the huge weight of guilt she carried from what she had done. Poor Olivia. It wasn't her fault she was a truffle pig any more than it was Daphne's fault she was an ant. How she longed for the boring human world one more time. But there was no more time. It was getting darker.

If she was going to lose, she was going to make sure she softened the blow for her old friend. Leaving Olivia in a better place would be the last good thing she could do. That was as close to a win as she could hope for. The thought made her feel a little proud of herself. Especially as, to do it, she was going to do something a little witchy.

Her mother would have been so proud.

'Come with me,' Daphne said to Olivia as she stood, then calmly led her by the hand to the kitchen. There, she pulled out an old stool, stood up high, and reached to the top shelf of the spice rack. She picked up a small pot and climbed back down. She poured a pinch of the tiny white crystals onto Olivia's palm. They stuck to the tears on her hand.

'Eat this,' Daphne said.

Olivia looked at her, confused.

'Eat this. It'll make things better. It'll all be over soon. Go on. Lick it.'

Olivia stared back at her, not knowing what that meant.

'Trust me, Liv. You'll be fine. It'll help you through this. I'm sorry I have to go.'

Olivia nodded and licked her palm. She squeezed her eyes with the horrible taste. 'It's salt?'

'It's love,' replied Daphne. 'From me to you. I have to go.'

Daphne ran out of the house without a plan.

The child stood in the middle of the road.

Chapter Forty-five

THE SUN DIPPED A little lower in the sky, the shadows lengthening across the leafy lane. Daphne approached slowly, her hand ready to grab Gugwana's knife concealed in her top. The evil child just stared back, grinning.

'Would you kill a child to save yourself?' hissed the demon. 'There is nothing wrong with self-preservation.'

Daphne paused, fingertips near the handle of the blade.

'Your pig friend could not do it,' said the demon. 'Now, when the child is dead, you will know that she is better than you.'

Daphne stood, frozen.

'I raise you this then,' said the demon. 'If you do not kill the girl, then when you are dead, I will. We'll jump into the river and I will leave her body as she drowns. She will feel the full panic. And that will be your fault. You could painlessly put her out of her misery, free her from her torture, and save yourself, ant.'

Daphne had lost. If she killed the demon, and the child with it, she knew she would never cope with the guilt. She'd break and leave room for another demon to come through the woods and take her. They surely waited, watching. Perhaps they were already there. The fungus would get the ant, and that would wreak havoc in the world. Or she could do nothing, and she would die, and then the child too. But at least the world would continue without a possessed witch. No mushroom sprouting from a zombie ant to kill the rest of the ants. A night witch. That's what Gugwana had called it. How she would have loved to have Gugwana with her now.

The child hit the stick in the palm of its hand. 'The sun creeps low, Daphne Locke. Make your decision. A life for a chance at life. Or if you die, she will suffer before I dispense with her.' The child raised her left hand forward, palm down, then gave her own knuckles an almighty whack with the stick in the other hand. The traces of the demon instantly left the young girl's face. She burst into tears and clutched her knuckles in agony. Daphne felt her heart breaking for her. Then the red eye glow returned to the child and it hissed.

'The little shit sobs because it hurts so much.'

Daphne dropped her hand to her side, and turned around. Fighting her own tears, she rushed to Sara's front door and banged hard, but no one came to answer. She banged again. And again. She knelt on the floor and shouted through the letterbox.

'Sara, please.' There was no sign of movement. 'Sara, the fucking demon is out here.' The flap dropped shut and the door opened. Sara stepped forward, and the demon child hissed at them both, continuing towards them.

'I've lost, Sara,' said Daphne.

'I can hear you,' hissed the demon from within the child, stepping closer again.

'I know,' said Sara, her eyes gently filling with water. 'I'm sorry. There was nothing I could do. I tried. The agreement was made and the sentence has to be carried out. I tried everything, I promise.'

'I know,' said Daphne. 'Listen, I need to tell you something that might help when I'm gone.'

'Okay,' said Sara.

'The truffle pigs, remember, I asked you about truffle pigs? They're demon hunters. You can get help from them.'

'I'll find them, thank you,' said Sara.

'No need,' smiled Daphne through a tear. 'There's one in my house.'

Sara stood tall and gripped Daphne by her arms, looking her right in the eye, and she suddenly looked like her terrifying mother. 'The sirens are dangerous, Daphne. You should not have done that.'

Daphne's jaw dropped and she looked back at Sara. She stood, shocked, as the sun dipped a little lower. 'You knew? Again.' Daphne stared at Sara, suddenly no longer seeing a best friend, a rock to rely on, a mentor. Instead, she stared at a woman she didn't feel she even knew. She looked so strict. Daphne felt the responsibility of dealing with this demon flood to her, and only her. Sara knew everything and was again refusing to help.

'Why?'

'There is no time for that now,' said Sara with a steely face. 'If there is a siren in your house, I will need to protect that young girl. These are things you should not have played with.'

'Why not, Sara? Why does it matter? You can tell me now. It's not like I have more than a few minutes anyway.'

'We do things the way we do for a reason.'

Daphne was used to feeling anger now. But when it was aimed at Sara, it felt different. It came with sadness. 'I thought you were my friend. But all along, you just thought I was stupid.'

'You were not ready. I had hoped you were, but you were not.'

The demon girl was creeping up, now only a few metres away, grinning up at Daphne, slopping sounds coming from inside its mouth. 'They do not trust you, Daphne. They do not like you. You are finally right about something. They do think you are stupid.'

'That's not true,' said Sara.

'Because I can't do magic. You've killed me.'

'No.'

'You have killed you, stupid,' spat the approaching demon through a laugh.

Daphne turned to the demon child, looking at the taunting expression on its face. In those few seconds, she'd never felt so pissed off.

Sara looked back at Daphne and her straight face crumpled into a cry. 'I'm just saying what Mum said to say. I'm so scared of her and I don't know what to do, and now I've ruined everything.'

Daphne looked back to Sara. She understood. Agatha Hunter was utterly terrifying. And yet she felt somehow disappointed that her friend, someone she always looked up to, was unable to stand up for herself. Daphne looked over at the approaching demon child, then back to Sara.

'That's a male demon, right? The father from last time?'

'Yeah, kind of.' Sara brought her crying under control.

'Honestly,' said Daphne, looking deep into Sara's eyes, finding the friend she'd always known behind the weird combination of sobs and attempted steel. Just for a moment, on Sara's face, it flickered though. A look of love. A look she hadn't truly seen since they had played together as small children in their garden. She looked deeply into the eyes of her old friend and gave her the faintest of smiles. 'Sister, it's like the set of Harry fucking Potter round here.'

Then Daphne charged. She ran straight into the child, her momentum forcing them both back, tumbling across the garden and into the road. The girl stood and wrestled back hard, and Daphne pushed and shoved the girl across the leaves that carpeted the concrete.

'That's right, ant,' hissed the demon. 'Hurt the girl. It's fun, isn't it? Hurt her! Make her bleed.'

Daphne pushed her again, right across the road and into the bushes that edged the garden opposite. The girl raised her stick to hit back, and Daphne pounced, forcing the young girl into a short bush. There, they wrestled, but the fight felt like it was getting easier and easier, and Daphne knew that Sara had understood the message.

Tendrils and vines from the bushes grew longer and started to entangle the child as it still swung its stick into Daphne. As Daphne wriggled free and stepped back, the bush continued to grow, constraining the child by all four limbs and body. Daphne moved towards her house and looked up to Sara, who was concentrating hard on the bush and the demon child in its grasp.

Daphne looked at Sara. Looked at the demon child, entwined and trapped. 'Keep her there,' she shouted before running to her own house and banging on the front door.

'Olivia,' she called, 'come out. Keep your eyes on the floor and come to me. It's okay, I promise.'

'That's not a good idea,' said Sara, a look of concern spreading across her face.

Daphne stepped away from the door towards the child. 'I don't have a lot of choice now, do I?'

Olivia stepped slowly out of the house. She looked terrified, eyes down, fighting back tears.

'Keep coming, Liv, don't look up, just keep walking this way.'

The sun was almost touching the treetops when Olivia reached Daphne, who took her hand and led her up the short path to the roadside, a single lane of leaf-covered concrete between them and the child struggling to escape the bush.

'I've got you,' Daphne said to Olivia, before repeating Olivia's college days mantra, 'It'll be okay. Everything always is. Always.'

Daphne grabbed Olivia, pulled her into a tight hug, and smiled gently. Olivia squeezed her back, and for the first time in an embrace, Daphne felt warmth instead of the compulsion to break free and run. Daphne hugged tighter with one arm, then pulled her other back and covered Olivia's eyes firmly with her hand.

Daphne whispered, 'Sing, Liv.'

'What?' Olivia sobbed, a look of terror on her face.

Daphne pulled her other arm forward and covered both of Olivia's eyes tightly as she felt Olivia squeeze harder.

'Sing, please.'

'I'll kill her.'

'You won't. Just sing.'

Olivia started to hum a tune. After a wobble from the jerking sobs, the tune started to take shape, and the temperature dropped.

Daphne held Olivia's eyes firmly shut and looked over her shoulder at the trapped child, gripped hard by the bush that was still pulling tight.

'Just hug me and sing, Liv.'

The singing was beautiful. The temperature fell further and the wind came in cold and strong. The way it whistled through the trees made a sound reminiscent of the sea. The sun dipped lower as drops of rain started to fall. And the singing was beautiful.

Sara looked terrified.

Daphne glanced over her shoulder while Olivia clutched her firmly as she sang. Sure enough, the demon's true face was coming out from the head of Penelope Pengilly, slowly moving towards the women, drawn to the siren's song.

'Keep singing, beautiful,' said Daphne, checking her hands were fully covering Olivia's eyes. 'Keep those pretty eyes shut, and just sing. Just keep singing.'

Chapter Forty-six

OLIVIA SANG, EYES FIXED shut. But as always, when her eyes were closed, there it was, an image flashing bright in her brain. That innocent face of the man on the beach crumbling away under the force of her fist and the rock she held tightly as an unnatural anger unleashed from within.

And there it was again. That rain-pocked brain. Skull crumbling away. The remaining eye had looked at her right as it died. She had seen it focus and then the life drain from within. That memory had stayed hidden from her in the daytime ever since, and had only come back in her nightmares.

'Keep singing, beautiful,' said a whimsical voice from right in front of her face, the sound somehow shimmering.

The horrors remained in Olivia's mind. The rain-pocked brain. The eye that died. And then there was a feeling. A beautiful feeling of love washed through her as if pushed by the sound of the wind that mimicked the sound of the sea as it blew briskly through the trees all around. It blew in forgiveness. Her friend felt so soft and warm as she hugged her. Her own voice sounded so magical as she sang.

The feeling that flooded in wasn't anger and bloodlust like she had felt on the beach. This was pure love. The arrival of the feeling confused her, but it felt so warm and welcome.

'Just keep singing,' said the sparkling voice right in front of her, so beautiful and soft and gentle. Olivia felt such love for her old friend. And then, with her eyes firmly shut, she peered further into her own mind as she sang, and the effect of whatever was in the salt that Daphne had given her really simmered up with a light and loving warmth. Where before she would see battered brains and crumbling skulls, now, feeling so soft and gentle and warm, she watched the horrible pictures fight for their place in her brain like they knew they shouldn't be there, yet somehow still wouldn't leave.

If only they would leave. They tortured her.

And then the shimmering magical voice came again from outside, 'Are you coming or what?'

The images, the crumbling skull and the rain-pocked brain agreed to go, and she watched them shrink and disappear from view, shrouded by a feeling of love that felt like it had come from nowhere. Remnants remained, tiny pieces of fractured, safe memories, but they weren't scary. They weren't to be feared. They held no power. Instead, she felt acceptance for herself and who she was. It wasn't her, Olivia Merrigan, who had done those terrible things.

It was a part of nature and something even beyond that. It was something that worked through her for the greater good of the world. Something that wasn't her fault. Wow, that salt was strong.

She felt her friend's breath by her ear, her hands pushing a little more firmly against her eyes. What a lovely friend Daphne was. She'd never realised how soft she was before.

'I've got you, Liv.' The beautiful voice softly wavered magically through her ear and lingered in the beautiful scenes in her memories and imagination, the scenes of everything inside her vast mind, all the parts of her stepping forward to give and receive gentle forgiveness. A kiss on the cheek made her smile and cry with a soft beauty she'd never felt before. 'Just keep singing,' said the shimmering voice as if from a magical sky. And so she did. And it was beautiful. Thunder boomed, somehow gently, and she felt its power lift her as she gently smiled, and as the thunderbolt rumble subsided, it felt like it carried away all the evil she felt about herself, as if it were being taken away by a withdrawing wave. When one eye opened, she thought she saw an angel. And then it closed again, and she looked deep inside her own mind, the source of her song, her pain, and her healing, all gently dancing in the soft, fluffy cloud of the salt.

Then the waves of pain sailed out on her song.

And she found her peace that was there all along.

And the wind made the sound of the sea.

Chapter Forty-seven

DAPHNE SQUINTED OVER HER shoulder again as the cold rain smashed down harder. The bitterly cold wind blew strong and howled through the trees, which all bent inward, taut, towards the screaming child on the street as if they were stretching to grab onto the girl or the demon themselves. Leaves blew from the branches onto the women and child below. The demon was now half out of Penelope Pengilly, moving slowly towards the beautiful singing. Sara stepped closer, watching the child thrashing around in the bush as a first roar of thunder rolled in.

Daphne kept her hands on Olivia's eyes, tears streaming out from under them. 'I've got you, Liv,' she said, and gave Olivia a small kiss on her wet cheek. 'Just keep singing.'

The tune was so, so beautiful, but Daphne couldn't help but notice the demon seemed to be refusing to come any closer, hesitant to get too close to the beautiful source of the song. Daphne looked over her shoulder and smiled at it.

'You coming or what?'

That was all the invitation it needed, drawing it closer to the song. Olivia now seemed to be grinning as she sang. Daphne stayed firm and blocked Olivia's eyes, even when the demon's front tentacles almost reached her feet. A slippery tip moved inches from her ankles, and a slippery tongue slid out towards her. The body of the demon closed in, its rear tentacles still inside the child screaming in the bushes. Daphne looked back to Olivia and brought her face closer.

When she was just a few inches away, eye to eye and sure to obscure the child from view, she gently parted her fingers and looked into Olivia's eye. The pupil gaped wide, bringing Daphne memories of seeing her mother dance alone that night and memories of herself looking into the mirror at herself with love. The love salts were working their magic.

Daphne gave Olivia a look of reassurance and trust and, somehow, received a message of love through that one wide eye before closing her fingers back firmly as Olivia continued the ethereal song. Daphne firmly pushed her palms into Olivia's eyes and felt a sharp pain in her legs as a tentacle wrapped around it, squeezing the bruised shin hard as the demon pulled itself ever closer to the song and its beautiful singer. Daphne felt the pain shoot up her leg as the tentacle squeezed tighter, and a disgusting tongue slipped around the back of her knee as another tentacle felt its way forward, and yet another wrapped around her thigh and pulled hard.

'Don't let go,' Daphne said quietly to Olivia. 'Until I say, okay?'

Olivia nodded and smiled peacefully, still singing, though the tears had stopped falling under Daphne's hands.

'Squeeze your eyes closed. You've got this.'

A tentacle reached Olivia's face, and a tongue slipped out and licked her cheek.

Olivia nodded and squeezed her eyes hard, and Daphne looked back over her shoulder. A black plastic bin blew down the street, scraping and clattering into the old black lamppost and bouncing off, skidding across the road. Leaves swirled around them in the wind, and thunder rolled in again. Olivia's voice somehow blended in with the roar of the sea-like wind and the sky's roar that shook the ground.

The final back tentacle slid out of Penelope Pengilly, who dropped like a stone and cried in the bush as the tendrils and vines started to retreat. The demon's face drew close behind Daphne, another tongue-led tentacle encircling her thigh, pulling the demon ever closer.

Sara, with one hand raised towards the grappling flora, crept towards the demon silently, poised to attack.

Daphne saw her. She didn't care. This one was hers. She reached into her clothes and grabbed the knife firmly in her hand. She looked back at the disgusting face of the demon, who paid her no mind, besotted with the song and its beautiful singer, squeezing her eyes hard. It raised another tongue-tipped tentacle to caress Olivia's perfect cheek.

Daphne wasn't going to let that happen. She gripped the knife hard and looked the demon right in the eye.

'Now who's stupid?' she said as she swung the knife into the side of the demon's head, right into the ear. The demon screeched an almighty noise and fell hard to the floor, tentacles flailing, tongues quickly retracting into the tips. But, looking like it had awakened from its trance, it didn't disappear like Daphne had expected.

'Open your eyes, Liv. She's safe, I promise.'

Her eyes stayed shut.

'Come on, beautiful. Peekaboo.'

Olivia opened her eyes and the look of love switched to rage in a heartbeat, and a mass of rainwater rushed down the lane like an ocean wave.

Daphne smiled at her old friend and held out the knife handle.

'Go get him, piggy.'

Olivia flew into the demon in a fit of rage, rushing past the knife and grabbing its throat, pinning it helplessly to the ground, her other fist raised high to deliver a killing blow.

'Wait!' shouted Daphne.

Olivia halted her strike and looked over at her old friend, who walked over calmly and stood over the demon, the fungus, the pathetic stuck truffle about to meet its end. Daphne looked at it, struggling fruitlessly on the floor, and felt the anger. All the pain and fear it had caused her, all the damage to Penelope Pengilly and God only knew who else, now filled her up in the form of an anger she would be very happy to let loose. She kicked it. It felt good. And kicked it again. That felt good too.

Kick after kick rained in, each one more satisfying than the last as the demon screamed and roared, and Daphne stopped kicking and screamed and roared back. And it felt good.

Then the kicks turned to stamps, and Daphne's screams turned to a giggle and a sob until her legs grew tired and the anger's energy finally dwindled and trickled away. She looked at her friend Olivia, panted, and stepped back. 'Okay, Liv, it can fuck off now.'

Olivia smashed her hand into its throat and ripped it out with ease. Again, the demon roared an unnatural roar, the sky lit up, and as the light from the bolt faded, so did the demon.

It was gone. And so was the cold.

And it felt good. Not just the winning. Not just the safety. Something else. Something darker. The revenge.

Olivia collapsed to her knees, soaking wet and shaking. Sara ran forward and cradled the distraught Penelope Pengilly as the rain stopped falling and the clouds started to retreat across the sky, revealing a beautiful late sunset.

'Did you do it?' asked Olivia. 'Did it work? You're not going to die, right?'

'I don't know,' said Daphne.

'Wow,' said Olivia, staring at her old friend. 'You're really beautiful.'

Knowing that the love salts were responsible for that comment, Daphne almost managed a smile. But that seemed trivial right now.

Sara placed a hand fully over Penelope Pengilly's infected eye and closed her own. When she took her hand off, the eye was healed. Sara turned her head to Daphne. Her own eye was bloodshot and swollen.

'Will she be okay?' asked Olivia.

'She will,' said Sara. 'But there is something I must do. Please, look the other way. Turn around, both of you, now.'

Daphne and Olivia obeyed and turned to face the house, Daphne worrying about what might be happening behind her. Number two looked older than it had just two years before, when Daphne had returned. As if it were tired.

'Okay,' said Sara, and the pair turned back around together.

Penelope Pengilly stood, little life left behind her eyes, with an expression on her face that looked exactly the same as the women Daphne had seen on the news report and in the psychiatric hospital guest room. As they had followed her down the corridor and chased her out of the building. The girl stepped forward with a small jerk and lifeless eyes, her expression an exact match for the freckled woman with the blonde bob.

'She won't remember a thing,' said Sara. 'She'll be like this for a few days – but she's safe – then she'll be good as new. Till then, stay away from her, Daphne. She'll get a bit upset around sisters.'

'It was you, wasn't it?' Daphne said to Sara. 'Those poor women on the beach. It was you.'

'For their protection.'

'And again, you didn't tell me.'

'For yours, Mum said. I'm so sorry.'

'That's not really working out, is it?'

'You were the woman on the cliff?' asked Olivia, pupils like saucers.

'And the hare on the steps, right?' said Daphne, and Olivia giggled.

Sara looked back at Olivia as she approached, guiding the shell of Penelope Pengilly by the hand.

'*Hare*. They weren't saying "hair" at all, were they? They were saying "hare". You. You did that to them, and they knew I was the same as you. That's why Bright said they smelled ant. Jesus, Sara!'

Sara looked stumped for an answer. 'I didn't know what to do. I wanted to tell you. And I really was trying to help. Every minute of every day. I tried. I honestly tried. I tried so desperately hard. But Mum said not to tell you. I'll do better. I'm sorry.'

'Wait. For a few days?'

'What do you mean?'

'You said stay away from her for a few days. You think I have a few days?' Relief trickled into Daphne's stomach.

Sara stared back, a look of sympathy taking her face.

The sun sank behind the top of the hill. Twenty minutes.

'Did it work?' asked Daphne. 'The thing you were working on? Does that matter now it's gone?'

'I don't know.' Daphne could tell that Sara was fighting back tears as she spoke.

'I have to go.' Daphne squeezed Olivia's hand one more time and ran into the darkening shadows of Hanging Hill Woods.

Chapter Forty-eight

SARA GENTLY LED PENELOPE Pengilly to Olivia.

'Never, ever do that again,' she said, with a firm look in her eye. She passed the girl's hand to Olivia, who crouched down and gave her a hug. As she hugged, she closed her eyes tightly and could feel the warmth returning to the thin torso of the girl, while the fading effects of the witches' salt brought some extra warmth.

But Olivia noticed most of all the strong feeling that something was gone from her mind, and in the gap left by that something, a feeling of beautiful relief. Behind Olivia's closed eyelids, there was no rain-pocked brain. No skull crumbling away. No visions of William Head illuminated by a giant lightning flash or fractured image of a spine hanging down over a rough sea. Nothing.

Nothing but acceptance for herself and affection and hope for this poor girl. It was over. There was peace.

'The state of this road,' said Sara, pulling Olivia out of her connection with the girl and her first moment of peace in days. 'You lot are always so dramatic. Anyway, call the police. Let them deal with the little one. Tell them nothing. And stay away from Hanging Hill Lane. And I mean it. Never do that singing thing again.'

'Were you really the hare?' asked Olivia, staring back at Sara, wondering how she could be so fond of this woman.

'Call the police now. They won't take long.'

Sara stormed away into her house, and when she got to the doorstep, she turned around and looked at Olivia. Olivia looked back and studied Sara. She looked like a kind, gentle woman who somehow wore the mask of someone who was terribly confused, although the mask didn't really fit. Perhaps she would now say thank you or well done. She didn't.

'I mean it. I'm sure you're a lovely woman, but you have no idea what harm you can do. And keep the clothes.' Sara disappeared into her house, closing the door behind her without a touch, leaving Olivia confused about the clothes.

But about one thing, Olivia was clear. She never intended to sing again in her life. She'd get the young girl to safety and then work things out. She had no idea what her new life might look like, but one thing was as sure as sure could be.

She would never see Heidi and Nina ever again.

The moon shone from low in the sky.

Chapter Forty-nine

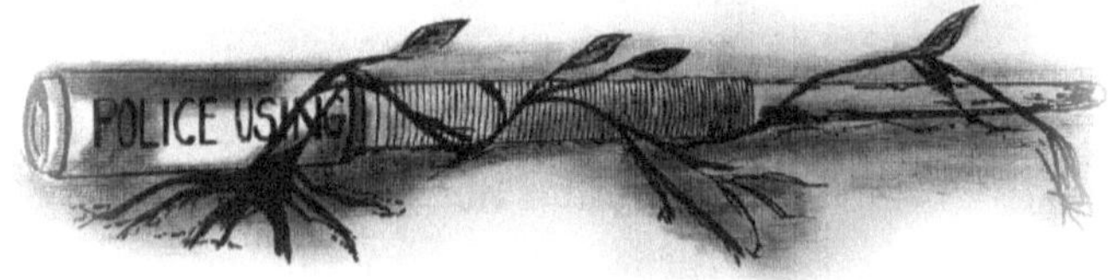

Joanne Bach sat drinking tea with Beverly Trevithick, who brushed biscuit crumbs from her chin. A couple of highly experienced and intimidating officers had been to the Blue Horizon Bar, hoping to get some information out of Nina and Heidi, but came back sure they knew nothing.

'Is this normal?' asked Bach. 'Like, this long with almost nothing? A complete mystery.'

'Honestly, we know she left and never arrived. That's more than we find for some people.'

'That's shit.'

'Yeah.'

'So what do we do?'

'Worst case, keep looking until she turns up dead or something bumps her off priority and she becomes a historical case. Best case, the phone rings and she's solved it herself and come home all ditzy with no idea what a stir she's been causing.'

'We both know that call ain't coming.'

With impeccable timing, the office phone rang.

'Surely shitting not,' said Beverly Trevithick. Detective Ovary answered. The policewomen watched him, trying to work out if there was anything useful coming in. It was a short call.

'Well, that's the most ridiculous hoax we've had for a while. A woman claiming to be Olivia Merrigan.'

'Why a hoax?' came the croak.

'Because she also claims to have found Penelope Pengilly, and says she'll await collection from us at... wait for it... Hanging Hill Lane. Idiots, it's not like we're not busy.' Oliver Ovary turned and walked to the door. As he opened it, he turned to the women. 'And no, you don't have to respond to that one.'

'I wanna go,' said Joanne Bach, her hands starting to shake.

Detective Ovary looked back sternly. 'No.'

'I wanna go,' she said again.

Ovary stared back and didn't waver. Joanne Bach stood and picked up her coat.

Ovary raised his voice. 'Constable Bach, I suggest you sit back down if you—'

He was stopped in his tracks by a stare back from Beverly Trevithick. She really was the whole station's mother. Ovary just glared at Bach.

Bach's emotions were boiling up. 'Do you know what day it is today? Anyone?'

The room looked back silently.

'No. So I'm going.' She had to get out before she boiled over and got herself in trouble.

It was only Beverly's glare that was stopping that as it was. Trevithick didn't take her eyes off Ovary while she said softly to Bach, 'You heard what he said, Jo. If that one's not a hoax, I'll tell you why I call the Sergeant Lance.' Her face softened, and Bach calmed just a little. 'But if you want to go, then go. And of course I know what day it is.'

'Thanks, Bev.'

This was a surefire hoax, but Joanne felt herself fast heading for a meltdown, and the idea of it happening in her car on Hanging Hill Lane somehow felt that it might be cathartic. She hated the look of sympathy on every other officer in that room, even Bev, and the giant elephant that followed her around every time she wanted to go with her gut to Hanging Hill Lane. She walked out of the silent room and the elephant stomped out with her.

Chapter Fifty

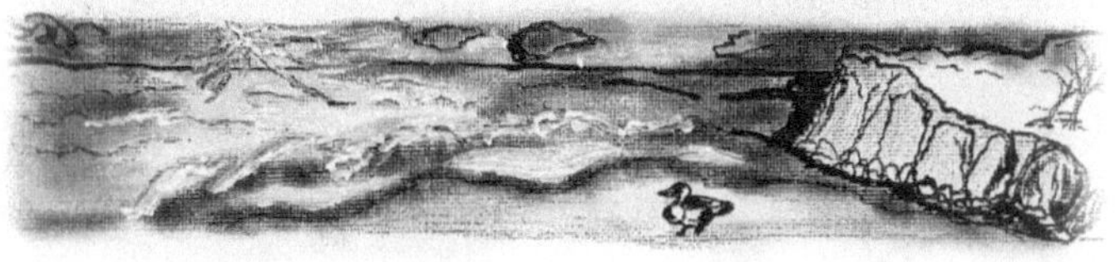

OLIVIA SAT ON THE small garden wall, gently hugging Penelope Pengilly, who stared into space. Olivia felt somehow okay. Okay with herself and what she had done, or rather, some kind of monster had done through her. Now that she had seen a demon face-to-face and knew what she had really been fighting that day, it made more sense. She even understood Sara's hostility. She knew she would have been out of control if Daphne hadn't been there to keep her in line and hold her eyes shut. She would have to come to terms with who – and what – she was in her own time. But she felt affection towards who that might be, even if she knew the witches' salt had seen to that.

But right now, she would wait for the police, get the young girl safe, and tell them a story about her finding herself with some meditation in a beach hut alone for a few days, with no idea the world was looking for her. She had a reputation as being a bit of a hippy. They'd believe that for sure.

As she waited, she watched the clouds clear, and the moon grew brighter in the sky. The light faded and the old dim streetlights of Hanging Hill Lane flickered and lit up.

And then, in the dark shadows of the woods at the bottom of the lane, stood a small creature. As it stepped into the dim light, she saw it more clearly. Was it the witches' salt playing tricks on her eyes? It was barely three feet tall and all dressed in green. Then followed another, its mouth curving up into a lopsided grin that screamed mischief. Olivia squeezed Penelope Pengilly harder and looked over to Sara's house as a sense of worry overtook her. Daphne's neighbour would surely know what these strange creatures were and if she was in trouble. A third creature appeared, and the three approached her. The mischievous grin seemed to fill itself with more aggression with each small step, and soon, sharp teeth glinted. But the thing that worried Olivia most was that these were clearly female. Whatever power she had, whatever monster had worked through her, it had completely ignored the women on the beach while it ripped apart every male there. She felt nothing stir. Whatever crazy power she was learning she had would not help her from these tiny females that clearly meant harm. Olivia protectively moved the child to the other side of her. She felt scared and helpless and looked back towards the house at number four, which stood dark and quiet.

One of the creature women shouted, 'Give her back,' before retreating a couple of steps towards the woodland as the sound of its voice echoed up the lane. Then they stepped forward again.

'Excuse me,' Olivia shouted weakly in the direction of Sara's house. The house stayed still and quiet as the creatures crept closer, three steps forward and two back like a spooked squirrel investigating an abandoned delicious nut, like they were afraid to leave the woods, yet intent on kidnapping the dazed young girl.

'Give her back, now.'

Sara's house stayed quiet. Olivia looked around. She was completely alone on that small wooded street, all aside from a young girl in some kind of trance and three small monster women that were skittishly approaching.

And then, from the top of the hill, luck came.

A car.

The headlights carved a gentle pool of light that swerved around the hill, and before the car came into view, the creatures scampered back into the woods and disappeared into the dark undergrowth.

Olivia squeezed Penelope Pengilly to her side, looked up at the approaching headlights, which gave a twirl of blue to announce its arrival, and waved.

✴ ✴ ✴ ✴ ✴

Joanne Bach had a short but emotional drive to Hanging Hill Lane. The drive alone had given her brain some space to think about her wonderful fiancé. The memory of him seemed to stave off the inevitable breakdown. But, for the very first time, she was accepting that her obsession with

Hanging Hill Lane was just what the psychologist had said. A trauma-filled, open psychological loop she was desperate to close. Perhaps if she could close the loop now she could start to recover from everything that had happened. And then she might even ask for that time off, after all. When she turned onto Hanging Hill Lane, it felt like that loop was alive.

Hanging Hill Lane. The women here centuries ago suffered from a different kind of loop. One made of rope. Perhaps she didn't have it so bad.

By the time she arrived at the top of the hill, she had readied herself and could almost feel the peace on the other side of this small moment, all the tension, sadness and grief that were about to boil over as soon as she pulled over and took the lid off. She would allow herself to say goodbye to Hanging Hill Lane and all of the recent past that had oppressed her and brought so much pain, even if it hurt as she did so. It was a good plan, and she felt like light was finally around the corner. It was a nice feeling, if a little sad. That hoax call might just work out brilliantly.

The whole feeling changed pretty quickly when she rounded the bend at the bottom of the hill.

Sitting on a wall at the bottom by the woods opposite number two was a blonde woman. A child, who appeared to be bulging out of her green school dress, stood motionless between the blonde woman's knees, a vacant stare on her face.

Joanne pulled up alongside them and the blonde woman looked through the car window and smiled. She looked tired but otherwise just like she did in the photographs in the misper office. The child stared into space with little behind her eyes. Anyone in the town would have recognised Penelope Pengilly. For a police officer involved in misper cases, it was like meeting an old friend. If only she hadn't looked so strange.

Joanne Bach caught her own jaw hanging a couple of inches too low for a professional officer of the law and closed her mouth before she got out of the car and walked around to the woman perched on the garden wall of number one.

It was Olivia Merrigan and Penelope Pengilly, together, on Hanging Hill Lane.

* * * * *

'Hi.' Olivia smiled with love in her eyes and heart, looking at the policewoman who looked truly beautiful in her majestic uniform. Her face looked so soft Olivia wanted to touch it. The young Police Constable looked back, studying Olivia and the eyes of Penelope Pengilly. It was then that Olivia realised that the salt Daphne had given her might actually be drugs, and now she was there with a police officer, high as a kite. Still, the police lady looked too adorable to arrest her.

'Olivia Merrigan, right?'

'Yeah. Can we get this beautiful one to some help?'

'Jump in.'

As Olivia helped the small girl into the back of the car, Joanne Bach pushed the send button on her radio and spoke to the station.

'I've got them,' she said.

'Call signs, please, who is this?'

Joanne Bach mumbled her call signs. 'I'm returning with Penelope Pengilly and Olivia Merrigan. We need a child health worker waiting, please.'

There was a long silence before a moment of pregnant static, then the reply came from an anonymous police voice.

'Fuck.'

Olivia watched PC Joanne Bach, seeing the human behind the uniform, feeling affection for her. Bach's attention was taken by an item lying on the pavement. It was just over a foot long, black and weathered, like a stick. A police issue baton. Olivia watched her as she walked around and picked it up.

'You're fucking shitting me.' The policewoman appeared to be talking to the stick. Maybe *she* was on drugs.

She turned and Olivia smiled warmly at her from the back of the car, stroking Penelope Pengilly's soft hair with a calm love. The girl just stared blankly.

The drive back was Olivia's first time in a police car. Still, she enjoyed the soft peace, and the car stopped again just a few metres up the road.

Olivia didn't know why the car had stopped and she didn't care. They had stopped just two houses away, and the policewoman was staring at number six. It was hard to tell from the angle, but she was sure she saw the beginnings of a tear. She was sure she made out a faint whisper from the officer, too.

'I found it,' the officer whispered. Then she looked at her stick on the passenger seat and whispered again. 'Happy birthday, Police Constable Knight.' It may have been the witches' love salt making everything feel that way, but just for a moment, the policewoman, as she stared at the house, looked like she was in love. And then she moved the car off up the hill. It was a strange and somehow beautiful moment that seemed to make sense, even though she had no idea why.

Immediately as the car turned out of Hanging Hill Lane, the effect of the witches' salt fell away and the colours around her dimmed to what they looked like in the normal world. But although the effect of the salt had evaporated, she was left with peace. She closed her eyes and breathed. There was no smashed face, no bare brain pocked by the rain, no death on the beach, no storm.

No pain.

Penelope Pengilly let out a small scream, spooked by a crow that bounced off the windscreen from the dark sky.

Olivia looked at her and gave a soft and gentle comforting '*Shhhh*', and stroked her long, knotted hair.

And her shush was the sound of the sea.

Chapter Fifty-one

DAPHNE RAN INTO HANGING Hill Woods, her limp barely slowing her down. Past the stack of stones and down the path towards where the old stone bridge stood and the bean-nighe sat doing her ugly work.

The full moon shone dimly and the sun had dropped. Nightfall had arrived. Daphne had beaten the demon set to kill her and was desperate to confirm that the bean-nighe's prophesying would come to nothing, that the agreement with the demon must surely be broken if the demon was gone. She had to check that her clothes were no longer on the pile. Then she would know for sure. She arrived at the bean-nighe's bridge panting and bleeding and straight away saw the pile of clothes.

A white frilly blouse, stained in blood, was right on top. Hers.

She was next.

She could feel the light of the moon glow brighter around her as her final minutes ticked by.

'I stopped it. I stopped the demon,' she said to the washerwoman who didn't show any signs of hearing her. Daphne shouted louder. 'Stop! I stopped it.'

The bean-nighe looked around at her with an ugly smile, and scratched a boil by her bottom lip that burst and oozed pus down her chin.

'What is on the pile is on the pile.' Some pus dripped from her chin onto the ground.

Daphne stepped forward, desperate, her breathing quickening, looking to snatch her blouse from the pile, her last and only hope. The bean-nighe hissed a disgusting sound, and the bushes ruffled all around as Daphne sensed the piskies ready to stop her.

She was beaten. She'd lost.

She'd done all she could and it hadn't been enough. The sun dipped further and the light from the moon glowed as it seemed to eat away at the last minutes of her life. Daphne stepped back and sank down against a tree.

'*Psst.*' It was a soft, friendly sound.

Daphne looked around. Peering at her from behind her tree was gentle Charl. Charl was hope. He beckoned her over, and she scurried to him as quietly as she could.

Charl produced a white garment, a little frilly and al-most new. It almost matched Daphne's blouse, which sat at the top of the pile as the bean-nighe strung up the final garment before it was the turn of Daphne's blouse.

'I'll distract her,' Charl said quietly. 'You swap the blouses, then run. Run fast, and I will delay them.'

Daphne took the blouse and looked back to the bean-nighe as the disgusting old woman walked back towards the pile of washing as Charl ran around in front of her and danced. It was a ridiculous dance and Charl was clearly well used to playing the fool. The bean-nighe watched Charl and started to laugh an ugly laugh. Her fat shoulders bounced up and down as Daphne crept closer behind her.

Daphne gripped the frilly top in her hand and noticed the pocket was full. Something soft made a small bulge. Something didn't feel right.

You've got to survive and keep going if you want to keep doing good. That's what the policewoman had said. So she kept going.

Charl danced, a truly excellent fool, and the washerwoman laughed and laughed as Daphne soft-footed towards the pile of clothes right behind her, watching for sticks that might crack under her feet and give her away. Charl didn't give Daphne a glance. Not the slightest clue that she was there. He deftly danced and the bean-nighe laughed as Daphne silently made the switch. Clutching her own blouse tight, she tiptoed back away from the bridge, desperately hoping that the piskies would not be watching and waiting to pounce. She stepped over the tripwire-like roots carefully and saw the path back home.

She kept walking, slowly and quietly. Behind her, Charl broke into song and the bean-nighe snorted out an uncontrollable laugh. Daphne looked back just in time to see the washerwoman stop laughing. She yawned loudly, waddled up to Charl, and kicked him hard. He arced up and down into a bush, and she turned back towards her pile of clothes just as Daphne ducked down from view, keeping low as she crept silently away.

When she knew she was out of view, she ran. Ran back up the path and found the hiding place where she had hidden with Charl the last time she was in trouble.

One day, if she ever dared enter the woods again, she would thank Charl. A few days ago, piskies had just been local folklore. Now, they'd both tried to ensure her death and save her life. Charl was different. Charl was one of the good guys, in this world that continued to grow beyond all she ever thought it to be. Perhaps he would make a good ally in the years to come. She would need all the allies she could get.

Her walk back to the lane was fraught with shadows and sounds that made her jump. When the stack of stones came into view in the moonlight, she knew she was home. And while she wasn't carrying a clock, it felt like twenty minutes had surely passed since the sun had gone down.

She had made it.

She was alive.

Chapter Fifty-two

ALMOST EVERY LOCAL OFFICER at the station must have been either at the entrance or staring out of their office windows to see the return of Penelope Pengilly. Joanne Bach walked across the car park with Olivia, coaxing Penelope Pengilly forward by her hand. As she stepped into the building, she looked around at the eyes all around her, looking at the young girl being led in by the county's current biggest misper case. If there was any news that could displace the news of the beach murders, this was it. A woman with a kind face stepped forward.

'Hi, I'm the social worker here for Penelope.' She crouched and looked at the young girl's blank face. 'Oh my God.' She looked around. 'Can we get her an ambulance?'

'She'll be fine,' said Olivia.

'Pardon?' said the social worker, not hearing clearly in the commotion around her.

'Nothing,' said Olivia. She crouched. 'You'll be fine,' she whispered to Penelope Pengilly with a scrunch of her hair before she was led into a side room by the social worker and two high-ranking officers.

In the crowd stood Tim and Jim with Oliver Ovary and Jason Cox, all staring in disbelief. Now that they were all standing, it stood out how Beverly Trevithick must have been a full foot shorter than the rest. She walked forward with a smile for Joanne and then looked at Olivia.

'We've been looking for you, Olivia. We've been worried. Where were you?'

'Finding myself. I'm sorry,' she said.

Trevithick turned to Tim and Jim. 'Would you boys mind taking Miss Merrigan and get the report done?' Joanne had never seen either of them move so fast, and Olivia Merrigan walked away down the corridor and out of sight.

'You're not gonna believe this,' said Joanne to Beverly. 'There's more.'

'More than our biggest two misper cases?'

'More,' grinned Joanne Bach with a lightness she hadn't felt for a long time. She reached inside her bag and produced the small stick. It wasn't smooth anymore, but still extended when she pulled at the tip. Her police baton was back.

'You're shitting me,' said Trevithick. 'Where did you find it?' The end had been smashed and ground into a point and it was dented and dirty, but it still had the little bit of nail polish by the handle that Joanne Bach had put there to identify it when she first received it.

'So?' asked Joanne as the crowd dispersed, a couple of officers giving her a little pat on the back.

'So what?' asked Beverly Trevithick.

'So why do you call him Lance?'

Beverly Trevithick started laughing and looked around to check that no one was in earshot. 'We started about the same time. Not long after, he seemed to move uncomfortably and then took a couple of days off for medical reasons.'

'Go on,' said Joanne with a smile.

'Turns out he was off sick with a haemorrhoid the size of a blue whale and was getting it lanced. We called him Lance ever since. But now he's a Sergeant, no one dares.'

'You do.' Joanne laughed.

'Mother gets away with everything. Perk of being an old sweat. Right. You've earned yourself a cup of tea and a biscuit. I'm somehow glad that's over.'

'It is, isn't it,' said Joanne Bach.

Beverly Trevithick smiled a motherly smile and walked away to put the kettle on and cut an extraordinarily large slice of cake. Lance approached Joanne and patted her on the back.

Joanne stifled a smile, and refrained from calling him Lance, however much she wanted to. 'Sergeant,' she said, 'do you have a minute?'

In the Sergeant's office, Joanne Bach sat down and caught her hands shaking. She didn't know why she was nervous.

Sergeant Cox looked at her, waiting.

Joanne Bach breathed and got herself under control, and said, 'I was thinking, sarge. About that time off. Perhaps I could use a couple of weeks.'

Cox looked back, thinking.

'Is that still okay?'

'And the psychologist?'

'Can we play that one by ear?'

'Can you finish the paperwork for your extraordinary work today? And then we'll see you in two weeks?'

Joanne Bach felt her mouth smile. She closed her eyes, leaned back, and breathed, and for the first time in a long time, felt peace. She couldn't believe nor control it, but the corners of her mouth would not stop reaching skyward. 'Thank you, sarge.'

Chapter Fifty-three

DAPHNE STARED AT THE moon as it shone bright through the only gap in the nighttime clouds. She was still alive. She held her blouse tightly and her breathing softened. Breathing had never felt so good. The first thing she would do was knock on Sara's door and show her she was alive. They'd done it. Relief shot through her with more power than any amount of fear ever had, forcing tears from her eyes as she gasped for breath. She'd never felt anything like it. Her life hadn't been taken from her. She was going to make it amazing. She was going to be the best witch partner Sara could dream of. She was going to be the best friend to Olivia she could. And Paulie. She was going to do everything she could to make things right with that beautiful man. Thoughts raced through her and disappeared. It was like letting go of a thousand tonnes of terrible thoughts all at once. It still kind of hurt, but in a good way. Paulie. She was going to make things good with Paulie. Their story had been cut short, but now it could start again.

Except that a blue spinning light illuminating the bottom of Hanging Hill Lane signalled that her terror might not quite be over.

An ambulance sat outside Sara's house at number four, a police car sitting quietly slightly up the hill from it. Sara was standing in her doorway, hands over her mouth in distress. As Daphne tried to step onto the road, an unusually pale police officer stepped out in front of her from the shadows.

'Could you just wait here a second, please?' said the officer, clearly upset.

'What's happening?' asked Daphne.

A paramedic was loading a small, still child onto the ambulance. She didn't want to believe it but it became clear as the body passed under the streetlamp. It was Alfie. Sara howled in anguish.

'I'm her best friend,' said Daphne. 'Tell me or let me through.'

The policeman looked at Daphne and tried to find the words. 'I don't really know. Sounds like that poor little kiddie ate some fishhooks. It's tragic.'

Daphne's jaw widened as she looked on in shock, and Sara started to move quickly towards the ambulance, tears streaming down her face.

An almighty crack echoed from the ambulance, and the vehicle began to roll down the hill. Paramedics and police scrambled towards the vehicle as it picked up a little speed.

Sara tripped and dropped. It looked almost as though she'd been shoved or that her feet had caught something on the ground. Except there was nothing there.

Nothing.

The sound of Sara's skull popping and the pulp of her brains showering across the road would be a memory Daphne would never forget.

As people in uniform ran to stop the rolling ambulance, Daphne stood and looked at her blouse in her hand and she knew this was her fault. She'd been tricked. Again. The bulge. Alfie's mitten. It suddenly all made sense.

A light flickered and flashed on in her mother's room at the front of her house and took her attention, and she looked up through a haze of shock. In the window stood a mannequin. It was dressed in her mother's clothing.

A thin voice called quietly from behind her, echoing distantly and softly through the woods.

'Stuuupiiid.' It sounded like Charl.

Charl was right.

As she sank to her knees and looked to the skies and felt herself tear apart, the moon softened then disappeared as a dark cloud cut through then slid across it, revealing a single gap to the heavens where five stars shone down brightly, twinkling and glowing as though there was nothing wrong with the vast and perfect world where Daphne knelt, alone and stupid.

And down on Earth under those five shining stars, though there was nothing near her, nothing alongside her, nothing in front nor behind, the nothing spoke in a close, whispering voice that burrowed into her ear and deep into her breaking mind.

'Gotcha.'

It sounded as if the nothing had smiled.

A note on this book

This book truly is the result of a worldwide collaboration. From the words landing on my laptop in my home in Southwest England, it's travelled to almost every continent before reaching you in its finished form.

A very early draft went to alpha readers: Isla in Scotland and Paula in Ecuador, before a new version went to Australia for some excellent development advice from Becker. After another draft, it went to Danielle, an American in Canada, for a thorough edit, before heading off to its final beta readers: Alex, a Romanian in England; Leigh in Ireland; Patrick in Canada; and Aimee in Peru. Then it got its final changes and another thorough edit by Kathy, who, like the bean-nighe, started life in Scotland and ended up in Cornwall. She hasn't edited this section and would definitely question those semi-colons.

But still the book hadn't finished its international journey. Its internal design and illustrations are by Vanessa from the Philippines, and finally, the cover was illustrated by Mino in Romania.

And now, wherever in the world you are reading, it has finally landed with you, the final piece of the international puzzle. Thank you for reading, and please consider leaving a review – they are really helpful to indie authors.

Thank you for reading.
Phil

Thank You

I have a long old thanks list for this one. But it's all truly deserved.

I have to thank the group Books of Horror, because it's the best online group I've ever known. Not only did the group propel the first book in this series to the number one seller in British Horror on a certain massive online bookstore, they gave me so much support and the confidence to follow it up with this one. So thank you, Books of Horror. Especially Tiffany, because, Tiffany, you are awesome!

The Brit authors who I regularly chat with, especially Jim Ody, and everyone there in our little group. Justin Boote for the work ethic inspiration (but I still don't know how you do it). Leigh Kenny for the support from Day One. I want to say more of you, but there are too many, and if I start listing I'll forget someone. You know who you are. You make my phone ping all bloody day.

MJ Mars, author of *The Suffering*, for letting me use your book in mine. Everyone should read it.

My cover designer, Mino, who is one of the most fun creatives I've worked with. Thanks for being patient with my endless revisions.

My editors: Becker, Kathy and Danielle, for making me look cleverer than I am. Daphne's mother's irrational love of semi-colons in all the wrong places is for you.

My support from across the pond: Patrick McNulty.

My sources of specialist knowledge: Detective constable Amanda Rowe for the amazing info about missing persons procedure in the Devon and Cornwall Police. I owe you another coffee.

Simon Gardiner for the info about the inside workings of a psychiatric hospital.

My alpha readers: Isla and Paula.

My beta readers: Patrick McNulty, Leigh Kenny & Alex Nisneru – thanks for finding the last bits of the story to fix (read their books).

Everyone who read and reviewed my first book.

My family for not putting their copies of my book in the bin yet.

And of course, my book illustrator, taga luto and wife, Vanessa. Salamat sa lahat.

About the Author

Philip Alexander Baker started his writing career as lyricist for indie band Lemanis, which released two albums, *Shell*, and *The Truth Behind the Push-Me-Pull-You*. Life as a filmmaker and screenwriter followed, including writing the award-winning *A Story for Happy*, and producing the British crime drama films *Killing Lionel* and *Card Dead*.

The Hanging Hill Lane series are his first books.

Twitter.com/Phil_Baker_
Facebook.com/PhilipAlexanderBaker
Instagram.com/Phil_Baker_